Rachel SINCLAIR
LA DEFENSE

VINCI
BOOKS

By Rachel Sinclair

Kansas City Legal Thrillers

Bad Faith

Justice Denied

Hidden Defendant

Injustice for All

L.A. Defense

The Associate

The Alibi

Reasonable Doubt

The Accused

The Hate Crime

Secrets and Lies

Until Proven Guilty

Vinci Books

vinci-books.com

Published by Vinci Books Ltd in 2026

1

Copyright © Rachel Sinclair 2017

The author has asserted their moral right to be identified as the author of this work in accordance with the Copyright, Designs and Patents Act 1988. This work is a work of fiction. Names, characters, places and incidents are the product of the author's imagination or are used fictitiously. Any resemblance to actual persons, living or dead, places and incidents is entirely coincidental.
All rights reserved. No part of this publication may be copied, reproduced, distributed, stored in any retrieval system, or transmitted in any form or by any means, including photocopying, recording, or other electronic or mechanical methods, nor used as a source for any form of machine learning including AI datasets, without the prior written permission of the publisher.
The publisher and the author have made every effort to obtain permissions for any third party material used in this book and to comply with copyright law. Any queries in this respect should be brought to the attention of the publisher and any omissions will be corrected in future editions.
A CIP catalogue record for this book is available from the British Library.
Paperback ISBN: 9781036703196

The EU GPSR authorised representative is Logos Europe, 9 rue Nicolas Poussion, 17000 La Rochelle, France
contact@logoseurope.eu

Chapter One

HARPER

"HARPER, you have to come out here. I can trust you. I can't trust this moron they got representing me out here." Ginger was sobbing as she spoke with me. I could barely understand what she was saying.

"Slow down, slow down," I said evenly. "First of all, what happened? What did you do?"

"I didn't do nothing, Harper. I didn't do nothing. This guy, his name is Robert something, he invited me to this fancy party. He invited all the girls to this fancy party with this big-shot movie producer named Ezra something. I don't know, Harper, I forget his name. Look it up on the internet. You'll see what happened."

I scratched my head and looked down at the floor.

"Are you looking it up yet?" Ginger demanded. "Look it up, Harper. You'll see."

I sighed as I walked into my office and booted up my laptop. "Okay," I said over the phone. "Ezra something." I typed in the word "Ezra with the words 'movie producer' and immediately saw what she was talking about. Ezra

Cohen was a Paramount development executive found dead in his Malibu home. I continued to read on and saw he was found in his bedroom, and, initially, it looked like death from natural causes. But the coroner's report came back and Ezra not only had cocaine in his system but also showed traces of arsenic poisoning, almost undetectable, so the death was ruled a homicide. Ginger was arrested for his murder because she was the last person with him before he died.

"Ginger," I said, "who is this guy to you?"

"I told you, I didn't know him. He was a john, that's all. My boss, Mario, he got me that gig. He had a party and I was there to service Ezra and his friends. I blew him, Harper, that's all, and not really even that, because he couldn't get it up. I blew his limp dick, and the last I saw, he was passed out on the bed. I took off and the next thing I know I got the cops at my house arresting me because I lifted some stuff from him, which I did. I lifted a pair of gold cufflinks and a ring and hocked them. They arrested me for that and then they arrested me for killing him. I didn't do nothing wrong, Harper, I swear."

"Well, you stole from him, so, technically, you did something wrong."

"Harper, if you seen this guy, if you seen his house, you'd know he won't miss that ring and those cufflinks. He won't even know they were gone, he had so much stuff in that house. I need the money because Mario hasn't paid me yet, even though I've gone on 10 gigs since I've been out here. I need to get rid of Mario and do my own thing."

"And Mario?"

"He's my agent. He gets the jobs for me. The jobs pay him and he pays me. Except he hasn't paid me yet, and, Harper, it ain't cheap living out here. I'm living in a little house by the beach with 6 other girls but it still ain't cheap. We're sleeping two to a room, but I gotta eat, so I stole those cufflinks and that ring and got $20,000 for both those things. I gotta pay that back, though, which is bullshit, because Ezra don't need those things no more and he don't need my money no more either."

"Ginger, here's the thing," I said. "I can't just up and leave. I have the girls. They're out for summer break, but I can't uproot them. I have two dogs, Stella and Sue. The girls have their friends here and have been making plans with their friends for the summer. I also have Axel to think about. We were on the brink of separating but we're good now. I can't just up and leave him to represent you in California. Not to mention my practice. I have a ton of open cases. Granted, none of my open cases are large or complicated, but I have a lot of them. I don't have an associate to take these open cases for me. I'm sorry, Ginger, but I can't represent you. I'm sure there are plenty of lawyers willing to take your case. Get some referrals."

"No, Harper. I trust you. Only you."

"Why do you trust me so much?"

"Because you don't judge me. You've been the only person in my life who's never judged me."

I knew she was right. I didn't judge her. I understood her. And, when I had her over for dinner one night and got her story, I knew why she was the way she was. She told me her mother had died when she was very little and her father molested her from the time she was five. By the time she was 13, she'd had two abortions after her father impregnated her twice and she'd had enough of living with him. So she ran away and lived on the streets. She didn't tell anybody about what her father did to her because she didn't want to end up in foster care. She'd spoken to enough people to know foster care wasn't for her.

When she ran away, she had no means of support. So, she burglarized a house and pawned everything she got from the house and used that money for a Greyhound bus ticket. Her intention was to go to her maternal grandmother's house and see if her grandmother, whose name was Addy, would take her in. Unfortunately for her, Vinnie Varagusa, the man who would become her pimp, spotted her in the bus station and struck up a conversation. Vinnie convinced Ginger to work for him. Since she didn't know if her Grandma Addy would take her in, Ginger went with the sure thing and accepted Vinnie's offer. Vinnie found her a place to stay and found johns for her. Ginger thought he was helping her out, not realizing how much Vinnie was exploiting her.

Now she was in L.A., and, from what little she told me over the phone, I gathered she was still being exploited. It sounded like this Mario character was treating her like Vinnie did. Vinnie didn't pay Ginger for all the work she did and neither did this Mario person. Vinnie paid Ginger for some of the work, but not all of it. I wondered if Mario was paying her for any of her work.

"Ginger, I can't. I'm sorry. I have a life out here. I'm really sorry."

At that, Ginger started to cry. "Harper," she said between sobs. "You can't do this to me. You can't. You told me you'd always have my back. Now I need you. I need you, Harper. They're gonna put me in jail out here, Harper, and I didn't do nothing to that man. I didn't do nothing. I just blew his whiskey dick and stole from him and left him on the bed. They're saying I poisoned him, but why would I poison him? I didn't know him. I didn't know him. I was only there because Mario got me that job. He said it was a good job. He said I'd make good money from that Ezra because Ezra is rich and could make me a regular girl. Ezra has regular girls and Mario said I could be one of them. I gotta eat out here, Harper, and Mario ain't paying me regular, so I wanted to become one of Ezra's regular girls. That's all."

"I understand all that, but Ginger, I have to draw the line. I can't leave here for months on end. I'm sorry."

Truth be told, however, my heart was melting just a bit for poor Ginger. The underdog could always count on me. If there was a hopeless case, I was the attorney to make it less hopeless. And Ginger, for all her faults, really was like a lost puppy. I could never turn my back on a lost puppy, and I had problems turning my back on Ginger.

Not that I would tell her that, though. I didn't want to sound like I was wavering at all, because if I did, Ginger would be all over that. She had enough street smarts to read people, and would know if I was changing my mind about taking her case.

She sniffed. "I understand, Harper. I gotta go."

And, at that, she hung up the phone.

Chapter Two

I WENT to work the next day but couldn't get my mind off Ginger. She sounded so desperate over the phone. So lost and alone. The one saving grace was that California's Superior Court had deemed capital punishment unconstitutional, so at least Ginger wouldn't face the death penalty if she got convicted.

Really, Harper? Really? That's all you can say to yourself – at least they won't kill her if she gets convicted?

"Pearl," I called my assistant. "Come in here. I need to ask you a few things."

Pearl came into my office. She was a beautiful black girl who always dressed more stylish than I ever could. She typically wore her long hair in braids and her skin was so flawless she never had to bother with makeup. I was envious of how effortlessly she put herself together every morning. I felt like a frump next to her. "What's going on?" she asked me. She had a pad of paper in her hand and a pen.

"Have you seen Tammy? I need to run something by her as well."

Pearl shook her head. "No. Tammy comes in this afternoon, though. I think she has a dentist appointment."

"Okay." I took a deep breath. "Here's the thing. I might have a case in Los Angeles I might need to tend to. It involves Ginger."

"Girl," Pearl said. "What trouble is that Ginger up to now? She's always up to her ears."

"You don't know the half of it. Ginger has always been in trouble, that's true. But not like this. She's been charged with murdering a studio executive for Paramount. She says she didn't do it, of course. And she also says I'm the only person she trusts."

"Well, that's probably true," Pearl said. "After all, she really bonded with you. She's told me on more than one occasion that you've been the only one who's tried to understand her and hasn't judged her for the things she's done."

"I know." I looked out the window at the people below. "I can't leave, though, can I? I have about fifty open cases, after all. I can't just leave."

Pearl cocked her head. "You could if you got an associate. You need one, anyhow. I never understood how somebody as busy as you are can handle everything alone. Find somebody to help you out on your cases. I can call all your clients and make sure they're okay with somebody else finishing their cases for them and then you can go to California and help Ginger."

Pearl made perfect sense. I'd been thinking about pulling the trigger and getting an associate for at least a year. Pearl was right – I was a busy attorney and was trying to do everything myself. It wasn't working out well. "Do you think my clients would be okay if they were passed onto another attorney?"

"Well, you don't have anything major in the pipeline,"

Pearl said. "I can give you your list of current clients, but, from what I can see, none of your current clients are being charged with anything more serious than a burglary. Most have plea deals being worked out. I don't see why they'd object to your hiring a good associate to finish the cases. Besides, you need a vacation, Harper. I know it wouldn't exactly be a vacation if you go out to California and work on this murder case, but it's probably as close as you'll get to taking a break. Find a house by the beach and relax with a glass of water on your patio while you listen to the ocean waves. That'll put you in a better frame of mind."

Pearl had another point. Granted, working a major murder case wouldn't be a vacation, but it was definitely something I could handle. And handling one murder case, as opposed to a murder case on top of my other open criminal cases, would certainly be my version of taking a break. I suddenly imagined myself finding a beach house and sitting on the patio with a glass of grape juice, listening to the seagulls and children playing, smelling the salt water and feeling the sand between my toes. In my mind's eye, I saw the sun setting over the ocean and felt the warmth of bonfires built up and down the beach.

I realized I was closing my eyes and Pearl brought me back to reality. "Harper," she said. "What are you thinking about?"

I shook my head. "Nothing." I opened my desk drawer and brought out my slinky, the toy I enjoyed playing with when I got stressed and needed to think. There was something about playing with that slinky that focused my brain more than anything else. "What about Axel? What about my girls? And my dogs?"

"Your girls are on summer break, starting next week. How perfect is that? If they were in school, you'd have a problem, but with them being on break, you can spend the summer in California. When is the trial?"

"I don't know. I can ask for a speedy trial and get it teed up within 180 days. Hopefully 90 days. I could be back in time for the girls' fall semester in school. But what about Axel? I can't just up and leave him. Can I?"

"Yes you can. You'll only be gone for the summer. He'll live, I can assure you." Pearl rolled her eyes and smiled. "You're overthinking this. Listen, I'll go to Zip Recruiter to find some people to interview for an associate's position. I'll line them up for you this week and you can have somebody hired by the weekend. Then I'll contact all your clients and tell them what's going on. Trust me, you've been needing this. This new case in California gives you a perfect excuse to get some help in here."

I took a deep breath. "Okay. Find some people to interview to be my associate. I need the help of an associate but I just don't know about taking Ginger's case. I'll have to think about it."

"Don't think too long and hard. Ginger can't wait forever for an answer. How would you like to be accused of a murder you didn't do and the person you want as your attorney is dilly-dallying about representing you?"

I didn't need to answer that question. Pearl was right. Ginger would need an answer. "Find some candidates for my associate and I'll think about it."

"Will do."

THAT NIGHT, I talked to Axel about my plans. "It'll only be for the summer," I said.

"I know, mate. I want you to go. I'll miss you but I can visit you from the time to time, right?"

"Of course. I want you to visit as much as you can."

"Okay, then. I don't want to put a leash on you and don't want you to put a leash on me. Of course, if you're gone for longer than three months, I'd have more of a problem. But three months really isn't that long."

I hugged him and he kissed me. "Thank you for understanding. Now, I have to tell my girls."

For some odd reason, I dreaded that more than I dreaded anything else.

Chapter Three

"NO," Rina said adamantly when I told her I was thinking about going to California. "I won't go and you can't make me."

"Rina, if I do this, and that's a big if, but if I do, I'm sorry, you won't have a say in the matter. You have to go with me. Obviously."

"No," she shook her head. "I got summer plans with Emma and Haley. We were planning on swimming over at Emma's house. She lives in Hallbrook and has her own pool. Emma has already planned five pool parties, Mom, five. All the kids will be at those parties and I have to be there, too, Mom. I have to be there. If I leave for the whole summer, Emma and Haley will forget I'm alive and that'll be the end of the world. My life will be over if I don't go to those parties and see Emma and Haley all summer."

I looked over at Abby, quietly looking down at a book she had in her hand. She was petting both Stella and Sue while she read. Stella the Golden Retriever and Sue the

Rottweiler loved Abby to death and she felt the same way about them.

Abby glanced up and had little tears in her eyes. "Abby," I said. "What say you? Are you also looking forward to swimming at Emma's house?"

She shook her head. "No. I'm not friends with Emma. She doesn't talk to me. I guess I'm not popular enough for her to acknowledge I'm alive."

I sat back in my chair. "Rina, Abby has a point. I know you're best friends with Emma, but I have to tell you, I'm not sure if I like that. Emma strikes me as a snob and so does Haley. You could stand to make different friends. The last thing I want is for my daughter to become a bullying mean girl."

"Who's a bullying mean girl?" Rina crossed her arms and glared at me. "Mom, Emma and Haley are the most popular girls in school. They know everybody."

"Don't you think it's odd that Emma doesn't speak to your own sister?"

"No. I don't think that's odd at all. Abby is a nerd and Emma doesn't talk to nerds. Nobody who's anybody at the school talks to nerds and Abby is a nerd. That's all. Emma's afraid that if she talks to Abby, people will stop talking to her. I don't blame her for not talking to Abby. If she weren't my sister, I wouldn't talk to her at school, either."

Abby's eyes filled with tears and I went over to her and put my arm around her. "Thank you, Rina, for making up my mind. You are coming to California with me for the summer, and, when you get back, I'll have some serious talks with Emma's mother about Emma's lack of respect for Abby and for others like her. You need a time-out from those girls. A summer with just me, Abby, Stella and Sue sounds like just the thing you need to bring you back to earth."

At that, Rina gave me the stink-eye to end all stink-eyes and turned and ran into her room and slammed the door.

"Abby, Buttercup," I said. Abby's big brown eyes turned to me. "You didn't say anything about going to California. What do you think about the idea?"

She shrugged. "It's okay, I guess. I'll miss Lily. She has a pool, too, in her apartment. She was hoping I could swim with her. She really doesn't have friends at school except me. I guess that's because her family doesn't have much money."

Lily Alderan was a girl who Abby bonded with. Lily was only at Abby's school, the exclusive private school called Pembroke Hill, because she got academic scholarships based on her entrance exam scores. In other words, Lily was poor and smart. Abby explained this made Lily an outcast at school, at least when it concerned the popular kids, and, since Abby was also an outcast due to her shyness and social awkwardness, the two girls became best friends. As far as I knew, Lily was Abby's only close friend and vice-versa.

"I understand," I said. "Lily will be lonely this summer without you. I hate to do that to you, taking you away from her. But I hope you'll be okay with all of us going to California for the summer."

She nodded. "I am. And you're right. If we go to California for the whole summer, Emma and Haley probably will drop Rina as their friend. They're that type, Mom. They're mean girls. They bully everyone who has less money than them and everyone not as pretty as them. I'd like to see Rina not be friends with them anymore."

"Then that settles it. We're going to California, and, hopefully Rina can find a different group of friends to hang out with when we get back. I don't want her hanging around girls like that." I shuddered. "I was bullied by girls like that when I was her age. Having been the victim of the mean girl bullying, the last thing I want is my daughter perpetrating it. I'm surprised, though, they'd choose Rina to pal around with. After all, we're far from rich."

"Yes, that's true," Abby said. "But you're a lawyer and you've tried all kinds of cool cases. Everybody knows Rina's mom is this big-shot attorney who tries all these cases that everyone has heard about, and that makes Rina cool."

I smiled. "Oh? I've suddenly become cool? That's a new one."

"Yeah, Mom. You're considered cool at school. It does me no good, though, Mom, you being a big-shot attorney. People still pick on me because I always manage to say the wrong thing at the wrong time."

"Well, Buttercup, I know you won't believe me, but you'll be the cool one someday. That's because you have smarts along with being beautiful. When you get older, you'll find being smart and kind will take you much further than being stuck-up and rich. Just you wait and see."

She smiled. "You really think so, Mom? You really think I'll be cool one day?"

"I know so." I tousled her hair. "And Rina will be angry with me. I know that. But she'll get over it. I predict we'll have a lovely time in California. Don't worry, I'll find somebody to be your nanny out there. After all, you girls will need somebody to take you to the beach every day."

"And Stella and Sue can come too?" Abby was petting the dogs who were sitting at the table, watching us and waiting for some food to drop off the table so they could scoop it up. I didn't like to feed them from the table because I didn't want them to get fat, but if any food dropped somehow, they were all over it.

"Nah. They can just stay here and fend for themselves." I smiled as I saw Abby's face drop when I said that. "I'm kidding, of course, Buttercup. Stella and Sue will come with us. I'll find some dog beaches where we can take them and they can run."

At that, Abby came over and gave me a hug. "I'm getting excited about this, Mom. You said we can find a beach house and everything? That sounds unbelievably awesome."

I nodded. "I have my work cut out for me. I'll have to find a place for us to stay. Maybe look on AirBnb and find out if anybody's vacating their beach house for the summer. Maybe we'll get lucky. Who knows? And I also have to hire an associate. We'll see how it works out and keep our fingers crossed."

At that, I kissed Abby's forehead and went up to my room. I wanted to call Ginger back and get on the internet to find our perfect beach house.

If I was going to spend the summer in California, I would do it right. And a beach house sounded just like heaven.

Chapter Four

THE NEXT DAY, after finding an AirBnb opening right on one of the beaches – it was a two-bedroom portion of a larger house and was the bottom part of the house, so there was a patio that faced the boardwalk – and snagging it, I called Ginger to tell her the good news. I was also ready to interview candidates for the associate's position.

This would happen, and, truth be told, I was getting excited.

But not nearly as excited as Ginger. "Woo hoo!" she screamed over the phone. "I knew you wouldn't bag on me, Harper, I knew it. I talked to this other girl, her name is Amber, that's her show name, but her real name is Megan, but Amber, she told me you wouldn't come through, but I told her she was wrong. I knew you would, Harper, I knew it. I knew it."

"Well, tell me more about your case," I said. "Have you been arraigned? I'm assuming you made bail. How did you do that?"

"I got read my charges," she said. "And I guess my case

will go through the Grand Jury, whatever that means. I don't know what's going on. I got this attorney, his name is Gavin something, I don't know, but he's a real creeper. I don't like him but Mario got him for me. Mario paid my bail, too, Harper. He wants me working for him so he got this lawyer and paid for me to get out of jail. Gavin's a creeper, Harper. He wants stuff and I don't want to give it to him. He wears his hair in a ponytail and chews tobacco and I don't like that. I think that's gross and he's gross too and I don't trust him. So, I'm glad you're coming out, Harper. So glad."

"This Mario paid your bail? How much was it?"

"A million dollars," she said. "Mario said he can afford it and he'll get it all back as long as I don't jump. He says if I jump, though, Harper, he'll find me and have one of his men kill me. So I won't jump. No way."

"Of course you won't jump. That goes without saying, even if Mario wasn't on the hook for all that money. And you can tell Gavin his services will no longer be needed."

"Good, Harper, good. I can pay you. I got money now. Mario still hasn't paid me or nothing for what I've done for him, but that's okay because I got a job with a real studio. It's an adult studio and all but it's a real studio. They hired me because my name and picture is in all the papers out here so they're cashing in on all that free publicity. They're paying me, though, Harper, a lot of money, so I can pay you."

"Well, good," I said. "That would be my next question but it's good to know you have steady income."

"I do. Have steady income. Anyhow, get out here as soon as you can, because I need to tell you everything going on out here and I don't want to go over all that on the phone."

"I have ten people scheduled for interviews," I said. "I need to hire an associate to take over my cases while I'm gone. As soon as I hire somebody and get packed, the girls, the dogs and I will be driving out to see you."

"I can't wait to see you," she said. "I got to talk to you about all this. This ain't right what they're doing to me. I didn't do nothing to that man. Nothing at all. Except suck his whiskey dick. That's all."

"I know," I said. "I believe you." If I didn't believe her, I wouldn't take her case.

OVER THE COURSE of the next week, I interviewed applicants. I finally settled on Harvard law grad Liam O'Neil. Liam spoke the best and was eager to get trial work. He'd been working for one of the largest law firms in the city, busting his butt 80 hours a week and never saw the inside of a courtroom. He was ready to jump and decided criminal work was the field for him.

"Okay, then," I said. "I know you have to give notice to your job. I'm leaving soon. I'll continue all my cases for two weeks and you can start working for me after your two weeks are up. We'll go over all these cases so you know what you'll be getting into. Most will plead out and are almost ready to plead, but there will be a few stragglers that might go to trial. Try to get the trial date in the fall. That way I can help you try them, at the very least."

"Sounds good," Liam said with a smile. "I'm ready to get into that courtroom."

"I like your spirit."

I took him to lunch and found out more about him. It turned out he was an openly gay man living in a Downtown

Loft with his boyfriend Tristan. They were looking to possibly get married but Liam was getting cold feet about the whole thing.

"Well," I said. "If you get married, maybe you can have a double wedding with my dad. He's getting married this fall to a Russian guy he met."

"Oh, really?" Liam asked. "How interesting. Do tell."

"There's not much to tell. He fell in love with a man. They're getting married in September and are having their reception at the Mission Hills Country Club. It is what it is."

Liam grinned. "You're taking it very well," he said. "I don't think I could take my dad marrying another guy half as well. He's my dad."

"You just have to let people live their life and don't judge. That's the best way to get along in this world. If somebody makes my father happy, who am I to judge?"

By the time lunch was over, I knew Liam pretty well. I also thought he'd be an excellent addition to my law firm. He was smart, capable and eager.

Most importantly, he was available. And I needed somebody right away.

I was really doing this. I was going to California and defending Ginger on a murder charge.

And, for the first time in a long time, I was really looking forward to digging into a case.

Chapter Five

FIVE DAYS LATER, after screaming at Rina to get packed, I loaded everybody and the dogs into the SUV to make the drive to Los Angeles.

I arrived at the new beach house we would call our home for the next three months.

Just as advertised, the apartment was the bottom portion of a large house right on boardwalk of a Malibu beach. The entire structure was two stories and our part was a bit cramped. It had three small bedrooms, with a small kitchen, a small living room, and two small bathrooms.

Rina, upon going into the house, immediately scrunched up her nose and gave me the stink-eye. "Mom, I hate this place. I hate it. Look how tiny it is. And you didn't say that me and Abby would be sharing a room. I can't share a room with her, Mom. You can't make me. We're not babies, you know."

The girls would have to share a room because I'd have my own room and so would Mia, a girl I found willing to be my live-in nanny for the summer.

"I know you're not babies, but I'm sorry Rina, this is just how it'll be. There are two beds in there, two dressers and a walk-in closet. You girls will be fine."

"We won't be fine," Rina said dramatically. "This place is like a tin can compared to our house back home. A tin can. I can't stand being here, Mom. I hate this place."

Abby put her arm around Rina. "Look," she said, pointing to the patio. It had a patio set and a small pit of hot rocks in a large granite bowl. "It looks like fun to sit out there and watch everyone. And listen to the sound of the ocean."

Abby walked out on the patio. Rina reluctantly followed her as did the dogs. While I unpacked our kitchen items, I watched them. Within a couple of minutes, two cute boys on the boardwalk were talking to them. The boys were carrying skateboards. I raised my eyebrow as I watched Rina flip her hair and prance around flirtatiously. I smiled.

Something told me Rina would take to this place after all.

I WANTED to get right into the case, but, before I did anything, I had to meet my local counsel. Pearl found an attorney willing to sign my pleadings and appear with me at my court appearances. This was necessary, as I didn't know the local rules of the Bar as well as local attorneys and I was unfamiliar with the procedures. I knew the basic rules and laws of the state though. I studied them before coming out. Nonetheless, any attorney not duly licensed in a state cannot practice law in that state unless they have local counsel.

David Jenkins' law practice was in a high-rise in Downtown Los Angeles. His bio indicated he'd been practicing law for the past 15 years and his specialty was white-collar crime. He also had many clients involved in organized crime and racketeering. He had more than a few drug kingpins as clients, as well as some low-level Italian mafia *Capos* and some Russian Mafia *Pakhans*.

And he'd be my local counsel. I wondered what that said about my case. Maybe nothing. Maybe everything. Pearl said David was interested in Ginger's case and eager to help. I thought that odd. David represented the city's big cheeses and Ginger wasn't his typical client.

I got to his office and his receptionist showed me in. It was on one of the top floors of The Wilshire Grand, which, at almost 1,100 feet, was the tallest building in Los Angeles. I was slightly apprehensive when I got to his office because he'd quoted to Pearl a rate of only $150 per hour. He probably charged up to 10x that for his other clients. You don't rent an office on one of the top floors of a building like the Wilshire without making the big bucks.

Curiouser and curiouser.

I went into his office after he summoned me. I swallowed hard as I looked at his distractingly handsome face. His hair was dark, his eyes were hazel, and his body, beneath his green button-down silk shirt and fitted slacks, looked muscular and hard. I bit my lip, hard, remembering Axel's equally handsome face and feeling guilty I was so mesmerized by this man.

He grinned when I walked in. "Harper Ross," he said. "David Jenkins. Damn glad to meet you."

I smiled and extended my hand. "Glad to meet you, too," I said. "Thank you for doing this for me."

He raised an eyebrow. "Sit down, sit down. I guess I

should be thanking you, Harper, for letting me on this case with you."

"I'm sorry?" I said. "I guess I don't understand. You have quite a practice from what I can gather. Lots of wealthy clients who pay top dollar. I don't think you need the exposure from this case."

"Yeah," he said. "I guess I don't. But I still wanted on this case." He shrugged. "And with the rate I'm charging you, it'll practically be *pro bono*. Anyhow, where are you on this case? Have you begun discovery yet?"

"No," I said. "I have to get the lay of the land and try to figure who might've done this. Then I can send discovery requests over to the prosecutor's office. At the moment, however, I don't know what I'm looking for. Or who I'm looking for. I only know this studio executive was found dead in his bed, my client was apparently the last person who saw him alive and he had arsenic in his system. That's all I know right now. I'll do some investigation to find out more about the party and I'll interview witnesses to find out more about the victim's close contacts. I've only just begun."

David nodded. I had the feeling he knew more than he was letting on.

"So," I said. "Do you mind telling me the real reason why you're so interested in this case that you're willing to work it for a tenth of your asking price?"

"Aw, Harper," he said. "I can call you Harper, right?"

"Of course. We'll be working together, so I wouldn't like you calling me Ms. Ross."

"Harper," he said, "I have connections you'll need. I'm tuned into everyone in the business. I know just about everybody Ezra knew and I'm not talking about his professional contacts. You need me on this case."

"That's all well and good but why are you working so

cheap?" I raised my right eyebrow. Something wasn't sitting right with this guy but I couldn't put my finger on it.

"I can work for my going rate if you'd rather. It's $1,000 per hour." He smiled, knowing I wouldn't pay $1,000 per hour. Not for him and not for anybody in Los Angeles. All he had to do was sign off on my pleadings, appear at my pre-trial hearings and be my second-chair at trial. His part of the case would be relatively minor. I'd do most of the heavy lifting.

"No, no, that's okay," I said. "Let's just go with the stated quote of $150 per hour. I just didn't know why you were willing to work for that little money, that's all."

"I thought so," he said. "Now, Harper, what can I do for you?"

"Well, I'll have to get a read-out of what hearings are scheduled for this case. I'll need you to go to the courthouse with me on those days. And-"

"You have your first pre-trial conference scheduled for two weeks from today," he said. "In the Malibu Courthouse. Division 18. June 25, 1:30. I already have it on my schedule." He grinned and I looked down at the floor. "Anything else you need, Harper?" He raised his eyebrows flirtatiously and I felt uncomfortable.

Very uncomfortable.

"How did you find all this out so soon? I don't even know what hearings are scheduled yet."

"I'm efficient. And I have a great assistant. Sherry. I think you met her. She keeps me on top of things."

"Okay, then. I guess you'll be at that pre-trial conference on June 25 at 1:30. Other than that, though, I don't really know. I have to get cracking on this case."

"I have a feeling you'll be calling me a lot once you find

out what was going on with Ezra Cohen. This wasn't some squeaky clean guy."

I felt a pit in my stomach grow as I spoke with David. There was something about this case that made me extremely nervous although I couldn't figure out what it was.

"I have to ask – do you know Ginger at all? Have you come across her? She makes adult movies and guess she's still prostituting even though she might be a high-priced call girl as opposed to just working the street. Have any of your clients come across her somehow?"

He shook his head. "No. Nobody I know, including my clients, have heard of her before this happened. Now, of course, her name is everywhere. Ezra Cohen was a big fucking deal in this city. His murder has shaken everybody in this town. In the movie industry, everybody knows everybody. When one of their own has been murdered in cold blood, it attracts a lot of attention."

I wrote this down. "And that's why you want on this case so badly? You want justice for this guy? Do you have a lot of friends in the movie industry?"

"No," he said. "I mean, yeah, I know people in the industry, but I don't run in those circles. Neither do my clients." He looked at me and I could somehow see the wheels turning in his head. "But it's an appealing thought that I can make some contacts in the movie industry. Getting clients from that industry would allow me to transition away from what I'm currently doing. I'd be trading one booming industry – the drug trade – for another – the movie industry - but my clients wouldn't be quite as scummy." He laughed. "Then again, maybe that's not true. People involved in film aren't exactly angels themselves."

I nodded. "True that."

He looked at his watch. "I have court coming up soon. Is there anything else I can do for you?" He reached into his desk and pulled out a large file. "Here. This is what the prosecutor's office gave me on Ezra's murder. That can get you started on your discovery process."

"Thanks for that," I said. "And, if you don't mind, I'll just show myself out."

I left and took the elevator down to the lobby. My mind was on David and the slight degree of apprehension I felt in his office. He made me uncomfortable even though he couldn't be nicer. It could've been that he was extremely handsome and I was physically attracted to him. That made me feel guilty, because I had a great, loyal guy waiting for me in Kansas City.

Whatever. I'd have to shrug it off. I was getting a real bargain with this guy. He was one of the most prominent members of the Los Angeles Bar and would help me at a bargain-basement rate. I'd have to take him at his word that he wanted to get involved because he wanted a foot in the door of the movie industry. Nothing in this guy's background told me he wasn't anything but above-board. I did my due diligence on him and he'd never had a Bar Complaint against him. He didn't have a criminal record.

His background was better than mine.

AFTER I SPOKE WITH DAVID, I went to see Ginger. She was living in a three-bedroom house in West Hollywood. This apparently was her new house, as her old place was getting too crowded. I didn't think she was trading up with this place because the West Hollywood area was notorious for criminal activity, but it wasn't my call.

Ginger wanted to live in this neighborhood, which was all that mattered.

I knocked on the door and looked around. Her house was cute, really, and well-maintained. It had a picture window in the front. Around the house were small palm trees that looked like bushes and flowers surrounded her porch. Also on the lawn was a 50-foot date palm tree – my favorite kind of tree in California. It was majestic, with the fronds fanning out on top and a sturdy and strong trunk.

Surprisingly enough, there was nobody on the street.

She opened the door and immediately hugged me and started crying. "Harper, Harper, Harper, I'm so happy to see you. I don't know what I'd do if you didn't come out here."

I hugged her back and walked into her house. The front room had two old couches, a big-screen TV and a coffee table that had nothing but a bong and a bag of pot on it. I was relieved to see there weren't lines of coke on the coffee table. There were colorful pictures on the wall taken from different film festivals over the years – an origami film reel in red with yellow background and the words "Asian American film festival May 6-18," and a poster with an eye in the middle that apparently was from a London Film Festival. There were several others from different locations, such as Paris and San Diego. Each of these posters was in a solid black frame and were strategically placed around the room. In the corner of the room was a cat tower, with three different levels and a cat sleeping on each level. The cats all eyed me warily and the one on the top of the tower rolled over on her back.

I smiled. This place looked aggressively normal, aside from the bong and the pot on the coffee table, but I figured that, if you think about it, the bong and pot were pretty normal items as well. Especially since pot was legal in California.

I sat on the couch and Ginger lay down on the other couch. "Goddamn Mario wants me to work today. He wants me to work every day, but Imma tell him to fuck off. I'm tired of him telling me what to do and not paying me."

I looked in her eyes and saw how high she was. Her eyes were tiny slits and her pupils were dilated. I hoped and prayed she was only high on pot. This was a safe assumption because pot was the only thing I saw around the place, but I couldn't be completely sure.

"I thought you're working for a real studio?"

"I am. They're trying to get me exclusive but Mario won't let me off. I signed a contract with Mario and he doesn't want me to work for just that studio. He wants a cut from everything I get from that studio, too, even though I found Dark Angel on my own. I don't know what to do, Harper. I'm afraid this studio will fire me if Mario keeps pestering them about him being my manager and him saying he has the say on what jobs I take and what I do."

"Tell me about this Mario character. Who is he and how did you find him?"

"He found me. In Kansas City. I was working the street and he told me he was a talent scout looking for good girls to work in L.A. I knew what kind of work he wanted for me and was excited about doing it. I was tired of the johns back home. You never knew when you might find somebody who's gonna beat on you or do things they don't pay for like anal. Mario said that in the movies, the girls know what will happen. If you want to get beat up, you can. I don't, but some girls do. It's your choice and they pay you extra. They pay you extra for anal, cream pies and facial abuse. And bondage. All that stuff is extra. I like that idea, Harper because I know I'll get paid extra for these things. Before, when I was working the street, I was never sure if I would get extra money for these things."

"Cream pies? Facial abuse?" I wasn't sure what these terms meant.

"Yeah. Cream pie is when the guy shoots inside you and you spread your legs and the stuff comes out your pussy. Facial abuse is when the guy beats on your face while he fucks you. Bondage is-"

"I know what bondage is," I said with a smile. "I saw *Fifty Shades of Grey*, same as everybody else. Or I should say I read the first book. Couldn't go onto the second one, though. Not my cup of tea."

"Yeah, well, it's not like in that book or nothin'. It's worse than that. I don't do that right now. My new boss tells me I won't have to do all that. He said only girls who get desperate do that stuff, bondage and beatings and stuff, or the girls that like it. He said I have such a name now I can get away with doing the usual threesomes, gang-bangs and girl on girl. None of this beating and bondage bullshit."

"And what is Mario's last name?"

"I don't know. I just know him as Mario." Ginger shrugged. "I'm bad about getting last names sometimes. It comes from always being with johns. Johns don't usually tell you their names, and when they do, it's probably fake. So I don't know Mario's last name."

"You never got a business card or anything like that?" I was talking to the wind in asking that question, and I knew it, but I had to ask. There was a chance Ginger did *some* diligence on this Mario guy, however slight.

"If I got his business card, I'd know his last name, right?"

She made a point.

"What does this Mario guy look like?"

She stood up. "Yay high," she said, putting her hand slightly above her head. Ginger was around 5'6" and seemed to be indicating he was slightly taller. Maybe 5'7" or 5'9." "Bald head except around his ears. Big bushy eyebrows. Ear hair. Not fat, not skinny, just kinda there. I think he might have dentures." She shrugged. "I guess he's in his 50s, maybe older. I'm not real good at knowing people's ages just by looking at them."

"And he works out here, right? He found you in Kansas City but he has a home base here, right?"

"Right."

"And what was he doing in Kansas City? Do you know that?"

It seemed somewhat unusual to me that a Los Angeles adult film scout would be looking for girls in Kansas City, but, then again, maybe he was specifically looking in the heartland for that wholesome look. Not that Ginger was necessarily wholesome looking, with her bleached-blonde hair and tons of makeup, but I could imagine the right hair and stylist could make her look that way. At any rate, she had a certain naïveté that could be very appealing on-screen.

"He just said he was looking for girls, that's all. I wanted off the street because of Cooper hassling me all the time so this looked like a good opportunity. It's worked out, too, because I still get johns, but they're classier johns than the ones I got back home."

I made notes as she spoke. "What is this studio? The place where you're working now?"

"It's called Dark Angel," she said. "It's in Van Nuys in the Valley. It's a new studio, trying to get its name out there, and my new boss, his name is Dale Thompson, he tells me

I'm his lead girl. He tells me he wants to build his studio around me." She smiled. "I never thought I'd become popular like that, Harper."

"Ginger," I said. "You might be popular but you're also facing a murder charge. I don't want you to lose sight of that."

"But you can get me off, can't you, Harper? Like you did with that Darnell kid. You can help me beat this charge." Her big blue eyes got wide as she looked at me. They were bloodshot and her pupils were dilated but she still looked like an innocent school-girl when she gave me that look. I could see her appeal. She probably starred in the kinds of movies where her hair was in pigtails and she was dressed in a short Catholic school uniform – plaid skirts that barely covered her ass and a cropped button-down that tied around her midriff, like an early Britney Spears. Probably sucking a lollipop seductively while she licked her lips and talked about how she wanted to get spanked.

"I'll do what I can, but I'm not a miracle worker." I took a look at the coroner's report, the first document in the file David gave me. "The poison in his system was apparently given at the same time you were with him, so that complicates things."

"What does that mean?"

"That means he was poisoned at the same time you were in the room. It sounds like somebody set you up, although I don't know who. You're new in town. I'm assuming you haven't yet made any real enemies. So why would somebody go through all that trouble to set you up for this murder?"

"I don't know Harper, but I know you can probably figure it out."

"Tell me everything that happened. Did you bring him anything to drink?"

"Yeah. I brought him a glass of scotch."

"And that glass of scotch is what poisoned him," I said, looking at the coroner's report. "Says so right here."

Ginger shook her head. "That's not possible. I didn't poison him. I didn't do it, Harper. I didn't."

"Somebody did. Somebody put that poison into that glass of scotch before you gave it to him. Obviously. Either that or you did it. If you did it, just tell me. I'll get you a good deal. I promise."

"I didn't do nothin'," Ginger protested. "I promise you."

"Okay, okay. But tell me who gave you the glass of scotch you gave to Ezra."

"I don't remember."

"Think. Was it a man? A woman?"

"I don't remember."

"Come on, Ginger, you have to give me something."

She shook her head.

"You can figure out who did it, can't you Harper? You can figure it out."

I sighed as I looked at the file David gave me. It had the name of the private investigator David was using on this case. "I hope you're right. In the meantime, I'll give this investigator a call and see what he knows. And I'll do a background investigation on Ezra. See who he knows and what he was up to. From what David tells me, Ezra wasn't a choir boy."

"Who's David?" Ginger asked.

"David Jenkins. He's a prominent defense attorney in town. He'll be helping me with this case."

Ginger shuddered. "I don't want no man attorney, Harper. Not after that last creeper. That Gavin creeper."

"He won't be your attorney. I will. That hasn't changed. I just need local counsel to practice law in California. I'm not licensed out here. He's a very high-powered attorney, very respected. I don't think he's a creeper like Gavin was. He'll be an asset, I promise."

"Well, you better not get off my case and leave me with him, Harper."

This was getting a bit strange. "I won't do that. I promise. But why do you believe I would?"

"I don't know. I'm just telling you not to do that, that's all."

"I won't. But David will be good for this case. He seems to know his way around the city and the players in it. I don't know this city or anybody in it. He knows the prosecutors, the judges and all that. That's very important, more than you know. He can tell me what makes one judge tick and another one tock. He'll know what evidence will fly with one judge and what another judge will shut down. He doesn't know the people in the movie industry but he knows shady people who hang around the movie industry. Without him, I'm flying blind."

Ginger seemed satisfied with the information. "Well, okay, then, Harper. I guess it's okay you got this David guy on this case. As long as you don't leave me with him and go back to Kansas City, it'll be okay."

I frowned, suddenly realizing that Ginger's abandonment issues were getting in the way. And why wouldn't they? She never had anybody who cared about her. She only knew people, mainly men, who used her.

I put my arm around her shoulder. "That won't happen," I said. "I came out here to help you. I won't cut and run."

"Thank you."

"Now, if you don't mind, I have to meet with the private investigator assigned to this case and find out what he knows. He can hopefully get some witnesses lined up for me and can tell me what direction to go. I like to do a lot of the investigation myself, usually, but in this case, I'll have to rely on the PI."

"I hope you can get information you need from that guy, Harper. That PI guy." She nodded. "I seen those detective shows. Those PIs always know what's what."

"I hope you're right about this one. I hope he knows what's what. In the meantime, lay low. Stay away from people in the non-adult movie industry. Don't go to parties or anything like that."

"I will, but I like having johns in the industry. They pay good."

I left Ginger's house and called the PI, whose name was Tony Marinaro. He wasn't in, so I left a message for him to call me.

In the meantime, I decided to speak with the cops on the case and see Ezra's home to see what I could glean from the crime scene.

But I never quite made it there.

Chapter Six

I WOKE up on my patio. I had no idea what happened or how I made it there. My head was absolutely throbbing. I squinted and saw it was nighttime. I swore I left Ginger's house when it was still daylight, yet, here I was, laying on the chaise on my patio in the dark. I could hear people walking by on the boardwalk, could see people building bonfires and could hear the sounds of the ocean. I could tell it wasn't all that late because the beach usually cleared out around midnight during the week.

I looked down and saw vomit on the patio next to me.

And a half-drunk bottle of scotch.

I picked up the bottle of scotch, wondering about it.

It was then that I became aware of my body. Aware of how I was feeling. It was a sickening feeling yet also a feeling of coming home. It was a feeling I'd known for twenty years, a feeling I was desperate never to feel again, yet a feeling I knew I would somehow, someway, always return to.

I was drunk.

I got to my feet, feeling unsteady, and tried to piece

together what happened. I was driving from Ginger's house to Ezra's house, where I would go to get a feeling for what happened the night Ezra died.

I left a message for the PI and then…and then…

I went into the house and saw Rina and Abby were sitting on the couch with Mia. Stella and Sue were also sitting on the couch with everyone. Mia stood up when she saw me come in. "Late night, huh?" she asked me. "The girls told me you work late a lot so I shouldn't worry."

I felt like the room was spinning and everything was blurry. Everything seemed like it was a different reality.

It felt like the reality I lived in when I was a heavy drinker. I used to take a shot in the morning, a shot in the afternoon and then spend my evenings getting blasted in front of the television. I would turn on TCM, my favorite station, because I adored old movies, and would drink the night away while I watched Katherine Hepburn's pratfalls or Steve McQueen's capers.

I pointed ineffectually towards the patio. I saw worry on Abby's face and annoyance on Rina's.

The girls didn't know about my background. They didn't know I was a recovering alcoholic. I took my last drink several months before they came to live with me permanently.

Mia's eyebrows scrunched. "I don't understand?" She shook her head. "You were just pointing to the patio but I'm not quite sure what you're trying to tell me."

"Did you see anybody out there with me?" I asked her. "On the patio with me? Drinking scotch with me?"

At that, Rina shook her head. "I knew it. I knew Mom was drunk. I could tell. She has that look on her face, that look like our Mom used to get when she came home from the bars. Wasted."

I was a terrible role-model for her and Abby, but I didn't know what to do about that. I was always lecturing them on the evils of alcohol, always admonishing them not to go down the road I went down. I never used my own experiences in these lectures, but I used other people as examples of what not to do. I had a hard time admitting to the girls I had such a weakness, such a dark corner of my psyche I tried never to acknowledge.

"No," Mia said. "In fact, I never heard you out there at all. We've been sitting here watching TV. I took them to the beach today. Don't worry, I made sure they both wore sunscreen and I put that umbrella up. The girls had a blast riding their boogie boards while I kept a close eye on them."

I felt somewhat impatient while she spoke. I didn't want to hear the details about their day. I just wanted her to tell me what she knew about how I ended up on the patio.

I put my hand on the back of my head and it felt wet. I looked at my fingers and saw blood. Somebody had hit me on my head and, somehow, must've forced me to drink alcohol while I was unconscious. Who would do that to me? And how could they get a drink down my throat while I was unconscious? Was that even possible?

I shook my head rapidly. "Okay, Mia, you took the girls down to the beach and they had a great time. I'm glad to hear it. But I need you to tell me how I got here because I don't remember. I don't remember and I have to assume my car isn't here, either." A garage was attached on the side of the house. I went out there.

My car *was* there.

What the hell was going on?

I turned around and Abby was standing right behind me. She pointed to the car. "You didn't drive like this, did you?" Her little hands were wringing in front her, over and over again. Her lower lip quivered and tears appeared in her eyes. "Tell me you didn't drive like this."

I opened my mouth but nothing came out. I wanted to tell her I didn't drive in my condition, but, truth be told, I didn't know if I did or not. I didn't think I drove in my condition but did I? When I was an alcoholic, there were many, many times when I made it home not having remembered driving. I always was amazed I could make it home in such a condition without killing somebody or going to jail.

I didn't think this was the case this time but was it? Did I drive while drunk enough to have blacked out?

"Abby, honey, I didn't drive like this," I said, not knowing if I was being truthful. "I would never drive like this."

"But you're drunk and you just said you didn't know if your car was here or not. In fact, you just said you assumed your car wasn't here. That would mean you didn't remember driving home."

I had to admit, at 13, little Abby was too smart for her own damned good. I put my arm around her. "Abby, please believe me. I didn't drive like this. Somebody must've driven me home. And then that somebody must've taken a cab to his or her own house or maybe an Uber car."

I put my hand on the back of my head again and still felt the warm blood. My hair felt matted. "I need to take a shower," I said, going back into the house.

Mia stood up again when I went back in. Stella and Sue, for their part, got off the couch, came over and softly whined. "Are you okay?" Mia asked. "You look a little pale."

I nodded. "I'm taking a shower." There was a small bathroom attached to my bedroom. "Do you mind coming into my bedroom with me? I need to talk to you," I asked Mia.

She looked worried, but nodded and followed me into the bedroom. "What's going on?" she asked.

"Um," I began. "I don't know how to tell you this, but I don't remember how I got this way. I didn't want to talk to you in front of the girls because they don't know this about me." I sat down on the bed and looked at my shaking hands. The blood on my right hand was dried and I licked my finger to taste it. I wanted to make sure it really was blood. I knew right away that's what it was. Blood. From my head.

Mia sat on the bed. "They don't know what about you?"

"I'm a recovering alcoholic," I said. "I've been off and on the wagon for the past few years. The last time I had a drink, though, was years ago. I haven't had a drink since before the girls came to live with me. I'm not very strong when it comes to that, so I can't have even a single drink. And…" I shook my head and suddenly realized I was crying. "And…I'm drunk right now, really drunk. I don't know how I got this way, though. All I know is I was driving from Ginger's house. I wanted to go to Ezra Cohen's house to check out the crime scene. I put in a phone call to the private investigator on this case, Tony Marinaro, and…" I shook my head. "I don't remember much after that."

I scratched my upper arm and suddenly had to vomit. My body wasn't used to alcohol so I had a very low tolerance for the drink. Because it had been literally years since I had a drink, I was easily susceptible to its effects.

"Excuse me," I said and ran to the toilet and heaved into it.

I hung my head over the bowl and more tears started to pour. Goddammit, I fought so hard for my sobriety. So hard. I white-knuckled it the whole way but got through it by showing myself I was stronger than the drink. I got through it because I knew if I didn't I'd possibly lose the girls. And, even if I didn't lose them, I'd surely lose their respect.

Now, here I was, heaving into the toilet. I never thought I'd be here again. Yet I somehow knew this was only the beginning. This feeling I had, this feeling that reality was gauzy and the world around me hazy, was a feeling I craved.

I didn't know why I craved this reality. I only knew I did.

Mia looked confused. "I don't understand. You don't know how you got drunk?"

"No," I said. "I don't. I haven't willingly taken a drink for years. I have this nasty bump on my head and it's bleeding. That's why I asked if you saw me come home. Somebody brought me home, dumped me on that patio chaise and left a half-empty bottle of scotch so I knew what poison is coursing through my veins. I know that sounds bizarre, and, believe me, it sounds just as bizarre in my ears. You probably think I'm absolutely crazy and that's okay. I just need to know who did this and why. It had to be somebody who knew about my problems, though. That much is absolutely certain."

"I don't understand?" Mia asked, looking utterly confused.

I nodded. "Okay, let me break it down to you. Somebody obviously wants me off the wagon. I'd think this person, whoever they are, wants me to do a shitty job on Ginger's case. That's the only thing I can think of. Somebody knows I have a real problem with alcohol, and if I get off the wagon, I'll end up screwing up Ginger's case. So, this person, whoever this person is, has to not only know I have a problem with alcohol but also has an interest in ensuring Ginger goes down for killing Ezra Cohen."

Mia made a face. "Who would go through all that trouble?"

"That's what I'm trying to figure out. See, the weird thing is, the last thing I remember was being in front of Ginger's house. Somebody must've come behind me as I stood on her sidewalk and hit me on the head. Then they must've taken me somewhere and poured alcohol down my throat. That's the only thing that makes sense."

"You're not making sense," she said. "Listen, I know it's difficult to admit when you've messed up and started drinking again. I had two alcoholic parents. They were always trying to stop drinking. They would quit drinking, sometimes for years, just like you. Then something would happen that would knock them both off the wagon. My father lost his job through no fault of his own and started drinking again. My brother drowned in our backyard pool and they both started drinking again. It was always something. They could handle life sober when life wasn't throwing curveballs but once life started throwing those curveballs, they couldn't handle it."

"I'm very sorry to hear about your brother," I said.

"Oh, it's okay. I shouldn't have said he drowned. I mean he did, but they revived him and he recovered completely. But even that scare was enough for my parents to start drinking again. They blamed themselves for that happening. I always told them that not everything in life was their fault, but they never quite believed that."

I shook my head. "That's just it. I mean, I know what you're saying – it's attractive to handle stressors with alcohol. But that's not what's happening. I'm not under great stress. I mean, I am, but no more than usual. Seriously. I have this big case with Ginger but I've had plenty of murder cases these past few years, including one involving my beloved uncle. In the process, I found out things about my uncle I never knew before – he has multiple personalities and was kidnapped, held hostage and raped by a serial killer for years when he was a young boy. I represented my college rapist in a case recently. In my last case, my client was a perfectly innocent 18-year-old African-American boy facing the death penalty. I've gone through a lot of stress these past few years and haven't broken down. I certainly wouldn't be breaking down now."

I was sobering up and becoming agitated. To my horror, the bottle of scotch on my patio was summoning me in a way I hadn't experienced in a long time. I knew that one drink, just one drink, was enough to send me into a tailspin.

So did the person who did this to me. That much was clear.

Who? Who would've known my weakness? It was a secret shame, something I didn't share with my closest friends and family. Tammy, my law partner, knew about it, but she was the only one. My father didn't know about it, neither did my mother nor my brothers and sisters. I carefully hid my addiction from everyone I knew.

Who else would know about it? Let alone who would know about it in California?

I wracked my brain as I told Mia I needed to take a shower. She left and I undressed and got into the stall and let the warm water rush over me. I shampooed my hair and soaped up and was startled to see the water turn red with my blood.

Was that gash on my head so bad I'd need stitches? It certainly seemed that way. It was still bleeding. It shouldn't still be bleeding.

After I got out of the shower, I looked in the mirror and parted my hair. I saw a large gash. I got a bottle of NuSkin out of my medicine cabinet and I carefully applied it. I wouldn't go to the emergency room just yet. I first would see if this NuSkin patched up the wound enough that I could avoid that trip.

I was still feeling drunk and the last thing I needed was to get in my car and drive to the hospital. I could call an Uber but didn't want to bother with that, either.

I knew what I wanted to do.

I went into the living room and saw Mia had apparently put the girls to bed. She was in the kitchen, doing dishes from dinner, and the girls and dogs were nowhere to be found. Stella slept with Abby while Sue slept with Rina.

"They were tuckered," she said. "From all that sun. They're in bed."

I nodded. "I'll go down to the beach."

She smiled. "Have fun."

I went out to the patio and picked up that bottle of scotch.

And then I walked to the beach and stood in the cold water. It lapped around my toes as the tide went in and out, in and out.

While I stood in that surf, I opened the bottle of scotch and poured some down my throat. It was tingly and bitter, yet smooth, as it was high-dollar.

It was like welcoming an old friend.

Chapter Seven

THE NEXT DAY, I had a hangover to end all hangovers. My body just wasn't used to alcohol, so my head was pounding, my hands were shaking, and every single cell felt filled to the brim with scotch. My stomach was churning and I went into the bathroom to vomit.

I felt like I always used to whenever I had a severe bender. Back then, I ended my hangovers with the hair of the dog.

Which is what I did. I walked out of my bedroom and saw everybody eating breakfast. I had a shot of scotch I put in my robe pocket before I went into the kitchen. This shot was still in my pocket when I got a cup of coffee. Coffee was something I never liked to drink when sober, because I didn't like how it made me feel – jittery and slightly high. But coffee was the only thing I wanted after a night of drinking.

Especially coffee with a shot of scotch.

I poured the cup of coffee, turned my back and got the shot of scotch out of my pocket and poured it in the cup.

Then I turned back around and sipped my coffee while I watched the two girls eat their cereal. "What are you guys planning for today?" I asked them.

Rina shrugged. "Go down to the beach, I guess," she said. "Unless Mia wants to take us around."

"Actually," Mia said to the girls, "I'd like to take you guys to Rodeo Drive so we can look around. Maybe have lunch. That's something that's always fun even if we can't afford to shop there so much."

I sipped my coffee some more. "Excuse me," I said. "I'll be right back."

I went into my room, poured myself another shot of scotch and put that shot into my robe pocket as well. Then I went out, poured myself another cup of coffee and put that shot of scotch into it. It slightly burned as it went down my throat, or maybe it was the coffee that burned. Either way, something burned, and I shook my head rapidly. "Woooo," I said under my breath. "That coffee hit the spot."

"You going to join us for breakfast?" Mia asked me.

"Um, no," I said. "I have to start working Ginger's case. I've submitted a motion for a speedy trial so we can get back to Kansas City in time for the girls to go back to school. That means everything will be on a lightning fast time-table. There can be no dilly-dallying. I have to figure out what happened to Ezra so I can put together a decent defense for Ginger. Otherwise…" I shook my head as I thought about poor Ginger going to prison for something she didn't do. "I can't think about that."

I was feeling slightly buzzed, which took the edge off my hangover and relaxed me. That was the feeling I always craved before – the feeling of being relaxed. That was always an elusive feeling. I was Type-A to the bone and tended to feel anxious. When I was sober, I always second-guessed everything I did. I knew why – I had suffered from bi-polar disorder my entire life. The meds I took to balance my emotions helped me immensely but alcohol always helped me more. Of course, the problem with alcohol was that it caused all kinds of other problems.

So be it. I knew alcohol would affect how well my mood stabilizer worked, which I wasn't looking forward to. But, right at that moment, I was buzzing just enough to be mildly euphoric. That wouldn't last, so I surreptitiously filled a small water bottle with scotch and put it in my bag. I made a mental note to buy a flask at the first sporting goods store I could find. Putting scotch into a water bottle seemed trashy.

I got dressed, put one sunglasses and put my wild red hair in a high pony. Then I went out into the living room and gave Rina and Abby a kiss on their cheeks. "I'll see you two girls later, after I get all my investigation done for the day. Maybe we can go to the beach tonight, build a fire and roast wieners and marshmallows. Would you like that?"

Rina shrugged but Abby nodded eagerly. "That sounds like fun, Mom. Let's do that after it gets dark."

"You got it," I said. "Anyhow, I'll be out for the rest of the day, but I'll see all you girls when I get home." I looked at Mia. "I'll call you and let you know what time I'll be home. Don't expect me home before 6, though."

And, at that, I went into my car, got out the water bottle, swigged back some scotch, backed my car up, and immediately thought better of it.

What was I doing? Driving drunk? Seriously?

No. I wouldn't drive drunk.

I got on my phone and summoned Uber.

And then drank a few more shots while waiting for the Uber to pick me up.

While I waited for the Uber, I went back in the house. "Uh, I won't drive today," I said. "I'm nervous about driving after what happened last night. I don't remember driving home last night and I don't want something like that to happen again. So, I'm calling an Uber to pick me up."

Lying was coming easy agin. When I was drinking, I constantly lied to everyone, including myself. When I worked for a firm and everybody would go to happy hour after work, I never went. I wanted to get smashed on my own so I always told everyone I was tired and wanted to go to bed early. If I was invited to dinner with my family and was having a bad day and wanted to drink alone, I'd call and tell them I was sick. I was always being asked out on dates, but I never went, because I couldn't be good company unless I was hammered. I felt I had nothing to add to anyone's life. So, if somebody asked me out, I would always tell the guy I was already in a relationship.

Those were some minor lies I habitually told. I was always so careful to ensure my addiction wasn't apparent to anybody but me. I went to just enough family dinners that nobody questioned me. I always drank alone – if I happened to be out in public where there was alcohol around, I wouldn't order a drink, because I knew it would start me on a bender. For years, I didn't have a social life, at all, because of my alcoholism.

Now, here I was, with everything to lose – Axel, my girls, my career. Well, not necessarily my career, because I always functioned just fine when I was drinking. And I couldn't literally lose my girls because I'd adopted them.

I bit my lip, a voice in the back of my head telling me this wasn't true at all. I *could* lose my girls if I got bad. They could be taken from me and put into foster care. That's where they were when I adopted them – they were in foster care because my former client killed their mother.

I shook my head.

The Uber car picked me up and I got in.

"Uh, I need to change my destination," I said.

"Sure," my driver said.

I got on my cell phone, immediately found the location of an AA meeting happening in my neighborhood and put it in.

I would nip this in the bud this time.

Chapter Eight

BEFORE I WENT into the Malibu Bluffs Park Center, also known as the Michael Landon Community Center, I longingly looked at my scotch-filled water bottle. 90% of me wanted to down that entire bottle before going into the Center. 10% of me knew this wasn't the right thing to do. I could trash myself and my life but I couldn't risk losing the girls. After all, their guardian *ad litem* told me that if she found out I was drinking again, she wouldn't hesitate to recommend that the girls be removed from the home.

It occurred to me that those two girls actually saved my life, because I had no doubt that, if not for them, I'd end up going down the same road as before.

One last glance at the water bottle of scotch and I poured it on the ground. "Alcohol abuse," I said with a smile. That was always a joke drunks would tell – if somebody spilled their drink, everyone would say it was "alcohol abuse."

Then I went into the building. I found the meeting room and went in.

This was a 7 AM meeting. It was safe to say that many of the people in the room were professionals just like me. Most of them were dressed for some kind of professional job – the women in dresses and pant-suits, the men mainly in button-down silk shirts and ties. Some of them had suit-coats resting on the back of their chairs. There were also some people who looked like they were heading to the beach or perhaps going to a job waiting tables or to Starbucks, for they were wearing shorts and a t-shirt, or jeans and a casual short-sleeved shirt.

I didn't look around the room too much so I was more than surprised when a now-familiar face got up from the long table and came and sat next to me. "You too, huh?"

I turned my head and saw David Jenkins sitting next to me. I laughed lightly and extended my hand. "Yeah," I said. "But this wasn't my fault. I've been on the wagon for several years, and, you won't believe this, but somebody hit me on the head yesterday and apparently force-fed me alcohol." I felt silly saying that to him. It sounded like I was completely joking or making an excuse.

David just nodded, though. "Really? That happened to you?" He furrowed his brow and looked concerned. I wondered if he was genuinely concerned or just trying to make me feel better about being there.

Everybody was milling about the room, chatting while getting coffee, water and donuts , but when a large bald-headed man in a golf shirt cleared his throat, everyone took their seats. And then everybody stood up and held hands.

"God grant me the serenity to accept the things I cannot change, the courage to change the things I can, and the wisdom to know the difference," we all said in unison and then we all sat back down.

The bald-headed guy smiled at everyone. "Hello," he

said, looking around the room. "I see a couple of new faces. If you're new and want to introduce yourself, please do. But before you introduce yourself, I'd like to tell you the rules of this meeting. They're pretty standard, but our rules are that nobody interrupts anybody else while they're talking; everybody will have the chance to speak; if you don't want to speak, you don't have to, you can pass; everybody will be respectful of everybody else, which means there will be no judgments on what people have to say; and, of course, whatever is said in this room must stay in this room."

I nodded. I was familiar with these rules, having been in AA meetings in the past.

Then, one by one, new people introduced themselves and told why they were there. But when it came to me, I didn't know what to say about what prompted me into this place. I couldn't tell the truth – that somebody did this to me. Somebody who apparently wanted me to fail in my defense of Ginger. That was still the only thing that made sense to me.

"Uh, my name is Harper and I'm an alcoholic," I began.

"Hello, Harper," everyone else said in unison.

I took a deep breath. "I'm here because I was recovering from my alcoholism and then something happened last night and I took a drink. Once I got going, I didn't really stop. I drank a quarter of a bottle of scotch last night while I stood in the sand, the waves crashing around me. I probably could've drowned last night, that's how wasted I got. Then I woke up and felt like crap, so I started drinking again immediately. I almost got into my car to drive in that condition, but I knew I couldn't. But I filled a water bottle up this morning with pure scotch and I wanted to drink it throughout the day. I was even going to buy a flask I could take around with me." I hung my head. "I have two girls at home I adopted. They were in foster care because their mother was murdered. I can't lose them, so I came here, instead of doing what I wanted."

Everybody was interested in what I was saying. They were all looking at me, their faces transfixed. Most of them were nodding their heads knowingly. They had all been where I was – sneaking around, putting alcohol in their morning coffee, carrying alcohol with them to work so they could take a sip throughout the day, getting hammered at night after work. Most of them were probably functioning alcoholics, just like I was – they had work and family responsibilities and they might've met these responsibilities admirably. Probably nobody knew just how buzzed they were throughout the day because they could pass as normal.

Just like I did for all those years.

I was in a room of people who really understood me, and I realized I'd have to continue these meetings even when I went back to Kansas City. I had gone along, white-knuckling it the entire way, without going to meetings, but seeing these hopeful and understanding faces made me wonder why I always wanted to go through it alone. I was still so ashamed that it was hard for me to admit failure to others. It was doubly-difficult to admit failures to myself. I couldn't really verbalize them to anybody.

"Glad you're here, Harper," the bald-headed leader said. "My name is Frank Lorenzo, and I'm the facilitator of this meeting. Just as an FYI, there are no professional mental health workers in this meeting. Everybody is here for the same reason you are – they've had a problem with alcohol abuse in the past." He paused. "Now, last week, everybody was given a homework assignment. I asked everyone to write down what they are grateful for. I'd like to hear everyone's response to this, but if anybody just needs to get something off their chest, or would like to share some kind of milestone, that's fine too. We'll start with Patty."

Patty was 20-something and dressed in a pant-suit, a leather briefcase by her side. She had blonde hair pulled in a chignon, and her nails were painted a pale pink and perfectly manicured. She didn't wear a ton of makeup – it was just subtle – but she was pretty and looked like a fresh-faced college student. Fortunately for her, the ravages of alcohol hadn't yet shown up on her face.

She spoke about what she was grateful for and also told the group what was stressing her that week. "I just found my boyfriend is having an affair, and the ironic thing is, he's having an affair with my girlfriend." She shrugged and smiled. "The crazy thing is, I've offered a three-way with me, him and my girlfriend, whose name is Sharon, but he always refused. Now he's seeing her behind my back and I'm pissed at both of them, so this whole thing means I'm maybe losing both my girlfriend and my boyfriend at once. That's devastating." She took a sip of coffee and didn't meet anybody's eyes, but everyone else's eyes were transfixed on her and what she was saying.

One by one, everyone offered sympathy or advice, and then Patty started to cry and somebody passed her a box of Kleenex and put her arm around the sobbing Patty. "I guess Rob will get his things today and if he moves in with Sharon, I'll want to kill them both. I have stalking tendencies anyhow. I've had restraining orders against me because I get so obsessive with people who dump me. All I want is to go to Sharon's house and wait to see if Rob shows up, and I want to be drinking a bottle of whiskey while I do my stake-out. I know that sounds crazy, and I think I might have to go to multiple meetings every day and tell my story so I don't do that. I also just want to die. I want to go home, take a razor to my wrists and get into the bathtub. Make Sharon and Rob regret what they've done."

When she said that, several people told her that if she was tempted to harm herself or others, she had to check herself into a facility until that feeling passed. Of course, there was a 99.9% chance that poor Patty was just blowing off steam, but you could never be too careful…

After Patty told her story, everybody gave their advice, and she'd calmed down a bit, it was onto the next person, and then the person after that. Everybody started out with something they were grateful for – one person was grateful to find a parking space in front of the courthouse when he went in for his DWI (a miracle!); another was grateful her mother had stopped nagging her to get married and have children (she finally accepted it wasn't for me, so we're speaking again); some people talked about how they're grateful to God, others expressed they were grateful they could surf whenever they wanted.

It was finally David's opportunity to speak, and I got the feeling he was a regular at this meeting. Somebody asked him about how things were going with his daughter, who apparently was living with his ex in Seattle, while somebody else asked him how things were going with a particular court case he was worried about.

David nodded and looked at me nervously. "Bella is doing fine with her mother now, but still wants to live with me. I got a court date to make that happen, but it's in Seattle, and her mother is fighting me tooth and nail. As for that other case I was talking about, I ended up pleading her out, so I guess it turned out okay."

He turned to me and whispered. "Of course, I can't

name names when I talk about my cases, but I just generally talked about what was going on last week."

I nodded. I wondered how much he'd divulged to the group about a court case. These cases were supposed to be confidential, just like this meeting.

"Okay, um," he said. "I'll pass this week. Things are going in the right direction so I don't have much to add."

"What about what you're grateful for?" somebody asked.

"I'm grateful that Bella wants to live with me," he said. "That must mean I'm doing something right."

Everybody nodded and it came down to me. "Uh, well, let's see. I'm grateful to have recognized I was about to fall into a pit and got myself out before things got too far. Other than that, I'm grateful for my two daughters, because if it weren't for them, I have no doubt I would've kept drinking. Because I like drinking. I forgot how much I enjoy drinking until last night."

I stopped there. I wouldn't tell the group about how I started drinking again. They all would've thought I'd gone insane. I mean, what kind of a person does that? Who gets smacked on the head and force-fed alcohol? That sounded like a complete joke. The dog ate my homework and somebody force-fed me that scotch, honest. They would think I was dodging responsibility and I didn't want them to think that about me.

Then I bit my lip and realized I was doing it again. I was already answering for them. I was already making assumptions that they would judge me in their heads. That was a terrible trait I had – I always thought everyone was looking at me and thinking about what a loser I was. No matter how many accomplishments I had under my belt, no matter how many huge cases I tried and won, no matter how many appeals I prevailed on, it never seemed enough.

I was quiet, but I didn't say I was finished, so everyone just looked at me as they waited for me to speak.

"Uh, the truth is, I don't know how I started drinking again," I finally said. "The last thing I remembered was standing outside my client's house, looking at my phone, and the next thing I know, I'm laying on my patio chaise. My head was bleeding and there was a half-empty bottle of scotch on the table next to me. I think somebody did that to me – somebody knocked me out and force-fed me alcohol. I know, I know, it sounds crazy. You all probably think I'm some kind of conspiracy theory nut with a tin-foil hat at home. But that's what happened. And once I had that feeling, that hazy, comfortably numb feeling, it was like coming home. It was like putting on a favorite pair of jeans or crawling into some fuzzy pajamas and sitting in a big easy chair with a cup of hot cocoa on a cold day."

Everybody was nodding along and listening intently.

I felt braver, so I continued on. "So, yeah, somebody did this to me, but it's some kind of defect that made me want to keep drinking. Somebody knows my weakness and they exploited it perfectly. I still can't quite figure out why. I suppose that will become apparent sometime in the near future. But..." I shook my head. Most of the people around the table didn't really confess their deep, dark secrets. I supposed that was because they'd been to these meetings many times before and everyone already knew their back stories. It would get boring to everyone if somebody came in and, week after week, told the same back story. I was interested to know why each of these people chose to drink in the first place, because I wanted to know if everyone felt as defective as I did.

I realized I was crying, which was normal in this group – it seemed that everybody, men and women, ended up crying when talking. It was my turn to have the box of Kleenex pushed towards me. I took one, dabbed my eyes and blew my nose. "So, anyhow, that's my story. But life has gotten much better since those days. I'm a well-respected criminal defense attorney in Kansas City, Missouri. I'm out here working on a case for a client who I used to represent back in KC, and I have a great house I'm renting by the beach. I have a thriving practice at home and just hired an associate so I don't have to do everything myself anymore, and my girls are great. I mean, one girl is kinda princessy, but she has a good heart, and the other one is just as good as gold." I shrugged. "I have no reason to complain right now."

After I spoke, five more people told their stories and then it was time to stand up and recite the serenity prayer again while we held hands. After that, the meeting was over.

Most people got their things and walked out. It was 8 AM by the time the meeting was over and most of the participants had a job. So did I, but my day was much more unstructured than everyone else's. In fact, it was, for the first time in a long time, unstructured. Back home, I was constantly getting clients coming in, or I would've court, and, in between all that, I was investigating various criminal cases. Here, I only had the one case. I didn't have court appearances for anybody else. I didn't have potential-client interviews, nor current-client meetings. I just had Ginger's case to work, and that felt …weird. Weird, but good. I had the nagging feeling I was missing things and really should be somewhere. However, I didn't *have* to be anywhere, and it was a good feeling.

Because I wasn't in a huge hurry to leave, I lingered

around the room. There were other people, a handful, who were doing the same thing. They were talking to each other, drinking coffee and laughing. Patty, the bi-sexual who had a girlfriend and boyfriend who apparently were hooking up behind her back, came over to me. "So," she said, holding out her hand. "You're new to town?"

I shook her hand. "Yeah. I mean, I don't live here. I live in Kansas City. I'm just here for a case." I motioned to David, who also was sticking around. He was in a group of people and kept glancing at me and smiling. "What do you do?"

"I work in development for Paramount Pictures."

Chapter Nine

I LOOKED at her and looked up at the ceiling. Somehow, someway, there seemed to always be a force guiding me towards the right person to talk to. The unseen hand that brought Ginger into my path when the Darnell Williams case was going on and it turned out she was the only witness to the murder. And now this Patty person who, no doubt, knew Ezra. She was apparently working in his department. She probably knew the inside players.

She was probably a goldmine.

I looked over at David, wondering if he knew Patty's back-story, too. He probably did because he was apparently a regular at these meetings. I could tell, just by looking at his body language, and the body language of the people he was talking to, he was comfortable with that group. I overheard snippets of conversation and it was apparent they all knew one another quite well.

So, surely, he knew Patty was somebody we probably needed. She was probably somebody who could tell me about Ezra and about who migh've wanted him dead. All I had to do was get her talking, get her to tell me who Ezra knew, and that could springboard me into looking at the person who might've really done this to him.

"So," I said, stirring my coffee, "do people in this meeting know what you do?"

She giggled lightly. "Oh, God no. It's such a cliché – movie executive who's a bi-sexual drunk. My life is a screenplay just waiting to be written. Only I'm not the one to write it. I've tried, believe me." She shook her head. "I would write it as a really dark comedy and then as a straight-up drama, but nothing seemed to come out right. I guess at heart I'm a frustrated writer who develops other people's projects for the screen."

I took a sip of my coffee. It tasted bitter and I knew I wouldn't like what it would do to my body – coffee tended to make me more jittery than most people and the crash from the caffeine was always ugly. Not as ugly as the crash from alcohol, but ugly nonetheless. "What do you know about Ezra Cohen?"

She shook her head. "A tragedy. I didn't know him all that well – he's in a different division than me. I'm developing projects for streaming and he was strictly developing the well-known franchises. So, I didn't know him personally."

I felt slightly disappointed, but still knew she might be a good connection. "You develop streaming projects? Anything I've heard of?"

"We're negotiating the rights to a couple of YA books. After the success of *The Summer I Turned Pretty*, my boss seems to think YA books are the place to go for projects. But I'm part of the development team for *American Gigolo*, *Ghost* and *The Truman Show*. I guess those are the things you probably know about. We're developing those movies for the small screen. And I'm always reading books, looking for the next great voice to develop for a new project. I'm so jealous of those people who find hidden gems that become these rocket ships – those books that come out of nowhere and make these amazing series. I wish I were the one who found *The Summer I Turned Pretty*, for instance. I have to develop my eye much better if I want to move up in the industry."

"So," I said. "Ezra was the big cheese over at the movie division, and you develop projects for streaming. And you're one of the executives with the streaming division?"

"Yeah," she said. "I have a development team under me. They report to me and bring me projects all the time. I'm on the board that goes over the different stories and scripts that people bring from the outside world, and we decide what's worthy for development and which ones are a pass. 99% of things get passed on the first go-round. You should see some of the scripts we get on spec. My little five-year-old niece could do a better job."

"Well…"

"Yeah. There's a lot of Duning-Kruger effect going on out there."

The *Duning-Kruger Effect* referred to the theory that some people were under a mistaken belief they were more talented or intelligent than they really were. Because they had generally low cognitive abilities, they were unable to recognize how inept they were. The *Duning-Kruger Effect* no doubt was responsible for all those awful singers trying out on *American Idol* and other talent shows where they were merely featured on television so others could make fun of them.

Apparently, it was also responsible for the dreck that came into places like movie studios and book publishers. I felt almost sorry for the people who had to read those scripts on spec or read those books that ended up in slush piles.

It was then I realized Patty was flirting with me, just a little. Her hand brushed mine and she smiled. "You know, back in the day, I used to see a girl like you and ask her to get a drink. Obviously, we can't do that." She laughed. "But I'm intrigued. I have a house in Amarillo if you'd like to hang out some time."

At that, another woman came over and put her arm around Patty. That new woman's name was Andrea, Andi for short, and she was a blue-eyed brunette with an amazing rack. I remembered her also talking about a girlfriend when she gave her "confessions" to the group, but didn't mention a boyfriend. She was wearing a sundress and tall Espadrille shoes and smiled at both of us. "You're already cruising this lady, Patty?" she asked teasingly.

Patty looked embarrassed. "Would it be oversharing if I told you I was part of a sex addicts support group as well?" She smiled. "Or would you just think I keep fulfilling stereotypes of what you imagine us movie industry Angelenos are like? You're from Kansas City, the heartland. You probably have this image in your head about what we're all about in this industry and you're not far wrong."

Andi put her arm around Patty and guided her away from me. Patty looked back and furtively handed me her business card. "Call me."

I looked at the embossed card that read "Patricia Miller, Development Executive, Paramount Pictures." I put that card carefully in my wallet and glanced over at David.

He was looking at me as if waiting for me to be free so he could speak to me. He came over to where I was standing. "Did Patty Barracuda get to you?" he asked with a smile.

"Is that what you call her?"

"Yeah. She hits on all the attractive women and men. Just between you and me, she's made her way around a lot of us. You're fresh meat."

I had to smile at that one. "Fresh meat, huh? Listen, she works at Paramount. She says she doesn't know Ezra but she's bound to know somebody in his orbit. I'm tempted to take her up on her offer to go over to her house in…Amarillo. Right? Have you been there?"

"Yeah," he said. "She has some amazing parties there for her AA folks. She doesn't invite people who aren't in AA, of course, as they're dry parties." He smiled. "I never would've thought, when I was a guy in college standing around a keg, I would ever mutter the words 'dry parties' without gagging. But it is what it is."

"I know, right?"

"So, what are you doing today? Where are you heading?"

"I want to head over to Ezra's house and check it out. I always like to go to the murder scene. And then I want to give a call to your PI, Tony, and see if he has a list of witnesses I can speak to. Other than that, I want to call the prosecutor and see what the offer is, not that I'll take any offer, but I want to see what they're offering anyhow. You know, just doing my usual investigation on this case."

I got on my Uber app and brought it up. David noticed me doing that. "What are you doing? You got an Uber here?"

"Yeah. I got up this morning and started drinking so I couldn't drive anywhere. After I got in the Uber car, I knew I had to come here instead of going to Ezra's house. I know it's still cordoned off as a crime scene but I wanted to call the cops and let them know I need to visit it."

"No need," David said. "To call the cops. I've already gotten clearance to visit the crime scene. You can come with me."

I raised an eyebrow. "Don't you have like a million other things to do today? Like court appearances, client intake and that sort of stuff?"

He waved his right hand at me. "What do you think I have an assistant for? As for court appearances, that's why I have associates. It all works out to where I get paid the big bucks but don't have to kill myself working 100 hours a week. I only work 80 hours a week." Then he smiled. "Just kidding. I work 50 hours per week, but I used to bust my ass before I made it this far. Trust me."

"I just got an associate myself," I said. "And I'll be looking forward to using him. Up until now, I've been doing it all myself, including my own investigations. I mean, I have an investigator, too, but I've always liked to do the legwork on my own. I've can't trust anybody long enough to delegate work."

"Delegation is an art form," David said. "And it's probably the number one thing you have to master to keep your sanity. Seriously. In this business, delegation is the name of the game. I'm glad you finally came to your senses on that."

"Okay then," I said. "Let me get rid of this styrofoam cup, and let's head on over to Ezra's place."

At that, I threw away my cup and followed David to his Land Rover. He opened the door for me, I got in, and we drove off.

Chapter Ten

"NOW," David said as he drove along the windy roads that apparently lead to Ezra's Malibu mansion. "Tell me again about what happened to you last night? I mean, you told the group about it and told me something about it, but I'm really confused. Somebody hit you on the head and poured alcohol down your throat? Who would do something like that?"

"Ah," I said. "You tell me and we'll both know. It was just the strangest thing. Apparently, somebody knows my weakness and are trying to destroy me. Somebody wants me to start drinking again so I'll do a piss-poor job on Ginger's case. That gambit might've worked if not for my two girls. I was fully prepared to start getting blasted again. I functioned pretty well before when I was drinking, but I doubt I could still function that well if I started drinking again."

As we drove along, I was thinking about how I dodged a bullet. Or, rather, Ginger dodged one. I was away from my home base and hadn't had a drink in years. Could I again be a "functioning alcoholic?" I thought about my last bender, where I went to a bar every day and blew off my court appearances. Tammy, my law partner, had to cover for me most days. I definitely wasn't functioning well then. I was hiding from life, avoiding the guilt and shame that followed me in the days after John Robinson was arrested for murdering Gina Caldwell. I blamed myself, 100%, for his murdering Gina, because if I didn't get him off on a technicality, he would've gone to prison and Gina would still be alive.

Gina would be alive and Rina and Abby would still have their mother. Granted, they were my world at the moment and I couldn't imagine life without them. Before I adopted them, I never wanted children. I didn't think I could handle kids. But I knew I had to do something to make their lives better because I felt responsible for their being orphaned. That's why I took them in initially. If it not for them, I probably would've fallen off the wagon long ago. And who knows where I'd be at the moment.

David nodded. "Who would know that you had a problem with alcohol? That would explain who would've done this. Then you go to the next step and figure out who would want you to screw up Ginger's case." He nodded. "From there, you might follow the trail of bread-crumbs back to who actually killed Ezra. Sounds like that's the best lead you have so far."

I put my hand in my hair, feeling where I put the NuSkin on the gaping wound. I felt the mound of NuSkin and looked at my fingers. I didn't see blood on them so I felt comforted. At least I finally stopped bleeding, a small victory. "Yeah, that's true. But I don't see how I could possibly figure that out." I shook my head. "And that's another weird thing. This happened right outside Ginger's house. I'll speak to Ginger to see if she saw who did this, but it's strange that they'd do that right in front of her house. Isn't that bold? They want to mess me up to screw up her case but they do it in front of her house? Where she could look out the window and see them? That makes little sense."

"A lot of what criminals do makes little sense," David said. "Or haven't you figured that out?"

"Well, maybe Ginger got a peek at the person and can tell me who did this. Maybe she was looking out the window."

David's car wound all the way up to the top of a cliff and then he got to a gate. A disembodied voice asked who we were, David gave a code, and the gate swung open. "They're expecting me," he said. "And I guess they'll be expecting you as well."

The car tracked a long way towards an enormous home built in the modern block style — all white stucco and glass. David drove over to an enormous parking lot next to the house. We were one of only two cars — the other car was a police SUV. The parking lot could easily hold 100 cars, however, and I supposed this was necessary. After all, this was a home made for party-goers who needed a place to park.

We walked to the enormous glass and steel door and David rang the bell. I could hear the sonorous chimes booming from inside the house. Ten seconds later, a woman dressed in a bullet-proof vest and blue pants opened up. "Come on in," she said. "We're still in here, looking for clues and processing the scene." She looked at me. "I'm Marissa Leoni," she said. "The lead investigator for the LAPD."

I took her outstretched hand and shook it. "Harper Ross," I said. "I'll be the lead attorney on the case."

She nodded at David and looked at me. "David told me

about you," she said. "Welcome. This case is shaping up to be a bit of a doozy."

"It is? In what way?"

"We've interviewed all 200 plus people at the party that night, and combed through all his associates and everybody he knew well. Even people he didn't know well. Ginger Perry has been arrested for this murder, but I sincerely doubt she's good for this crime. I interviewed Ginger and I doubt she could carry this out. I think she's been set up but God only knows by whom. It's frustrating when you meet so many people who wanted this guy dead and have to settle on just one."

My heart stopped when she said that. This was suddenly sounding good. "What do you mean? Who wanted this guy dead?"

"We're getting into the investigation more, but it seemed this guy had a multitude of ex-wives, girlfriends and even a few boyfriends he screwed over on his way to the top. Up until five years ago this guy was waiting tables at Spago. That was a decent gig because waiters make good money over there, but it certainly wasn't enough to pay for all this." She swept her hand in a gesture that said *just look at this place.*

I took a look around the front part of the modern mansion. The house was built in cubes that had fifty-foot ceilings made entirely of glass. This part of the house was minimalist, with a fireplace and an enormous chandelier. On the wall above us was an enormous painting that appeared to be an original Warhol. I moved through the house and came up on a giant foyer with a marble floor and palm trees growing on each side of the floor. Another room seemed to be built for entertainment. It had arched ceilings, a fireplace, and furniture surrounding a coffee table. Still other rooms had billiards and old-school video games such as Ms. PAC man and Frogger; a complete movie theater; an indoor pool and jacuzzi; and a bowling alley. Outside was a beautiful infinity pool surrounded by Greek and Roman statues.

In all, this place was probably 10,000 square feet. "I didn't know a development executive can make the kind of money that would buy a place like this. I mean, studio heads and movie producers live in a house like this. But a development executive?" I shook my head. "Something is rotten in the state of Denmark."

Marissa put her finger on her nose. "You catch on quickly," she said. She turned to David. "Where'd you find this girl anyhow?"

David smiled. "She came from Kansas City," he said in a low voice.

I furrowed my brow, suddenly feeling like a poor relation who came from BumFuck town. "Hey, if you must know, Kansas City is a very underrated city. Our football team keeps going to the Super Bowl year after year and has the best quarterback in the NFL. Plus, you should see our Downtown Arena and Performing Arts Center. People have compared our Performing Arts Center to the Sydney Opera House, I'll have you know. And we have plenty of beautiful architecture, including many buildings designed by Frank Lloyd Wright himself. Paul Rudd grew up in the area, Eminem spent much of early childhood in the area, and Walt Disney and Ernest Hemingway both spent many years in that area. Not to mention Thomas Hart Benton." For some reason, I felt the need to defend myself against these two Angelenos who seemed to think I was Dorothy from Kansas and imagined that Kansas City was a place surrounded by nothing but cornfields and cows.

What the hell was wrong with cornfields and cows anyhow?

Marissa just looked at me and said nothing.

As did David.

I started to feel self-conscious. I felt like I did when I was a kid in middle school and around the cool kids. I didn't feel I belonged then, and I started to feel I didn't belong here, either.

Shake it off. You got this.

"So," I said. "He obviously couldn't afford a place like this as a development executive, even for a huge studio like Paramount, so what would explain his sudden wealth?"

Marissa looked at David who just shrugged. "I'm guessing you didn't know about him inheriting a shit ton of money from his grandfather recently," she said. "Which would explain most of this house. But I'm skeptical this inheritance is the only reason he could afford this place. I'm a bit more than skeptical about that. We're looking at his ties to organized crime."

It was David's turn to look at Marissa skeptically. "Now why would you be looking at organized crime? Do you have any reason for doing that?"

"No, I'm just pulling that theory out of my ass," Marissa said sarcastically. "Listen, it's hard to track where Ezra's money was coming from, seeing as it was tied up with all sorts of legitimate businesses, including restaurants and real estate, but we're following up on a solid lead."

"What lead is that?"

"There's this Armenian kid, name's Alek Sarkisian. At least, that's his birth name. He changed it to Alex Sarks and has been looking to get into the movie industry. For some odd reason, our vic, Ezra, took a special liking to Alex. He's been talking him up as if he's the next hot thing. Been trying to convince the big bosses at Paramount to green-light several of Alex's movies. But Alex has no talent. None at all. He's written like 50 screenplays and has been shopping them around to every major studio, and, so far, every studio has told him no. He can't even get an agent. Yet Ezra was trying to convince the studio bosses at Paramount that this Alex kid is the second coming of Aaron Sorkin." She shook her head. "I just don't get that."

"Maybe Ezra sees something in Alex that others don't?" I asked.

She shook her head. "No, I don't think so. We've been following Ezra's financial ties and have traced his money back to several apartment complexes the feds suspect are funnels for the Armenian mafia. The Armenian Power is one of the most powerful gangs in Los Angeles. They have street gangs which are just the soldiers for the organization. That organization is into human trafficking, kidnapping, extortion, identity theft and drugs. It controls its turf by drive-by shootings and bribing officials to look the other way. These are some bad dudes. At any rate, Alex is the Godson of one of the *Pakhans* in the Russia mafia. The Armenians and the Russians are closely tied. The Armenians actually spun off from the Russians in this town."

I carefully took notes but wasn't quite sure where any of this was going. "Are you sure Ezra was involved with the Armenian Power?" I knew something about that organization, and, from what I knew about it, it shook down the legitimate businesses owned by other Armenians and Russians in the neighborhood. Ezra Cohen, from his name alone, was Jewish. I'd have to look at his background but it was clear he probably wasn't Armenian.

Something about this entire theory wasn't sounding right to me, for whatever reason.

My hunches were rarely wrong.

"This isn't the final answer, of course," Marissa said. "This is just one of the leads we're looking at. Ezra Cohen has multiple holdings with multiple properties owned by the Armenian Power. That could be circumstantial or it could be definitive. That's one area we're looking."

"What other areas are you looking at?"

"He has three ex-wives, all of whom despise him. The last one, Sasha, really had it in for him. She married him three years ago, right when he was coming into his inheritance. He was already working at Paramount. Sasha was quite the climber. She saw Ezra as a meal ticket, both because she wanted into the movie business and saw that Ezra could develop a project for her and also because Ezra would come into all this wealth. He inherited $50 million from his grandfather and he was his grandfather's only heir. Imagine that."

"His only heir? That seems rather odd."

"It *is* odd. But it's also because of bad luck. Both of Ezra's parents died in a plane crash about five years before Ezra's grandfather kicked off. He has some brothers and a sister currently alive, all of whom were cut out of the grandfather's will. Besides that, there were no other heirs. Ezra's father was the only surviving child of his grandfather Jacob. Ezra's father, Abel, didn't have any brothers and sisters who survived long enough to have children. They all died before age 17." She shook her head. "Bad luck followed that family around, I'll tell you what."

I scribbled notes furiously. "But Ezra had brothers and a sister. Right?"

"Right. They were cut out of the grandfather's will, though."

"And why were they cut out of the will?"

"That seems to be the $64,000 question. Suffice to say that all three contested being cut out of the will."

I made a note to get ahold of those pleadings. I knew something about will contests – my law partner, Tammy, did them all the time. I'd have to figure out what they were claiming. To contest a will, you have to show the person making the will wasn't in his or her right mind. Of course, another reason to contest a will would be undue influence.

"What are the names of his brothers and sisters?"

"He has one sister, Ariel, and two brothers, Eli and Daniel."

I wrote down their names. "Eli and Daniel have the same last names as Ezra, I'd assume?"

"Yeah. Ariel's last name is Rossi, though. She married a Guido."

"Okay," I said. "So we have possible Armenian mafia connections, we have Alex Sarks who has no talent and wants to get some projects developed, and we have Ezra's former wife, Sasha…"

"Hapsburg. Sasha Hapsburg."

"Sasha Hapsburg. Now, you said that Sasha hated Ezra. I'm so sorry, I'm just a little unclear on why Sasha hated him."

"Well, she was a climber. She wanted to get into the industry and thought Ezra was her way in. He made some promises to develop a vehicle for her to star in. That never came through. He didn't have the power she thought he did. She thought he could find a property to develop, a book or script, and could tell the studio they could only develop that property if Sasha starred in it. You know, like Sylvester Stallone did with *Rocky* – Sly gave them that *Rocky* script, the studio loved it, wanted to develop it, but Sly wouldn't give it to them unless he starred in it. Sasha somehow thought

Ezra had that kind of power. She didn't know he was just a schlub working for Paramount so any script or book he developed would be Paramount's property no matter what. He didn't have the right leverage to give her what she wanted, and she was too fucking stupid to figure that out."

"And…"

"When Ezra told her the truth, she got pretty pissed. And then she really got pissed when she realized she wasn't entitled to any money Ezra inherited. She somehow thought she'd get half that money when she divorced him one year after he inherited. Her divorce attorney had to explain to her that Ezra's inheritance money wasn't hers, it was separate property, so Sasha got nothing. She was only married to him for a year anyhow. Why she thought she somehow would get $25 million out of it, I don't know. Can't fix stupid."

I nodded. "What would she get out of killing Ezra?"

"Revenge. I mean, Ginger was the last person in his bed which means Ginger the prostitute was servicing Ezra at the time of the murder. Sasha would take great pleasure out of Ezra's name splashed across the papers in such a sordid way. Ezra was a prominent citizen with all his wealth and everyone in the movie industry knew him because of the parties he threw. He was also a powerful executive, even if not a studio boss. That makes his murder a big deal in this town. Believe me, Sasha is happy as a pig in mud that it's known that a prostitute and porn star was the last person in Ezra's bed before he died."

"It wasn't known that Ezra had prostitutes?" I asked.

Marissa shrugged. "People knew and nobody cared. However, it's in the paper, it's everywhere on the internet and social media and has made nationwide news. It's widely known, which is humiliating. Not that poor Ezra is humiliated now, obviously. But perhaps he knew he would die with Ginger in the room. That meant he'd feel humiliation before he died which would give Sasha a great sense of satisfaction. Other than that, though, I don't know what Sasha would get out of Ezra dying."

I nodded. "Sasha seems an outside chance. It doesn't seem she has too much motive to kill Ezra. But the brothers and sister would be a better bet. After all, with the laws of succession, they'd be Ezra's heirs, assuming he died without a will. That would be one way of getting their inheritance. I'll have to take a look at that will contest pleading and find out the grounds for the suit. Something tells me they claimed undue influence on Ezra's part. That would make them angry enough to kill Ezra. If he died and they inherited Ezra's wealth, they'd share the grandfather's fortune in equal measure."

"Who else would've had motive to kill Ezra?" David asked. "That you've found in your investigation?"

"His other ex-wife. She's low on my list, though. They divorced years before he had two nickels to rub together. She was pissed at him, though, because she found out he was sleeping with a man behind her back. He never told her he liked men so she felt she married him under false pretenses. She got an annulment on that basis."

"What's her name?"

"Angel Cody," she said.

"That's her actual name?"

"Yeah," Marissa said. "That's her actual name. She's not a porn star or anything like that, so there's no reason for her to go under an assumed name."

"And that concludes your list of people?" I asked. "For now, anyhow?"

"Yeah. That sums it up."

I raised an eyebrow. "So why, if there are all these other people who had motive to have killed this man, was my client arrested?"

She shrugged. "All those other people might have had motive to kill Ezra, but none of them was in the room when he died. That's powerful evidence that Ginger did it. The autopsy traced the ingestion of the poison to when she was in the room with him and they traced it to the scotch she brought him. Now, granted, somebody might've set her up by giving her that tainted drink to give him and she didn't know it was tainted, but none of those people I told you about was at the party that night. It stands to reason the culprit had to have been at that party to poison him because the poison was in the drink Ginger gave him. I've went through all the guests at the party and couldn't see anybody who had a clear motive to kill Ezra."

"But maybe somebody at the party was working with a person with motive to kill Ezra. Maybe there's a connection we're not seeing between the party-goers and somebody who wanted Ezra dead. Or maybe one of the party-goers had a secret motive to kill Ezra. That's a possibility," I said.

"Anything is possible. I'll be looking into all the people with motive. Ginger was arrested for the murder just because she was with him when he died. I personally think the most likely scenario was that Ginger was in on it but the mastermind was somebody else. I really don't see that Ginger had motive to kill Ezra."

I had to consider that possibility myself. Something never sat right with me about this whole scenario with Ginger and Ezra. As Marissa pointed out, Ginger had no reason to kill Ezra. She didn't know him. But would she have done it for somebody else? If so, what would that somebody else have promised her to get her to do it? Ginger would do anything for money. That much was clear.

The more likely possibility, however, was that Ginger poisoned Ezra but did it unwittingly. After all, she brought him the drink that killed him. Even she admitted that. However, she insisted she didn't know the poison was in there.

"Well," I said. "Thanks for meeting with us. I'd like to go to the scene, if you don't mind."

"Sure," Marissa said. "Go on up there. Not that going into that bedroom will tell you anything you don't already know, however. Unless you're a psychic or something like that. Sometimes those psychics can go to a murder scene and know just what happened. They know by the vibes of the room. It's creepy, but I've seen it happen."

I nodded and climbed the stairs to the second floor. I immediately knew which bedroom was his because there was a yellow crime scene tape blocking the door.

The room was apparently left intact. There was an outline of the body on the California King bed. The covers were still there, just the way they were when the body was found, for they were turned down and semi-strewn on the bed – as if somebody had been sleeping there. On the nightstand next to the bed was where the glass of scotch apparently was found. It had been taken from the room, obviously, for the contents had to be processed, and so did the glass itself.

I walked over to the balcony that overlooked the pool below. The view from this bedroom was something I'd only seen in movies. The house was situated high on a cliff, so I could see, in the distance, the outline of the city perfectly from this window.

I walked over to the bed. Marissa was right about one thing. Being in this room told me nothing.

Somehow, I'd have to figure out who at the party would've wanted Ezra dead. Or, probably more accurately, who in the party was working with somebody who wanted him dead.

And then I'd have to convince the jury about my alternative culprit.

I really had my work cut out for me.

Chapter Eleven

DAVID

"DAVID, you have Artur on the line for you," my assistant, Lisa, told me.

Ah, just the idiot I wanted to speak with. "Send him in."

To keep a lid on this Ginger case, I would have to rein Artur in. He had to keep his nose clean in this. I told him this, over and over, yet he didn't seem to get it.

That's why Artur was a soldier and not a leader in the Armenian Power organization. He wasn't smart enough to put together a decent strategy and he tended to free-lance and improvise too much for my taste. This wasn't the first time Artur had done something like this, either. This was just his latest screw-up.

He came into my office a few minutes later. Artur looked too on-the-nose for my taste as far as Armenian hit men went. Shaved head, tattoos on his bulging biceps, dressed in black, with a nose ring. He looked like the thug he was. "Hey," he said. "I hear you wanted to see me. Word on the street is you were looking for me." He spread his arms and smiled. "Well, you found me, so what's up?"

"I'd like to know what the fuck you think you're doing." I was pissed. If he fucked things up on the Ginger Perry case I would have to ice him myself. No questions asked.

"What do you mean?"

"You know what I mean." I swiveled in my chair. "You were supposed to keep an eye on Harper Ross not knock her out and pour alcohol down her throat. That was one of your stupidest moves. You apparently did that right in front of Ginger's home and in broad daylight. What the fuck were you thinking?"

Artur shrugged which pissed me off all the more. "Erik told me that would be a good idea. He got the idea from you, by the way."

"From me? What do you mean he got the idea from me?"

"You're the one who did your homework on that chick. You're the one who knew she was a drunk from way back. If you didn't want to use that, why did you tell Erik about it?"

"You stupid bastard. You have no idea how to finesse things, do you? That's why I regret giving you this job. I wanted to hit her weakness, which is alcohol, yes, but I would do it in my own way. Listen, there's a way to get recovering alcoholics drinking again, even if they swear they're never going to. I have all those tricks up my sleeve, but it's too fucking late now, because she's already gotten herself into AA." I knew she would be at that meeting in Malibu Bluffs. I had a tracker put into her car so I always knew all her movements. When I found she was heading to the AA meeting I knew there was already a problem. Ironically, it was the same AA meeting I always attended. Weird coincidence.

I wanted to exploit her weakness in my own time. My

plan was to get her to trust me. See me as her white knight. I knew she'd start feeling depressed and lonely because she was away from her routine. Away from her family and her boyfriend back home. Away from her life. I had been around enough drunks in my time to know that loneliness and depression are always catalysts for getting back on the bottle. I knew Harper was no different than any other drunk. She suffered from low self-esteem and an underlying mental illness – bi-polar disorder. I knew that, too. I'd handled women like Harper before. I knew just what made them tick and just how to get them to self-destruct.

Harper was a strong woman, but, underneath it all, she was really an insecure little girl with a weakness. Alcohol was her Kryptonite, and I knew just how to turn it on inside her.

Now this jackass came along and fucked everything up. He was like a fucking bull in a China shop, really. Bulldozing everything that came into his path.

He was looking at me smugly. His eyes were narrowed and he had a small smile on his face. A smile I wanted to wipe off with a knife. "What do you mean, I don't know how to finesse things?" he asked.

I sighed. "Do you know the story of the frog in the pot?"

"No, man. I don't know no story about no frog in no pot. But I'm sure you'll tell me about the frog in the pot, so…" He made a gesture that said *go on*.

"You can boil a frog in a pot without him even knowing about it." I paused, knowing that Artur wouldn't get my parable, yet I'd tell him about it anyhow. "What would happen if you boiled some water and threw a frog in there?"

"That frog would be jumping out of that pot and ribbiting his water-tight ass out of there, man."

"Right. But if you put the frog in cold water and slowly, slowly, slowly turn up the heat, one degree at a time, you get the frog used to the water gradually getting hotter and hotter. Before you know it, you're boiling the frog, and he doesn't even know what's going on."

Artur just looked at me for a few seconds. "Nah, man, that's bullshit, man. That frog ain't that stupid. He'll get out of the pot when it gets too hot." He shook his head. "That's the stupidest thing I ever heard."

"You're missing the point." Artur was right. I always thought the same thing – the frog won't stay in the pot if he gets uncomfortable, even if you turn up the heat gradually. But that was neither here nor there.

"What is the point? Enlighten me."

"My plan was to slowly get Harper to trust me. Get to know her, get to know her weaknesses, her desires. Her insecurities. What drove her to drink. Then I would slowly convince her she didn't need to take medication for her bipolar disorder. Tell her she can overcome her disease with her mind. Then I would encourage her to drink. I can be very persuasive. By the time I got through with her, she'd be going off her rocker and drinking so much there would be no way she could give Ginger a good defense. I had this entire thing mapped out, to the letter, and you go and fuck it up in one fell swoop."

"Ah, man, that sounds like a good plan."

"It does and it's a plan I gave to both you and Erik. Now, you're fucking free-lancing and fucking everything up. Harper already found her tribe of drunks at the AA meeting. The way I would've done it would've been so gradual she probably would've just slipped back into drinking and not taking her meds, and, since I would get her to trust me, she would've come to me for help, not a meeting. Now, I'll have to figure out a Plan B to get her to fuck things up on Ginger's case. I've done enough research on her to know she'll never fuck up on her own."

Artur stood up. "I'm sure you'll come up with somethin'," he said. "I have faith in you."

His flippant attitude enraged me. So did his smug smile. "Well, okay, then. Maybe I need to have a talk with Sargis." Sargis Gregorian was the leader of this branch of the Armenian Power and reported directly to Igor Kovalesky, the Russian *Pakhan* whose group partnered with Sargis's group. Together, the Russians and the Armenians ran their part of the city. I was surprised that Artur would do anything to piss me off enough to report him to Sargis, but he did.

Sargis was my biggest client and I promised him I wouldn't screw this up. I was tasked with ensuring that Harper lost Ginger's case. Sargis didn't need for the feds to come looking at him for killing Ezra, especially since he swore to me, up and down, he didn't have a thing to do with it. He knew it would look bad when the investigators looked too closely at who financed most of Ezra's real estate projects and owed millions of dollars when those real estate projects went bust. One thing was for sure – Ezra wasn't the one who lost all that money. It was Sargis.

Truth be told, I had no idea if Sargis killed Ezra. There was always rule number one with my clients – they had to give me plausible deniability when the feds came knocking on my door. Plus I had to have the option of putting them on the stand to take up their own defense, if it came to that, and I couldn't do that if I knew they were guilty. So, I always, always told them not to tell me if they really did it.

I suspected Sargis was dirty in this. He was just pissed off enough to have done it. Plus he was planning to shake down Eli, Daniel and Ariel, all of whom were expected to split Ezra's fortune. He would shake them down to pay Ezra's debts. Ezra wouldn't pay. He'd refused to pay. Ezra was a shady bastard that way and Sargis should've figured that out when he financed that apartment building several years back. One would think that when Ezra came into his inheritance he would pay Sargis back.

One would be wrong.

I didn't blame Sargis for being pissed. I wouldn't blame him if he was pissed enough to ice the fucking bastard. I didn't know for certain that Sargis was behind the murder, but I strongly suspected him. It was my duty to protect him. He wasn't officially one of my legal clients so I wouldn't be implicated in any conflict of interest if his name came up in connection with Ezra's murder. Well, that wasn't entirely true. He was one of my legal clients, but my relationship with him had always been strictly off the books. I always advised him but never put his name in my client database and never appeared in court for him. I never signed a pleading with his name on it. That was the only way I could continue to protect him when his name came up in connection with different murders around the city.

What I was doing to Harper was something I'd done many times before, all in the name of protecting Sargis. It usually worked, too. I always found a way to insinuate myself onto any case where somebody was charged with something I suspected Sargis had done. I always found a way for an innocent person to be convicted for the crime. I found various creative ways of doing this, but it invariably worked.

Once the innocent person was behind bars, the feds

stopped looking at Sargis for anything. It was an ingenious plan, really, and Sargis had gotten lucky thus far. There was always some fall guy or girl closer to the actual murders than he was. Once that person was charged it was just a matter of ensuring a monkey wrench was put into the works to make sure that person was convicted.

With Harper, it would be like taking candy from a baby. Pierce her shield, exploit her weakness, make sure she's off her game, and that would be that. Harper was an excellent attorney with a stellar track record. She knew how to win cases.

But would she know how to win Ginger's case if she was off the wagon, off her meds and off her rocker? It would be a close call, but something told me she would end up fucking things up in that situation. She might've been a rock star attorney but she was also human.

Artur was still staring at me, trying to figure out if I was serious about talking to Sargis about him. "Hey, I fucked up," he said. "It won't happen again."

"No, it won't," I said, raising my eyebrow. It wouldn't happen again because Sargis would take care of the matter.

I would see to that.

Chapter Twelve

HARPER

I RATTLED my ice in my glass as I sat on the patio of my home. Mia was grilling chicken next to me and I'd invited Patty from my AA meeting to come for dinner. After I spoke with Marissa about all the people who might've wanted Ezra dead, I was frustrated because I didn't feel I was getting the information I needed. There were plenty of hands in the cookie jar but none of those people were at the party.

Yet Patty worked at Paramount. She didn't know Ezra that well, but she might've been able to give me the lowdown on some of the people who attended Ezra's party. I had the guest list and it read like a who's who in the industry.

My plan was to have her over for dinner, ask her about all the people on the guest list and find out which were known to be a bit shady. That would be a good place to start.

I'd already checked out the leads Marissa had given to me and there wasn't anything jumping out at me. There was the suspicious Armenian connection and the boy, Alex Sarks, who wanted a project developed. What was up with that? Why was Marissa going there? My research showed Ezra was apparently mobbed up with some of his real estate projects because there was dark money funneling through an apartment complex that Ezra owned and dumped. But what did Alex Sarks have to do with it?

Then there was the postal ex-wife who thought Ezra somehow owed her a living. Sasha Hapsburg. Seen a million Sashas in my life and they were always the likely suspect in something like this. From the guest list, however, I didn't see she was on it. She might've somehow sneaked on through, but from what I understood, from talking to Tony Marinaro, David's PI, the security in Ezra's parties was always tight. Ezra knew people were gunning for him and made sure everybody who came to his parties was vetted.

For that matter, there weren't any Armenians at the party, either. I went through the guest list and painstakingly matched up every name on that list with somebody who had some kind of an on-line presence – this wasn't difficult since this was a movie industry party, and everybody on that list had connections with the movie industry in some way. Some were from the adult film industry, others from the mainstream movie industry, and some were involved in television and streaming. But everybody on the guest list, to a person, was *somebody* involved in the entertainment industry. Ezra didn't invite random people to his parties and random people didn't have a way to get in there. And he certainly didn't invite people from the Armenian Power to his parties.

I knew why, of course. He was protecting his image and was apparently protecting himself. He didn't want people knowing he had shady connections, and if there were shady people at these parties, the movie industry folks would gossip about him. He wanted to get ahead, from what I understood, which meant he wanted to eventually become a studio boss. The guy had ambition and money and wouldn't let anybody or anything stand in his way.

If that meant covering up his shady mob connections, that's what what he would do.

Abby came out to the patio. She had two glasses of water on a little tray and she sat down next to me, shielding her eyes from the sun. "You have a friend coming over tonight?" she asked me.

"Yeah," I said. "So Mia will take you and Rina down to the beach and out to eat. Maybe to a movie. Does that sound like fun?"

She shrugged. "Sure, Mom." She didn't seem to have much enthusiasm behind those words.

"What's wrong, Buttercup?" I asked her.

She turned her body in her chair and faced me. "Nothing," she said. "I miss home, that's all. I mean, it's fun being out here on the beach and all. Rina and me have had a great time boogie boarding every day and we love taking Stella and Sue to the beach. But it's getting old."

"I know," I said. "I miss home, too, in a way." I *did* miss home, to be perfectly honest, but, at the same time, there was a certain sense of calmness I experienced in California. Being so close to the water gave me some peace. I could hear the seagulls and the waves crashing, and being around so many people having a blast brought me out of my shell. There were people going past us on the boardwalk all the time – roller-blading, bicycling, walking their dogs, skateboarding. It was a very lively atmosphere and I craved it.

Plus I had no other cases to tend to while I worked Ginger's case. That was liberating and slightly weird. I was so used to so many things going on at the same time –

people calling, trying to make an appointment; going to court all day long; meeting with clients and other attorneys and judges; and working up trial cases. When I was in Kansas City, doing my normal practice, I constantly felt stressed because I was juggling so much.

Out here, though, there was just the one case to concentrate on. And that knowledge made me realize I could slow down and really try to focus on what I needed to do to ensure Ginger didn't serve a single day in prison.

Abby looked at me, one eye squinted. "Don't worry Mom," she said. "We'll have fun tonight with Mia. She's pretty cool. I'm glad you found her for us."

"Me too," I said. "She was a find."

At that, I heard the doorbell ring, and Rina answered it. "Mom," she hollered, "Patty's here."

"Send her on back."

Patty came back, a huge bottle of water in her hand. I made the introductions between her, my girls and Mia, and then Mia, the girls and the pups headed to the beach. The plan was to play in the water until the sun went down, bring the dogs back in and then get some dinner and catch a movie.

"Thanks for calling me," she said, "I was surprised to hear from you so soon."

"I wanted to talk to you," I said. "I liked what you said at that AA meeting and I thought you and I could team up to help each other out. Help each other with each other's sobriety. That kind of thing."

"That sounds like a good idea," she said. Then she took a sip of water. "You also want to pick my brain about Ezra, don't you?"

I smiled. "Well..."

"That's okay." She smiled, but it was the kind of smile

used to cover up her true feelings. I knew that smile anywhere. It was a smile that quivered, as if she was afraid to break down in tears at any moment. "I don't mind being used."

I put my hand on hers. "Hey," I said. "I don't want you to think that. I liked your vibe in that meeting. You put it all out there. Everything you're feeling and experiencing. I can't do that. I can't be honest with perfect strangers. I can't be honest with people who love me either. I can't even be honest with myself. So I admire your ability to put it out there."

"Well, you have to," she said. "You read that Big Book and you realize that being honest with yourself and everyone around you is one of the keys to recovering and staying that way."

The *Big Book* referred to the book passed out to everyone who attended AA meetings. It contained the 12 Steps to recovery. I had gone through that Big Book before, worked all the 12 steps, but found it was difficult for me. The difficulty was because I had a hard time admitting my faults and flaws to myself so I wasn't quite ready to identify them. Since identifying these character flaws was the first step in having the Higher Power remove them, I faltered on Step Four. Step Four called for me to make a searching and fearless moral inventory of myself and I couldn't look deeply enough inside to do that.

"I'm really glad you could make it," I said. I wanted to change the subject because it was veering into an area I didn't like. An area I wasn't comfortable with. My psyche was a black box and I always had to carefully conceal it.

She passed me a bottle of water unopened and I took it gratefully and sipped it. "That chicken smells good," she said.

"I'm sure it is. My nanny made it before she took my two girls to the beach."

She raised an eyebrow. "You were afraid I'd start talking about my lifestyle around your two girls, weren't you?"

I opened my mouth and nothing came out. To my surprise, Patty just laughed.

"Don't worry about that. I'm much more discreet in public. I don't tell just anyone about my slimy ex-girlfriend and slimier ex-boyfriend hooking up behind my back. I wouldn't have said anything to your girls, either."

"I know."

I got up and put some chicken and grilled veggies on two plates and we sat down at the patio table. "So," she said. "What do you want to know about Ezra? As I said, he was in a different department, so I don't really know him all that well, but I'm in the loop on the gossip going on since he died. I can help you figure out who to pinpoint for this crime."

I bit my lower lip. "I hate to even ask this of you…" I silently passed her a copy of Ezra's guest list. "Is there anybody on this list who stands out to you? I'm having a problem figuring this one out. I talked to the cop investigating this case and she seemed to say Ezra had enemies, none of whom appear on this list. There's the Armenian mob, two ex-wives, and his siblings. I guess that all those people had motive to kill Ezra. But not one of them appeared at the party."

She sighed and took a look at the list. "Well, let's see," she began. She carefully read the names on the list. "Okay. I read the list of the guests at the party. 250 of them, so that's a lot, even for Ezra. Most of these people are industry people, and I recognize quite a few actresses and models from different studios. I suppose you probably did a background check on most of them, right?"

"Right."

"The only thing that stands out to me is that there's one name I can't really place. This guy here, his name is Tom Dale. That's the only name I don't recognize as being in the industry."

I took the list and looked at it. "I thought I looked everybody up on this list and I found a social media presence for all of them. I tried to vet this Tom Dale, too, and didn't come up with anything at all."

Patty shrugged. "Well, find out more about him. That's the only person I don't know the first thing about. And if I've never heard of him, he doesn't exist. I know everyone in this town. That means I not only know people in the industry but know the ones waiting tables and serving coffee, waiting for their big screen-writing, directing or acting break. If they're in the industry or even wanting to break into the industry, I've come across them. Trust me on this. Everyone has come across them, especially people like me in development."

"Interesting," I said. I put a star next to Tom Dale's name. "So, is there anybody on this list who would be a likely suspect in your eyes?"

She laughed. "You might look at all the people who wanted Ezra's job in development. That would be a good place to start. And they were all at the party. It would be so easy to slip something into his drink and give it to Ginger to take to him. By the time Ginger did her thing with him, he was probably so high on blow and drunk on Jack he would've drank anything put in front of his face. Seriously. He was a sitting duck, really, if you think about it."

"And who would that be? Who wanted his job in development?"

"I would start with two people on this list. Adam Stilwell and Emma Black. They're both on Ezra's development team and both climbers like you wouldn't believe. Adam in particular is a climber and has reason to be pissed at Ezra. Last year, he found this YA book, *Dust and Sand*, and brought the book to Ezra. Ezra developed this book into a movie and that movie went on to become the sleeper hit of the year. It came out of nowhere and grossed $250 million domestic. Out of nowhere. Adam thought this would mean he'd get a major promotion, or, at the very least, acknowledged, but Ezra did none of that. Ezra pretended he found this book all on his own and took all the credit. So, yeah, Adam is pissed. He also told me he feels absolutely helpless because he works hard to find these gems. These diamonds in the rough. Then, when he does, he gets zero credit. I think he has motive enough to kill Ezra, and he was on the guest list."

I nodded. "And Emma Black? What is her motive?"

Patty smiled. "She was sleeping with Ezra, with the understanding her sleeping with him would lead to moving up the ladder to acquisitions. And then maybe moving up the ladder to development head. She's pretty far down on the totem pole at the moment. She's still where she was when she started working for Paramount three years ago, working as an executive assistant. So, she has cause to kill Ezra, as well."

"So, with Emma and Adam, they would kill Ezra because…"

"Revenge, I guess. Ezra was slimy with how he treated people under him. Made promises he could never keep. I don't know about you, but I'd be pretty pissed if that were me."

I sighed. "There were so many people who wanted this guy dead," I said. "And Emma and Adam sound interesting, but…" My gut was telling me something was off. I was missing something. Some clue.

My head was hurting. "How is the chicken?" I asked her.

"Delicious. Thanks for having me over. I hope what I'm telling you will help out."

"It will. By the way, do you happen to know my client, Ginger? You said you know everybody involved in the industry. I was wondering if you also knew everybody involved in the adult film industry."

"I don't," she said. "I know some of the girls and guys working in the adult film industry, of course. I come across them all the time. A lot of them want to move up to the mainstream film industry because they're tired of doing porn and know their days are numbered. They all want to be the next Traci Lords, but they have to remember that even Traci Lords never made it that big in the mainstream movie industry. She was the queen of the porn, but as far as mainstream films went, she didn't do much."

"Maybe not, but she's still pretty famous…"

When I said that, I stopped and shook my head.

"Yeah, she's famous," Patty said. "She's an adult film star most people have heard of. Jenna Jameson is the other one, of course. I don't know anybody who hasn't heard of Jenna Jameson. But other than that, who's known?"

"Well, there are the older legends," I said. "Ron Jeremy, John Holmes…" I had to laugh, realizing that my porn repertoire was extremely limited. To say the very least. "And after that, I got nothing."

"Exactly," Patty said. "And the adult film industry is a brutal business. The girls are pretty much out within a year. Either they quit because they realize the price they pay in being in the business isn't worth it, and neither is the money, or they're pushed out because people are tired of seeing them. Once they get out of regular porn they have to go on to niche stuff. The bondage scenes, the rape scenes, the golden showers and the Cleveland Steamers." She shuddered. "I can't even imagine that last one. The Eiffel Tower is bad enough, but the Cleveland Steamers? No, just no. I'd rather have somebody beat me up on screen."

"I'm sorry?" I said. "A Cleveland Steamer? Eiffel Tower? I don't get what those are."

She suppressed a giggle. "A Cleveland Steamer is when a guy shits on your chest and then rocks back and forth so it's spread all over the place. The Eiffel Tower is when there's a guy behind you and a guy you're blowing and they do a high five above you. The Eiffel Tower is pretty degrading, if you ask me, but the Cleveland Steamer is not only degrading, it's humiliating. Not to mention disgusting." She made a face. "Now, I'm not a prude who'll say porn, in general, harms or degrades women or anything like that. I'm all about empowerment and if a woman chooses to make money by having sex on screen, that's her right. Nobody will take that away from her. But to subject yourself to be shit on, or beat on, or pissed on, and filmed so that everybody can see it…" She shook her head. "Well, that's another ball of wax. And it's what a lot of girls are subject to when people get bored of them, so they're no longer getting any work in the more mild and mainstream porn movies."

I felt myself gag just a little as she was speaking. "Uh, that's…"

She nodded. "I know. Listen, I've lived in Los Angeles for most of my life. I've been in the movie business for the past 10 years. I've seen it all. There are so many people desperate to make it in the business that they'll do anything. Anything. For anyone. Never discount that. Everybody wants to be the next Chris Hemsworth or Margot Robbie, both Aussies, by the way. But you can never tell them their chances of making it in the mainstream movie industry are slim and none. As for the porn industry, it's the same thing. It's easier to get into than the mainstream movie industry but it's also much more brutal. All those girls are trying to get a leg up so they're not disposable. They're all trying to make their careers last much longer than what it's supposed to. They're making all this money and blowing it at the clubs or up their nose, so when the industry chews them up and spits them out, they have nothing to fall back on. I would say it's sad but it's more stupidity than anything."

"It's easier to get into the adult film industry than the mainstream movie industry?" I asked. "In what way?"

"Well, for one thing, there's so much churn in the porn industry that there's a lot more openings for those positions." Then she started to laugh. "Openings for those positions. I didn't mean to make a pun, but there it was. Anyhow, because of the industry churn, they're always looking for the next hot thing. And, let's face it, you don't have to take a method acting class to get a job moaning for the camera. You don't need much talent, in other words. You just have to have a pretty face, a rocking body and be willing to do it. Whereas, in the mainstream movie industry…" She shook her head. "You see so many incredibly talented people. People who have the right look, the right talent and the right drive. But they won't make it because there's 1,000 other people who have that same look, talent, and drive."

"So, everyone is looking for that one thing to make them stand out above all the rest."

"Right."

I got quiet and Patty noticed this.

"What are you thinking about?"

I shook my head. "Nothing." I stretched out in the chair. "Do you want to do something? Go inside, play a game, watch Netflix or something like that?"

"Sure," she said. "I can show you some of the TV programs I've developed over the years. Maybe you'll be impressed. Or maybe not."

We went back inside, did the dishes and watched some streaming series I'd never heard of but enjoyed all the same. I was happy Patty had come by. I needed a friend out in LA because I was feeling lonely and out of sorts and freaked out about my mini-bender that forced me into that AA meeting. Patty was a veteran of AA and could help keep me on the straight and narrow. She also seemed to know a ton about the industry and knew all the players.

She could definitely be an asset. No doubt about that.

Chapter Thirteen

I HAD my first pre-trial conference on Ginger's case that Monday, and I met David at the Los Angeles County Courthouse. I looked around and felt self-conscious, as I always did whenever I was in an odd situation that made me feel less-than. And this was certainly one of those situations.

Everybody around me was talking and chatting. I was not only a newcomer but a newcomer from the Mid-West. Plus, I was insinuating myself into this high-profile case involving a studio executive. It was a case everyone was talking about. It had all the elements that made for salacious gossip – the studio executive being done-in by the porn actress. The details of his life was passed around from person to person, and, here I was, dropping in out of nowhere to try to win this case for the porn actress.

I wouldn't use the term "porn star" to describe Ginger, because that term really didn't apply. She wasn't a star by any stretch of the imagination. She was only an actress. Granted, her new boss, Dale Thompson, did his level best to make her more of a star. But, at the moment, she was only an actress. One of many.

"Hey," David said as I walked into the courthouse. "How are you doing? I've been trying to get in touch with you. Haven't you gotten my emails?"

"No," I said. "I haven't checked them lately. Why? What are the emails about?"

"Just wanted to ensure you'd be here on time, that's all. The judge in this case, Judge Woo, isn't the most patient in the entire world."

"They never are."

At that, we got on the elevator and I smelled his cologne. I was uncomfortably close to him – my arm was touching his, just because the elevator was so crowded.

I'd Zoomed with Axel the entire week so I hoped he couldn't tell that there was this distractingly handsome attorney working my case with me. I didn't like it. I couldn't really control it, though, either. I needed David's assistance. If I didn't have his assistance, I'd be flying absolutely blind.

We got to the courtroom and took our seats. The prosecutor spied David and came up to him. "Hey," she said. "I see you're on the Perry case. Slumming, I see." She smiled coyly to show she was only busting on him, and he smiled back.

"Hardly slumming. Let's just say this case can bring me an entire different class of clientele."

"Hmmm…" She looked over at me. "I'm Adrian Jackson," she said, holding out her hand. I shook it. "Where are we on this case?"

"Well, we haven't exchanged discovery yet," I said. "I sent out some requests but haven't heard back."

"I'll get right on that," she said. "Are you interested in a plea bargain on this case? I can do 20 years, plus a reduction of the charge from murder one to manslaughter. I got the authorization for that. That's an absolute steal of an offer, if you ask me."

"No," I said uncertainly. "I don't think so, anyhow. But I'll be sure to bring Ginger that offer."

She shrugged. "Take it or leave it but that offer goes away in 72 hours. Otherwise we try this case and your client could possibly end up with life in prison without parole. As I'm sure you know."

"I do."

Our case was called and Adrian and I stepped forward. "Hello, Ms. Jackson," the judge said to Adrian pleasantly. "How is your son doing? I keep forgetting to ask you about that."

Adrian smiled. "Julian is doing great. His leg is healing and the doctors say that they got all the cancer. I feel blessed."

I inwardly groaned. Adrian was a prosecutor whose young son apparently was suffering from cancer. And she seemed very friendly with the judge. My sympathies went out to her, of course – I would never want to have to deal with something like a sick child, especially one that had cancer – but I also knew her story would make her sympathetic to the judge. Judge Woo could certainly ding me if he wanted to with his rulings. If he favored Adrian over me that would be something to put me at a distinct disadvantage.

David was standing next to me and Judge Woo didn't address him nearly so kindly. "Mr. Jenkins," he said, much more formally than when he greeted Adrian. "And I see that we have a Mid-West transplant, Ms. Ross. Welcome."

I smiled. "Thank you, your honor."

"Now," he said to everyone in attendance. "Where are we on this case?"

"We haven't yet exchanged discovery," Adrian said. "But we're in the process of doing that."

Judge Woo made notes. "Any movement towards getting a plea agreement?"

"None, your honor," Adrian said. "I've made an offer to Ms. Ross, but she has to take that offer to her client and see if her client will accept it."

"Is it a reasonable offer?" Judge Woo asked Adrian.

"Very reasonable, your honor."

"Okay, then," he said, looking at me. "And what are the chances you can get your client to take the offer Ms. Jackson is bringing to you, Ms. Ross?"

"I don't know," I said. "I'll have to speak with my client."

"Very well. I'll set this case for trial August 29 of this year, which gives the two parties just over two months to get discovery exchanged." He made a nod towards me. "I notice that Ms. Ross has filed a motion for a speedy trial, which is granted, as this trial has been set for under 180 days after the defendant has been arraigned." A time limit for a speedy trial for Ginger was 180 days because she was on out bail. For any other defendant, in pre-trial detention, the time-limit would be 90 days.

The judge set the time limit for discovery, ordering us to get our discovery into one another within 60 days, and he banged his gavel and called the next case.

"I'll be in touch," I said. "About Ginger. I'll ask her about taking that plea agreement, and I'll get back to you."

"Okay," she said. "Thanks."

At that, David and I got into the elevator and went

down to the lobby. "You want to get lunch?" David asked me.

I looked at my watch, thinking I never had time to eat lunch, then realizing I didn't have anyplace special to be. "Sure. Let's get some lunch."

He put his hand on the small of my back and I subtly moved away from it. I couldn't have David touch me in a flirtatious way. Not when Ginger's life was on the line, and not when I had a perfectly great guy waiting for me back home.

We walked across the street to a busy bistro, saw the hostess, and sat down.

Chapter Fourteen

"SO," David said to me, looking around the restaurant. "The prosecutor is offering you 20 years. Is that right?"

"Yes," I said. "You heard that right."

David whistled softly. "That's a damn good offer," he said. "Seriously. Especially for that judge."

The waitress came around and took our orders. I was dying for some pasta so I ordered the lemon spaghetti. David ordered a steak.

We sipped our waters and looked at each other. I was uncomfortable. There was just something about David that made me feel that way. Weird, out of sorts. It was partially because I felt somewhat inferior to him, as I was from a small Midwest City and David was this big-shot attorney in a huge city. I felt like small potatoes.

But it was more than that, too. There was an underlying unease I felt. A greasy pit was in my stomach as I stared at him and he stared back.

"Well, far be it for me to tell you what to do because Ginger technically isn't my client, but if I were you, I would take that deal. Take it, run and never look back. You won't see a deal like that again."

"You're not me. And you're not Ginger, either. Ginger will be the one serving that time in prison, not me and not you. Ginger. So, she'll have to say yay or nay to that."

David nodded. "Harper, I don't really know you all that well," he began.

"That's right, you don't know me. You don't know me at all."

"Well, I sort of know you. Remember, I was in that…" He lowered his voice. "Meeting with you. So, I have a handle on how you think and who you are. I just don't want you to be naïve about Ginger. I mean, she's a prostitute and a porn star."

"That makes her expendable, right? That means she isn't entitled to fair representation, right?" For some reason, this guy was getting my hackles up. I had no clue why. He just was.

"That's not what I'm saying," he said. "Don't put words into my mouth."

"Then what are you saying?"

He cleared his throat. "I'm saying I don't want you to be blind-sided by all this. Ginger was in the room when Ezra died. She was the only one in the room when he died. The Medical Examiner on this case traced ingestion of that poison to the time when she was alone in the room with him. There are witnesses who can attest she was in that room with him from 11:00 PM to 11:45 PM, and the Medical Examiner has said the poison was ingested during that time."

"You're reciting facts I already know," I said to him. "What's your point in telling me all of this?"

"My point is that you're spinning your wheels. It's pretty

clear who gave him that poison. Now the prosecutor is offering your client 20 years. It's malpractice to turn that down. It's malpractice to advise your client to turn it down. I hope you can see that."

I sighed. "This is all well and good but what's Ginger's motive for killing this guy? Seriously? She hardly knew him."

"Is that what Ginger told you? She hardly knew him? He was a rando?" He shook his head. "Now I know you haven't worked a case this big before," he said. "But you can't be taken in by what your client is telling you."

"I *have* worked a case this big before. I've worked plenty of big cases before. I represented a professional football player, and…" I trailed off. I had plenty of murder cases that were big back home. But they weren't cases that got national attention. This case was getting national attention. The media narrative was breathlessly reporting all about how this adult film star murdered the studio executive and Ginger's name was on everybody's lips.

Truth be told, most of my murder cases were those uncelebrated ones that flew under the radar as far as nationwide attention went. It was the curse – or blessing, depending on how you looked at it – of working in a small city. A small market. You made a name for yourself with the local bar but you would never be called as a legal expert on a cable news show. You never would make millions of dollars a year representing big-time criminals like David was.

There were lawyers making that much money in Kansas City but they were generally partners in large firms and personal injury attorneys. They cleaned up and lived in the mansions among the sports stars. The criminal defense attorneys who took the big cheese white-collar criminals were generally in those large firms. They got $1,000 a billable hour and up.

Here in Los Angeles, however, there seemed to be plenty of attorneys making that kind of money. Plenty of criminal defense attorneys out here were making seven figures a year.

I looked up and saw he was looking at me sympathetically. "You're out of your league," he said. "And you'll be doing your client a real injustice if you don't sell that 20-year plea deal."

I took a piece of bread off the table and buttered it. I needed to change the subject and quickly. "Tell me about some of your other cases. I think it's fascinating to hear the stories from the big-wheel attorneys representing these big Kahuna clients."

He shrugged. "My job isn't as glamorous as you seem to think. Seriously, criminal defense is criminal defense, no matter where you practice, no matter who your client is. I just have to be more of a ball-breaker when I represent my clients. You know, you get a Russian and Armenian mob clientele and you gotta be careful. You make a false move and you might be their next victim. They're ruthless, too."

"I can imagine. I mean, you lose a case involving somebody big, and what happens?"

"I watch my back. I hire bodyguards for several months. I make sure I don't do anything wrong in that case so they can't blame me for their cases going south. And I survive and go onto the next one. It's not a life I'd recommend to anyone, but it is what it is."

"And that's why you get paid the big bucks."

"Yeah."

The food came around and I dug in. For some odd reason, I was dying to just eat and get out of there. Go home and relax with my girls, my dogs and Mia. That was something I hadn't done for quite awhile – just relax at home with them. To my dismay, even though this whole trip was supposed to be like a mini-vacation, it didn't feel that way. I felt isolated and alone and…vulnerable. I hadn't felt vulnerable for a long time.

Yet, I knew I would have to make time to see Ginger. I needed to at least tell her the offer was on the table and see where it went. I wouldn't imagine she'd be dying to take that offer but I knew it was a good one. It was an offer I really should encourage her to at least think about.

The conversation between David and me was strained. I couldn't put my finger on why this guy felt off to me.

I only knew he did.

Chapter Fifteen

AFTER LUNCH, I decided to pay Ginger a call. I needed to see how she was doing, but I also wanted to give her the offer from the prosecutor's office. It was my duty to do that, anyhow. I didn't know quite how I felt about it. If I thought Ginger had a part in this guy's demise then I would probably have urged her to take it.

But if she was completely innocent….I might still give her the offer, especially since this entire case was shaping up to be something of a lost cause. I had plenty of other suspects but nobody I could wrap my arms around. Nobody was jumping out at me.

It looked bad that Ginger was the last person to see Ezra alive. She was in the room when he ingested the poison. There were plenty of witnesses prepared to back that up.

I called her on the cell phone.

"Hey, Harper," she said. "I'm at the studio. You wanna come down here? I'm at the studio in Van Nuys. Come on down here, I'd like to see you."

I suppressed a smile as I thought about going to the

porn studio to see Ginger. This wasn't something I would get a chance to do every day, so I might as well take this opportunity while I could. "Sure," I said. "I'll be there in a half hour."

I put the name of the studio – Dark Angel – into my GPS and drove to Van Nuys.

Van Nuys was in the San Fernando Valley and it came to be known as "The Porn Capital of the World." Apparently, at least at one time, the area was known for producing the highest amount of porn per capita in the world. The studios were in converted warehouses that dotted this part of Los Angeles county like monopoly hotels. I had done my research and found out that Los Angeles County had passed a law requiring condoms to be used in all adult films. This caused the porn industry to flee to other places that had less restrictions like Miami. Miami started to get the girls and the industry, but their industry mainly focused on amateur porn stars. Van Nuys still had the part of the industry that was more professional – producing quality DVDs, not just showing girls in porn clips on the internet.

Then, in 2016, there was an attempt by the state legislature of California to require all porn stars, state-wide, to wear condoms. That measure was defeated, and Measure B, the 2012 law that required condoms to be used on all porn shoots in L.A. County, was no longer enforced. That meant the porn industry in California returned after L.A. County started to see a 95% drop in permits for new porn locations.

I drove to the location of Ginger's studio which was nestled amongst other warehouses that weren't clearly marked. I got to the studio door, gave a password Ginger had given me, and they let me in.

"So, you're seeing Ginger, huh?" A uniformed security guard asked me. He was wearing a guard's uniform and a bored expression. "Let me take you to where she is. She's on set right now."

I was led through to a large room where there was seats that hovered above two sets. One set showed a living room, with a couch, television, rug and coffee table. There were paintings on the walls and a fake window. The other set was clearly that of a bedroom – there was a king-sized four-poster bed with a red bed-spread, along with a chest of drawers and a night-stand. I watched as a man and a woman entered through the door of the living room set. They said a few lines and immediately started kissing. There were several cameramen filming from several different angles and a director trying to position the two people.

Before long, there were several more women who came on the scene. Two of the women started to kiss each other, they pulled the man in, and the three of them made out.

I started to feel somewhat embarrassed about being there. As if I was a voyeur. I never felt like that when I watched an actual movie, but watching it live, it felt all kinds of wrong.

I felt even more wrong when I saw Ginger enter the scene. By this time, there was another guy on the scene and he was tied to a chair. This was known as a cuckold scene, where the husband or boyfriend is tied up and forced to watch his wife having sex with another man. In this case, however, the husband was tied up and forced to watch his wife, played by Ginger, having sex with another woman.

I decided I had had enough of watching all of this, so I wandered around and looked at the all the different sets. This was a huge warehouse and there were about ten different sets. I wandered by one and briefly saw there was a bondage scene being filmed. Another set had a gay orgy and still another had a reverse harem – five men and one woman.

Finally, I went into a room and Ginger came in. She was dressed in a tiny bikini and high heels. She apparently had a wig on, for her hair was white with blue and pink stripes. She had on even more makeup than usual and she was much thinner than she before. She looked like she had lost about twenty pounds since she left Kansas City.

I had seen her several days prior, so I imagined I just didn't notice her weight loss before. Now, as she stood there in a bikini, it was difficult to not see how much weight she'd lost.

She smiled and gave me a hug. "Harper, thank you for coming to see me. Can you believe it, did you see that hot guy I was paired with? God, it's so good to be with a guy that's actually hot, not some gross fat guy or some old fart. That right there makes this job better than the job I had in Kansas City."

I nodded and looked at her. "You've lost a lot of weight," I said. I noticed her ribs were poking out underneath her tiny bra-top. "I think you need a cheeseburger."

"What I wouldn't give for a cheeseburger," she said, "But if I ate a cheeseburger I would have to puke it up. I do that, Harper, when I overeat. Dale makes me do it. Dale, he tells me I can't gain even a pound. In fact, he wants me to lose even more weight. He tells me he'll fire me if I gain even one pound, Harper, he don't even care I'm really popular and everybody knows my name."

"Ginger," I said, feeling like a mother. "That's not healthy."

"I don't care about healthy," she said. "I'm making money, a lot of money. I'm making more money now than I ever have. All the girls are jealous of me 'cause I get top billing and top dollar, too."

I sighed. I wouldn't change her mind. She would do what she would do. "Okay," I said. "Listen, I have an offer for you to consider." I was starting to wonder if maybe Ginger *was* good for the crime. She certainly was acting as if she didn't have a care in the world. She was acting as if there wasn't the Sword of Damocles, otherwise known as a first-degree murder charge, hanging over her head.

"What do you mean by offer?" Ginger asked.

"I mean that the prosecutor has made an offer on your case. 20 years in prison, plus your charge will be reduced to manslaughter. That means you'll be pleading to a homicide, but you killed Ezra in the heat of passion. That means you didn't kill him with malice. Bear in mind if we take this to trial, you'll face life in prison and have a murder charge on your record." I really didn't think Ginger would understand the difference between murder and manslaughter, but I hoped she could figure out that one was considerably less serious than the other.

She furrowed her brow. "I don't understand, Harper. You're supposed to be representing me. You're supposed to be with me in court." She started to cry. "Why would you want to do me like that, Harper? Why would you want me go to prison, Harper? I didn't do nothing, Harper. All I did was suck his whiskey dick. That's all I did."

"I know that. I understand that. But I have to bring you any and all offers the prosecutor makes. That's my duty. You don't have to take it, of course. But I wanted you to know the offer is out there."

"Well, I say not just no but hell no to that offer," she said. "Tell that prosecutor she can take that offer and shove it up her ass."

"I thought you would say that. But I want to reiterate that if we take this to trial and lose, you won't be facing 20 years for a manslaughter charge. You'll be facing life in prison for a murder charge. Plus, if you take this deal, you have the possibility of parole after a matter of years. If we take the case to trial and lose, you could be facing life in prison without the possibility of parole." I paused. "The life of this particular plea offer is only 72 hours, which means that three days from now, the plea offer will no longer be on the table. I really only wanted to bring you this agreement because I wanted to see your reaction. If I thought for a second you actually killed that man, I would've strongly urged you to take it."

Ginger's reaction to the plea agreement momentarily reassured me that she didn't do it. But, then again, she was an actress. And she had always been shady.

"Well, take that offer and shove it up her ass. I'm not taking no deal." She crossed her arms in front of her and shook her head. "No deal."

"Okay, okay, no deal. I need to get a more active investigation underway on who might've done this. There are lots of suspects in this particular carnival, and none who were at the party. That's the whole problem, really."

"Figure it out, Harper. I'm paying you lots of money to figure it out."

"I know, I know. I'll figure it out."

Then she smiled brightly. Sweet Ginger was back. "I know, I trust you. I do." She gave me a quick hug. "I gotta get back to work. I'll see you when you come and visit me again, huh?"

"Sure."

At that, she turned and walked away, presumably to go and shoot another scene.

Chapter Sixteen

I GOT HOME and reviewed my list of suspects provided by Marissa, the police investigator and Tony Marinaro, the investigator hired by David.

Tony, for his part, told me to look closely at Ezra's siblings. "Ariel, Daniel and Eli had the most to gain out of killing Ezra," he said. "In fact, they were the only ones with something to gain in killing Ezra."

"What about Alex Sarks and the Armenian Power?" I asked. "It would seem the leaders of Armenian Power would also have reason to kill Ezra. He owed them a lot of money because they financed that apartment building he owned. Now it seems the leader, Sargis Gregorian, is shaking down the surviving siblings to get the money out of them." That was something else I had found out in the course of the investigation. It immediately made me suspicious that Sargis might be behind the entire thing.

Tony shook his head. "No, Sargis is clean," he said. "I've already checked that out. He not only had an air-tight alibi but didn't have any men at the party. You've seen the guest list – there wasn't a single person on that list of Armenian heritage. Not one person who associates with the Armenian Power. Not even somebody from the Russian mafia, which closely associates with the Armenian Power and bankrolls many of their projects."

Tony was speaking rapidly, which immediately gave me pause.

"Okay, then," I said, making a mental note to go after Sargis Gregorian, no matter what Tony told me. That seemed the best place to go.

After I checked out the family.

I had Tony make an appointment to see Ariel Rossi, Ezra's sister. After that, I'd see Daniel and Eli. Feel them out, see what emotions are let loose when I speak to them. Then, if I had suspicions, I'd call them for trial.

I went to Ariel's house that she shared with her husband and three children. The Glendale house was in the middle of a solidly middle-class neighborhood. I knew something about Los Angeles homes – they were much higher priced than Kansas City homes. In Kansas City, you could buy a decent house for $200,000. If you had a house worth $1,000,000, you had an incredible house. You had a mansion in a neighborhood populated by CEOs and sports stars.

But in Los Angeles, $1,000,000 buys you a modest three-bedroom ranch in an older neighborhood. And this was the kind of house Ariel was living in – her house was small with a stucco exterior and a pitched roof. I rang the doorbell, and a woman, presumably Ariel, opened the door. A tiny Shih Tzu dog, with ribbons in her hair, came up, barked and sniffed me excitedly, her little tail wagging a mile a minute. She barked again and backed up and continued to bark, her tail wagging the whole way. And then she lay on her back with her tail still wagging.

The house inside was very cute with hardwood floors. To the right was a small room that served as a living room. It had a fireplace, two couches and a small table with a lamp. To the left was the dining room, separated by an arched wall. Towards the back of the house were presumably the two bedrooms.

"Shhh, Bella, be quiet," she said to the barking dog. Bella was now on her feet barking away at me. Ariel picked up the dog and scolded her lightly. "Now, now, Bella, be quiet. This nice lady won't hurt you. No, she won't hurt you." She pointed at me. "See, Bella, she's a nice lady."

Bella, obviously not sure about me, growled, and Ariel laughed. "She's scared of new people," she said. "I have no idea why. I guess it's because she's such a little girl that everybody looks huge to her."

"She's adorable," I said. "I love dogs."

Ariel smiled. "Have a seat," she said, pointing to the couch in the living room. She handed me a glass of water. "It's hot out there."

I sipped my water and continued to be struck by how modest this house was compared to Ezra's behemoth. Maybe there was something to the theory that Ezra's siblings were behind his murder. I researched the issue and found that Ezra didn't have a will, for whatever reason, and that meant the laws of intestate succession would kick in for his estate. Which meant, in turn, his three siblings would get everything he owned. It would've been different if he had a will and cut his siblings out. But since he died without a will, his siblings were wealthy.

And Ariel, at least, wasn't wealthy at the moment. The money had to still go through probate, which was no-doubt why she hadn't yet moved into a tonier neighborhood. Not that she necessarily wanted to. I, myself, thought this neighborhood was cute. The homes mostly had tall palm trees in their front yards, along with different kinds of local trees such as eucalyptus, California pepper, olive and Chinese elms. Many of the houses had landscaping with a rock foundation, because of the long-time drought dogging California for years, along with strategically-placed succulent plants. Many of them looked professionally landscaped.

Still, when I compared Ariel's house to Ezra's, there was no comparison. Ezra lived like a studio boss. Ariel lived like somebody solidly middle-class.

"Thank you," I said, sipping my water. "For meeting with me."

"Of course," Ariel said. "You're working my brother's murder. I'll give you all the help I can. I've already talked to Officer Leoni and Tony Marinaro. I guess he was hired by…" She furrowed her brow. "Well, I guess you hired him, didn't you?"

"I didn't," I said. "The guy who's local counsel on this case did. David Jenkins. He's a white-collar criminal defense attorney. His office is downtown."

"I see," she said. "He's your co-counsel, then?"

"In a way," I said. "I'm from Kansas City, Missouri, so I can't practice law in California without the assistance of local counsel. But I'm the main attorney on this case."

She nodded. "I see," she said. "So, what do you need to ask me?"

"Well, I'm just trying to be thorough and figure out who did this," I said, almost apologetically. "And I understand your grandfather recently passed away and you and your two brothers were cut out of his will. You all were contesting that will. So I just wanted to get your side of the story."

She grimaced and sipped her water. "Our grandfather was very rich," she said. "That's true. And I won't lie. Ezra was a total bastard. None of us got along with him. I'll be straight about that." She sipped her water some more, her eyes not meeting mine. "I've been having problems talking about this. I'm sorry. You're the third person I've spoke with about this. So, I apologize if I seem a little...abrupt."

"No, no," I said. "I want you to speak frankly. That's the only way I'll figure out what happened."

She nodded. "I understand and I thank you for coming out here." She took a deep breath. "I have complicated feelings about what happened. I hated him when he was alive. But now that he's dead..." She paused, her face turned down. "Now that he's dead, I don't know how I feel. It's strange. One day, you're angry with your brother. You hate what he did. You hate what he's become. You hate that he suddenly thinks he's too good for you, that he's somehow above you, just because he's living in a big house in Malibu and knows all these celebrities. As if that's what makes a good life. You hate how much he's changed. You didn't know he was so greedy and money-grubbing that he'd change our grandfather's will to cut out his siblings. You're disgusted with the person he's become. Yet, when he dies..."

She started to cry and I put my hand on hers. "Take your time," I said. "Just take your time."

"Thanks." She cried some more. "I've been seeing my therapist about my feelings because I'm so confused about them. I guess I had unfinished business with Ezra. That happens when you grow up with your little brother, you love him, and then he dies when you aren't speaking to him. I just can't separate the Ezra who died in that house with the Ezra I knew when I was 10 years old and Ezra was 9. We always conspired to play practical jokes on our parents. I still see the Ezra who offered to beat up the boyfriends who cheated on me in high school. The Ezra who always had my back, no matter what. I still remember the days we'd sit on my parents' porch and look up at the stars, drinking a beer, talking about our lives and dreams. There are a lot of mixed emotions and I never got the chance to clear the air. It's difficult to process."

I made notes. I felt Ariel had nothing to do with the crime. Not that her brothers didn't do it. That was always a possibility. But Ariel herself? I was looking in the wrong direction.

"Now," I said. "You said something about him changing your grandfather's will. You mentioned that in passing. What do you mean about that? How did he change your grandfather's will?"

"He had his lawyer change it. Then he went to my grandfather's house, when he was delirious from late-stage Alzheimer's Disease, and had him sign it." She paused. "Our grandfather gathered all of us together before he got really bad and showed us his will. Our parents died in a plane crash five years ago, so we were to get everything equally. At that time, he was showing signs of Alzheimer's but they were minor. He was having memory issues but we weren't all that concerned. He'd forget what happened the day before, for instance, or would completely forget to meet us somewhere. Other than those glitches, he was of sound mind."

"So his will changed somewhere along the line?"

"Yes. I don't exactly know when that will changed because none of us found it was changed until it was read. Our grandfather had no reason to cut us out of the will. It wasn't difficult to figure out what happened."

"Who was the attorney who drafted that new will?"

"I knew you'd ask me that question," she said with a smile. "I keep forgetting the guy's name. I looked it up for the other investigators but I'll have to look it up for you, too."

At that, she got up from her chair and went into a different room. As soon as she left, Bella the dog growled at me, but then got a toy and brought it over. She barked excitedly and nosed the toy and I smiled and threw it across the room. Her tiny body bounded over to it and she brought it to me again. She didn't drop it this time, but kept the toy in her mouth and shook her head back and forth. I grabbed the toy and tugged on it. She growled and tugged on it harder.

Ariel came back before I had the chance to get the toy from the dog and throw it again. "Bella is such a sweetie," I said. "Did you find the paperwork you were looking for?"

"No," she said, her face perplexed. "I didn't. It's so strange, too. I have this filing cabinet where I keep important papers. The will was in a folder in that filing cabinet. It had the drafting attorney's name on it. I saw it yesterday." She shook her head. "That's weird."

"Well, I'll get a copy from the Los Angeles Courthouse," I said. "It had to be filed with the Recorder of Deeds for it to take effect."

"Yes, true," she said. "Anyhow, as I was saying, none of us knew our grandfather's will had been changed until it was read. And then all hell broke loose. My husband is not a patient man, to say the very least. He was pissed. Eli and Daniel weren't happy either. Me, I really didn't care. I have all I need and more. If I got one-fourth of a $50 million estate, I got one-fourth of a $50 million estate. If I didn't, I didn't. Nothing I could do about it and it wasn't like I was losing anything. But I was angry, too, because of the principle. That's what enraged me. That Ezra would do such a thing. It wasn't the money, it was the principle. All the way."

"Was your husband angry enough to…"

"No," she shook her head. "He wasn't. He wouldn't do something like that. Neither would my brothers."

"What do you know about Sargis Gregorian?" I asked her. "He's an Armenian mobster who's one of the leaders of the Armenian Power, a powerful organized crime syndicate in Los Angeles. It's my understanding that Ezra was in debt to Sargis because Sargis financed an apartment building Ezra bought right before your grandfather died. And…"

I chewed the end of my pen thoughtfully. I suddenly hit on an angle I didn't even think of before. Sargis financed Ezra's apartment project right before the grandfather died. And then the grandfather died, leaving Ezra the money. All the money. What if Sargis and Ezra were somehow in on killing the grandfather? After all, Ezra didn't have a ton of money before the grandfather died. He was working at Paramount in development but he certainly didn't have millions in his bank account. So how could Sargis have known Ezra would be good for that money?

"What are you thinking about?" Ariel asked me.

"I'm thinking," I said. "About how Ezra could secure financing for that apartment building. Why was Sargis so willing to work with Ezra when he was pretty much broke?"

"I don't know the answer to that question," Ariel said. "But I'm sorry, you were asking me about what I know about Sargis. And the answer is not much. I understand Sargis and my brother were partners on that apartment building downtown that went belly-up. I don't know who he is, though. The first time I've heard his name was when Marissa asked me questions."

I made a note about that. If Ariel was telling the truth, she obviously wasn't too involved in Ezra's business dealings.

I would have to follow-up on these questions if I ever spoke with Sargis. I had a feeling that wouldn't happen. I could issue a subpoena for court, which is what I resolved to do.

"How did your grandfather die?" I asked Ariel.

"In a car accident. He had a driver because he couldn't drive due to his illness. They were driving on a winding road in Big Bear and went off the cliff in the rain. Both my grandfather and his driver were killed instantly." She shook her head. "If you've ever been on Big Bear roads, you'd understand how treacherous they are. They're winding and many of those roads don't even have a guardrail. And the people who live on that mountain drive like maniacs. They'll tailgate you if you don't drive fast enough and the roads are narrow and one lane each way. I'm surprised more people don't die on that goddamned road."

"Did anybody examine the car after it went off the road? And why was your grandfather out and about during that period of time?" For some reason, I thought the grandfather was bedridden when he died. I imagined Ezra going to his deathbed and having him sign the phony will. I'd seen too many movies.

"The car wasn't examined, of course. It went down the

cliff in the rain. Nobody thought it necessary to examine that car. As for why my grandfather was out and about in a car, all I can say is he had good days and bad days. Some days, he was lucid and knew who everybody was. We'd visit him and he'd converse with us and call us by name. Other days, we'd see him and he wouldn't know any of us. Towards the end, he had more bad days than good ones. He didn't know us most of the time. Now, I don't know, this is just speculation, but I think Ezra saw him during those times when he didn't know us. That would've been the best time to get him to sign a new will."

"And the witnesses to this new will? Who were they?"

"The lawyer and the Notary Public. The lawyer was obviously shady because he made up the will in the first place. As for the Notary Public, I doubt she knew what was going on. Ezra could be sneaky. He probably got that Notary Public in and out of there so fast she didn't know our grandfather wasn't in his right mind when he signed that will."

It seemed like the entire story of the will was getting stranger and stranger. The grandfather was out and about when the car crashed even though he suffered from late-stage Alzheimer's? The Notary Public didn't question what was going on? The lawyer was shady?

I still wondered if somehow Sargis was behind all this.

I knew I'd be better off speaking with Sargis or somebody close to him before speaking with any other witness. Sargis seemed to be the biggest target although I was figuring out exactly how that all worked out. If Sargis was somehow behind the change of the will and the grandfather dying, what would that mean? That would mean Sargis wouldn't also have killed Ezra, right? Ezra was his investment, after all.

"Thank you," I said to Ariel. "I think I know who I need to speak with next."

We exchanged pleasantries and I left.

I would go and see David and see if I could get speak to Sargis. I needed to ask him some serious questions.

Chapter Seventeen

"NOW WHY WOULD you want to do that?" David asked me when I went to his office. "What the hell does Sargis Gregorian have to do with any of this?"

David shook his head and glared.

"I-"

"Seriously, I'd like to know your theory of the case with this." David seemed agitated when he spoke with me. His speech was rapid and his eyes were glowering.

"If you let me explain, I'll tell you what my theory of the case is with regards to Sargis Gregorian," I said. "Now, we know Sargis and Ezra were partners on this apartment complex downtown that ended up not happening. That entire deal fell through but not before Sargis put millions of his money into it."

"Right. That meant Ezra was on the hook for that money because he borrowed that money from Sargis. So why would Sargis kill him? Wouldn't that mean there would be no way for Ezra to pay that money back to Sargis?"

"You make a point, but that's what I'm trying to figure

out. I know Ezra had the money, and thensome, to pay Sargis back. You went to his house the same as me. You were right there with me, walking through that mansion. Yet he wasn't paying his debts to the Armenian mobster? Even though he clearly had the money? I'd think that Sargis would be goddamned pissed about that. Pissed enough to kill him."

"You're delusional," he said.

"Am I? Really? Listen, here's what else I found out through my independent investigation of this whole sorry matter. Sargis is shaking down Daniel and Eli to get that money. That's what your investigator, Tony, told me. Sargis sent his men to see Daniel and Eli. Daniel and Eli agreed to pay Sargis for his investment plus 10%."

That was true, too – Tony told me this was happening.

David's face started to get red. "Tony told you that?" He bit his bottom lip. "What else did he tell you? And what about Ariel? Has she also promised to give up part of her inheritance to Sargis?"

"No," I said. "In fact, she appears to not know who Sargis is."

"And does that make sense to you that Daniel and Eli would make a business arrangement to give Sargis a part of their inheritance but not Ariel? Does that make any sense at all?"

I shook my head. "No, I guess it doesn't." There was still another missing piece in this whole scenario. I just couldn't put my finger on it.

David made a point – why were only the brothers dealing with Sargis and not Ariel? That hardly seemed fair.

David seemed to calm down a little bit. "Okay, then," he said. "We'll go in a different direction, right? We're won't take a bat to that hornet's nest if we don't have to. Right?"

"The hornet's nest being..."

"Being Sargis Gregorian," he said. "We're won't go there with him. We need to go in a different direction."

"What are you thinking? What direction do we need to go in?"

"We need to look at Sasha Hapsburg," he said. "His ex-wife. The crazy ex-wife that Marissa was talking about. She sounds unhinged. She might be the most viable suspect in this. We can probably convince a jury that Sasha had motive to kill Ezra."

"The motive, but not the means," I said. "She wasn't at the party."

"Neither was Sargis," he said. "In fact, nobody on Marissa's list of suspects was at that party. That means you need to keep trying for a plea agreement on this. It looks like our girl is going down."

"That won't happen," I said. "I gave her the plea offer and she turned it down flat. She said, and I quote, that Adrian Jackson, the prosecutor, could take her plea offer and shove it up her ass. Ginger insists she did nothing wrong. She's sticking by that strongly."

"Look," he said. "You've looked at that guest list. You had Patty look at that guest list. You've done the research on the people on that guest list. You've seen nobody on that guest list who'd be a suspect in this murder in any way, shape or form. That leaves only Ginger. I agree it's odd that she'd kill Ezra, since she doesn't know him—"

"She not only doesn't know him but she's gotten nothing out of his death. So, explain that. For that matter, I'd like the prosecutor to explain that as well. Explain how a woman who had no motive for killing Ezra and who got nothing out of it would kill him? Especially since three people *have* gotten something out of his death – his three siblings – plus Sargis is finally getting paid for what Ezra owed him now that Ezra is dead. Ginger was in the wrong place at the wrong time, nothing more."

David was quiet during my rant. "Are you finished?" he asked me. "Or are you still mid-rant?"

"I'm not ranting," I said. "I'm passionately stating my case. And, I might remind you, you and I are on the same team. We're both Ginger's attorneys. I'd suggest you start acting like her attorney." I crossed my arms in front of me. "But go on."

"We're not going in the direction of Sargis, period. I still think we need to pressure our client into taking that plea agreement, but, barring that, I say we make the alternative suspect Sasha. She's the only suspect connected to the movie business. After all, she was an actress."

"From what Marissa told me, she wasn't much of an actress. In fact, I couldn't find an IMDB page for her, so that tells me she wasn't an actress at all."

David took a deep breath. "If you let me finish…"

"Go ahead."

Another deep breath. "Thank you. Sasha was a struggling actress but she has her SAG card. Granted, she hasn't used it, not even for a commercial, but that's not from lack of trying. At any rate, she works at Spago, where she met Ezra in the first place, which means she comes across a lot of people in the movie industry. Believe me, if she's somebody looking for a break and going to auditions, which she is, she knows people in the industry. A lot of people in the industry. That means she'd know most of the people at that party. That would also mean she had access to somebody with the opportunity to kill Ezra. Out of everyone who had something against Ezra, she was the only one with opportunity."

I nodded. "Okay. Sasha will be our fall girl on this case. No matter what. Is that what you're saying? She was in the industry and the three siblings weren't, and neither was Sargis, and nobody else had a reason to want Ezra dead, therefore we're nailing Sasha for this? Is this your idea of practicing law?"

He leaned back. "You have any other bright ideas? You're the one who doesn't want to plead this one out. You're the one rolling the dice and hoping to pull a rabbit out of a hat. If Ginger goes to prison for the rest of her life, when she could've gotten a 20-year sentence, up for parole in 5, that'll be on you. Not me."

He made a point. Was I committing malpractice by not being more persuasive with Ginger on this? If she got life in prison, she might be sentenced to life in prison without the possibility of parole. *Could* she be out in five years on a 20-year sentence? O.J. Simpson was sentenced to 30 years in prison for armed robbery and got out of prison in 9. If that could happen, anything could. It was possible for Ginger to get parole in a matter of years if she took this deal.

"Well, I don't have control on whether or not she takes this deal. Only Ginger does."

"That's right and you should be thinking long and hard about how you present this deal to her. It's up to you to bring all your powers of persuasion to tell her she's passing up the deal of the century."

"It's only the deal of the century if she's guilty of killing Ezra. Obviously. Otherwise, that's no deal at all. You've seen Ginger. You've seen how little she is. And she's having the time of her life making movies out here. She's happy. Even if she serves, say, 5 years in prison for killing Ezra and gets out on parole, where will she be when she gets out? She'll be 5 years older, which means she'll be 30, because she's 25 right now, and that's too old for the adult movie business. She'll be competing against teenagers and women in their early 20s."

"Where will she be in five years if she serves time in prison? I'll tell you where. Exactly the same place as if she hadn't served a day in prison. In either scenario, she'll be 30 years old in five years and the porn business won't have a thing to do with her by then. It's not like she'll take the money she's making at that Dark Angel studio and sock it away for a rainy day. She won't put that money into a retirement fund. She'll put that money up her nose or in her arm, just like they all do in that business. So whether or not she goes to prison for five years, it won't matter. When she turns 30, either way, she'll still have no place to go, no way to make money and will be back to turning tricks. If she's lucky."

I nodded. What he said was the God's honest truth. Ginger's days as a porn star were numbered no matter what she did. And he was also right that, whether Ginger spent the next five years in a prison or spent them "working" on adult movies, it wouldn't matter. She would no doubt end up broke and without prospects by that time. She would end up in the same place no matter what happened.

But that didn't make it right. It would never be right for an innocent woman like Ginger to go to prison. It wasn't right and I resented David pressuring me about it.

"Way to stereotype," I finally said. "You make it sound like all adult film stars are strung out on drugs."

"Aren't they?"

"No. I admit Ginger is on drugs and has been for as long as I've known her, but that's not true for all adult film stars. I saw this documentary about porn stars in Florida and all those girls in that documentary were nice girls who wanted to make a buck. I don't think any of them were on drugs."

He shook his head. "Irrelevant. What's relevant is that our client, Ginger Perry, is on drugs. Hell, if she goes to prison, she might be better off. Maybe she'll get off drugs that way."

"Nope. You and I both know there are more drugs behind bars than on the street."

He took another deep breath. "Okay, then. If you don't want to plead Ginger, then I say we convince the jury Sasha did it. I say we find enough evidence that she had motive to kill Ezra. The only other thing we need to show is the vehicle. Sasha wasn't at that party so she had to have found somebody at the party willing to do her dirty work. The best place to find that vehicle would be somebody who knew Sasha well."

I shook my head. "This is getting stupid," I said. "So we'll put two suspects on the hook here, Sasha and the mysterious person who poisoned the drink. Neither of which, I might add, had a decent motive for killing Ezra."

"You got a better idea?"

"Yes. Sargis. He's a mob boss with many more murderous contacts than a struggling wannabe actress like Sasha. He has motive, because Ezra wasn't paying him. Yet, here he is, successfully shaking down Daniel and Eli. Motive, means and opportunity. Sargis has it all."

David looked like his head was about to explode. "No more talk of Sargis. You don't want to go there. Trust me on this."

"I *do* want to go there if he did it. I personally think he not only killed Ezra but also Ezra's grandfather. I see no reason to give a struggling waiter like Ezra the money to buy an apartment complex unless he knew Ezra would soon come into money. Sargis gives Ezra money for the apartment complex, and then, poof! Ezra's grandfather gets into a car accident and dies. Then Ezra comes into all that money. Why would Sargis make a deal with him in the first place?"

David stood up. "Okay, Harper, here's the deal. You stop going down this road. You don't know who you're dealing with. Sargis Gregorian had nothing to do with this murder. If you think he did, you better well fucking prove it. And I mean prove it. Not just beyond a reasonable doubt, but definitively prove it. With concrete evidence. Not speculation. Not conjecture. Concrete evidence. Otherwise, back the fuck off."

"I-"

"Back the fuck off. You forget, I represent guys like Sargis all the time. Russian mob, Armenian mob, Italian mob, Mexican cartels, Japanese Yakuza. I represent guys from all these organizations. You don't want to fuck with them. Trust me. Don't go there. That's all I have to say."

As I looked at his handsome face, I started to hate him.

I wanted, more than anything else, to fire him. Yet I couldn't do that. David was valuable because his contacts and connections. And I didn't feel confident that I could find somebody else at such a late date.

I was stuck with him.

Chapter Eighteen

ON THE WAY HOME, I started to feel depressed, and, worse than that, I had an overwhelming urge to take a drink. So even though I had to be home, because I promised the girls I'd have dinner with them, I took a detour to another AA meeting. The meeting was at 6:30 at Our Lady of Malibu Church on Winter Canyon Road. I called Mia and lied about working late and drove to the church.

From the outside, this church didn't really look like a church. It was too modern and it was small. The roof was Spanish tile, the outside was stucco. In other words, it was a modern California vision of what a church might look like.

Going in the door I saw the interior was just as nontraditional as the outside of the church. The ceiling was made up of wood beams and the pews were also wooden. The altar, as Catholic Church altars go, was fairly plain. I wondered if this church was built in such a spare manner because of the whole Jesus-was-a-carpenter motif.

I followed the signs that directed me to where the meeting was, found the room and went in.

I saw a couple of faces that greeted me from the last meeting. I apparently wasn't the only one who needed to go to regular meetings.

We all stood up when the group leader came in, held hands, and said the serenity prayer. Then we all sat down again. The group leader, a slight blonde woman who wore her hair in a tight bun and was wearing heavy makeup in a futile attempt to disguise her aging skin, addressed the group. "Welcome everyone," she said, looking around the room. "I'm Barbara. I see some familiar faces here. I see some new faces here. If you're new, please raise your hand."

I raised my hand.

"And your name is?"

"Harper Ross."

"Welcome, Harper," she said.

"Hello, Harper," everyone said.

I felt braver in talking to this group than I did the last one. The last meeting gave me my sea legs. This one seemed more old hat. I was a veteran by then, a veteran of Malibu AA meetings. I'd tell the group about my issue with my client because I didn't know what to do.

Except I did know what to do. I needed to go after Sargis Gregorian. He was most likely person to have done this. Yet David was adamant I let that go. That contributed to the stress and confusion I felt. Stress and confusion, paired with a brief episode of falling off the wagon, made me mentally foggy. Mental fogginess was not something I wanted to experience right at this moment.

Everybody gave their stories. This meeting seemed to be more of a free-wheeling meeting than the one at the Michael Landon Center in the Malibu Bluffs Park. There wasn't a certain theme that everybody was supposed to have spoken about. At the last meeting, the theme was gratitude. This meeting, the topic was open. Everybody talked about their stressors.

Eventually, the meeting got to me.

I cleared my throat. "I'm Harper Ross, and I'm an alcoholic," I said, echoing what everyone else said by way of introduction.

"Hello, Harper," everyone said in unison.

"It's been one week since I've taken my last drink," I said. "Before that, it had been several years since I had taken a drink. And I've been doing okay with not drinking. But today I had the overwhelming urge to get shit-faced in a bar." I shook my head as I looked at everyone's faces. They all were smiling and nodding along. They obviously felt the same way I did. "I don't know why I had that urge except that I'm feeling out of sorts."

I didn't give them the story about alcohol being poured down my throat. It was too weird. I started to think it didn't happen. Maybe it was all in my head. It was just so strange.

"Why are you feeling out of sorts?" Barbara asked.

"I'm here on a case," I said. "A criminal case. And…it's not going so well. My local counsel, David, has been pressuring me to get my client to take a deal. I know it's not the right choice. At the same time, I don't know where to turn. I have my ideas on who might've done this but David is pressuring me to lay off that angle. I want to fire David but feel it's too late. I'm feeling under the gun, stressed and lost. That's why I wanted to come to this meeting. It was either coming here or going to a bar."

"Have you been working the Big Book?" Barbara asked me. "The Twelve Steps?"

I wasn't working those Twelve Steps as much as I

should've been. I tried to work the first step – admitting I was powerless over alcohol and my life had become unmanageable. I was having issues with that and couldn't work that step on a deep level.

"I'm trying," I said.

"I see," Barbara said. "Can I ask what step you're on?"

"The first," I said, feeling embarrassed.

"Do you think you have a block?" asked somebody else around the table. It was a 20-something guy with wild curly blonde hair, a deep tan and a tight t-shirt that showed his 8-pack abs. His name tag read "Matt." He hadn't yet spoken so I didn't know his story.

I shrugged. "I don't know. I'm still absorbing that first step into my psyche. I'm powerless over alcohol. The next two steps will be hard for me – I'm supposed to turn over my problems and my life to a higher power. And the fourth step will be the hardest. I can't admit my failings, even to myself. But I'm trying. I'm trying hard."

"That's all we can ask for," Matt said. "It's hard for all of us." He grinned, showing his dimples. "I mean, are you kidding? We're a bunch of drunks. We've all failed, lied and cheated. Some of us repeatedly. We've all had to take stock of our lives. I can't speak for anybody else, but working those 12 steps was the hardest thing I've ever done in my life. Working those steps involved a lot of shame and embarrassment. A lot of acknowledging shit I never wanted to think about again. Just thinking about what a screw-up I've been made me want to take a hundred drinks."

When he said that, everybody laughed nervously. They all knew just what he was talking about, I was sure.

I nodded. Was I the only one who felt that when I failed meant I was a total failure in life? That a specific failure meant I was a global failure? I knew I wasn't alone but certainly felt like it. I was with all these people who knew just where I was coming from. Yet I still couldn't move past the first step.

"Thank you for that," I said. "I'll keep working the 12 steps. I'll keep trying to get past the first step."

"I'm sorry," Matt said. "To interrupt."

"No, no, that's okay," I said. "I just wanted to come here and be around people with my same issues. That's why I came here in the first place. But I'll pass and listen to everyone else from here on out."

By the end of the meeting, I was feeling a lot better. I wasn't alone. I was in the same boat as a lot of people.

Now, if I could just work those 12 Steps.

THE NEXT DAY, I woke up determined to get Ginger's case back on track.

I left a message for Sargis Gregorian to come in for an interview, which would be held in David's conference room on Friday of that same week.

David had asked me not to go there, but I was going there anyhow. For my money, Sargis was still the most likely suspect.

Not a half hour later, I got a phone call while driving. It was David. "What the fuck are you doing?" he demanded.

"I'm interviewing Sargis. I need to ask him some questions."

"Shut the fuck up," David said. "I'm canceling the interview."

"You will not."

"I've already done it. Don't bother coming to my office on Friday. This interview won't happen."

I took a deep breath. "Listen, David, I'm thinking this whole partnership has run its course. This is my case. The only reason why you're on this case is because I need local counsel to sign off on pleadings and appear in court with me. I never intended for you to have significant input on this case. Nor is it welcome. I need to defend my client the way I want to defend her, and you aren't allowing me that. It's time to part ways."

"You do that and your name is shit in this town. Nobody will agree to be local counsel for you. There's no way you can try this case without somebody willing to sign your pleadings and appear in court with you. If you fire me, you're on your own. I can't protect you. And trust me, if you drag Sargis Gregorian into this case, you'll need protection. That's all I'll tell you."

"I don't understand what your problem is. I really don't. All I want to do is interview Sargis. That's it. I think he has information that will lead me to who killed Ezra. All signs point to him. Ginger will end up in prison if I can't defend her how I want. I can't let that happen. I'm sorry."

At that, I hung up.

He called right back, but I ignored him.

He kept calling, but I kept ignoring him.

I found a coffee shop and went in. I needed to use my computer to find somebody to help me out. Somebody willing to get on this case with me and let me do what was necessary to win.

My nerves were frazzled, however, and I had a hard time concentrating on the task at hand.

I got a cup of tea, sat down and closed my eyes. My heart was racing. I was so damned angry. Angry at David and at myself. I didn't vet David properly like I should've. I should've interviewed attorneys to find the right one. I should've gone with my gut. When I met David, every fiber in my being knew he wasn't right.

Why didn't I listen to myself?

I clicked away on my computer, my hand shaking wildly. I didn't know how to find an attorney to help me. I could just Google attorneys and start cold-calling them one by one. Surely *somebody* could step up to the plate and help me out. Surely somebody would be willing to make a name for themselves. This was a big case. Surely somebody would want the free publicity of appearing in court on this case.

I was lost in thought, looking at the computer and jotting down phone numbers. I would have to start cold-calling to find somebody.

Then I looked up and saw a man sitting across from me.

I looked around the coffee shop and saw empty tables.

The man was staring at me. He had piercing green eyes and long brown hair pulled back into a pony tail. I looked at his hands and saw tattoos on his knuckles.

I went back to my computer, hoping this guy would get the hint and go away. Maybe move to another table. He was invading my space and I didn't like that one bit.

I tried to concentrate on my computer but looked up from time to time and saw him still sitting there. Still staring at me.

I finally took a deep breath. I shut my computer and put it in my bag. I'd have to move to another table, or, better yet, go to a different coffee shop. Or maybe go home. However, I was a half-hour away from my house and was anxious to find another local attorney to enter an appearance on this case. Then I could officially fire David and do things my way.

I stood up and the man stood up as well.

I tried to ignore him as I packed my bag and headed for the door.

I got out into the parking lot and used the clicker to unlock my car.

But I never got into my car.

The man came up behind me and stuck a gun in my back.

An icy chill went down my spine as he whispered into my ear.

"You're coming with me," he said in a thick Eastern European accent.

Chapter Nineteen

"WHERE ARE YOU TAKING ME?" I demanded as I sat in the back of the man's black SUV.

He just drove and said nothing. He hid his eyes behind a pair of mirrored sunglasses, but, from time to time, he looked into his rear-view mirror and looked at me.

"You won't get away with this," I said, trying to sound braver than I was. "People are expecting me home this evening."

"I know," the man finally said. "Your two little girls are at home. Beautiful young girls. And that beautiful lady who looks after them. Mia, I think her name is?"

I bit my lower lip and tried to hold back tears. It was one thing for my own life to be threatened. It was quite another to threaten my family.

"What do you want?"

"I'll let you take a guess," he said in his thick accent. "I think you are an intelligent lady. I think you can probably figure it out. I have faith in you."

I looked out the window. My thoughts were stubbornly

focused on the fact I was in the back of an SUV going God-knows-where. I refused to think this entire episode had anything to do with Ginger's case.

A part of me knew I was stupid for ever thinking this kidnapping wasn't related to Ginger's case. Of course it was.

I had a feeling I was about to meet Sargis Gregorian himself.

I sighed. A part of me cheered that this guy hadn't already killed me. If Sargis wanted me dead, then this goombah, who was obviously one of Sargis' soldiers, would've driven me to the desert and put a bullet in the back of my head.

You've watched too many Tarantino films. I started to bite my nails as the car made its way through winding roads. We were obviously climbing to the top of one of the cliffs that overlooked the city.

At some point we arrived at a gate that opened the second our SUV got to the edge of it. The driver drove another thousand feet or so and arrived at a home that made Ezra's magnificent mansion look like somebody's servant's quarters.

This place was more like a compound than a home. It resembled the homes owned by some of the biggest celebrities in town. I always remembered seeing, say, Madonna's home from the arial view, or J. Lo and Ben Affleck's home. People like that.

The place looked more like a hotel than a home.

If Ezra's place was around 10,000 square feet and would probably sell for $10 million, this place was five times that and would probably sell for $50 million.

"Is this a hotel?" I asked the guy now walking next to me, his gun poking the small of my back. "Or an apartment building?" Truth be told, it resembled an apartment building. A luxury apartment building with luxury units.

It certainly didn't look like a residence.

The guy said nothing. He just continued to prod me forward to the front door of the estate. He opened the door without even knocking.

The door opened up into a grand foyer that had seventy foot ceilings and marble floors. About a hundred feet into the foyer were two leather chairs. On either side of the foyer were staircases that went into a point, and, above my head, was a giant chandelier.

"Is this a hotel?" I asked the guy again.

He smiled and just shook his head.

His phone rang. "Yeah, boss," he said. "I've got her right here." He nodded. "Will do."

"What's going on?" I asked him. "Where will you take me?"

He said nothing but stuck his gun in my back and led me to the back of the foyer. To the right was a heavy door covered with an ornate gold pattern.

He opened the door and shoved me into the room.

This room also had really high ceilings, although the ceilings weren't nearly as high as those in the foyer. They were only about thirty feet high, as opposed to the super-high ceilings in the front of the house. To the left was a wall of arched windows and to the right was a wall adorned with priceless artwork.

And, sitting at a desk, was a man. He was around 50 years old and was dressed elegantly in an expensive suit. He wasn't very tall – he couldn't have been more than 5'8" or 5'9" - but I could see he had rippling muscles beneath his fitted silk shirt. He had a full head of salt-and-pepper hair, a wide face with prominent cheekbones, and blue eyes. He was pale, as if he hadn't been in the sun all year, and his lips were puffy.

I knew just by looking at him he was Eastern European.

Nobody had to tell me who he was.

In front of me was the infamous Sargis Gregorian.

Chapter Twenty

I SWALLOWED hard and tried not to panic. My thoughts were going a mile a minute, yet my survival mechanism was kicking in. *Just do what he says and maybe, just maybe, you'll get out of this thing alive.*

He smiled warmly, his light blue eyes lighting up. He looked genuinely happy to see me, although I knew that wasn't true. No, he wasn't happy to see me. At all.

"Harper Ross," he said with evident glee. He clapped his hands together. "Sit down, sit down." He motioned to a leather chair right in front of his desk. "Make yourself at home."

He spoke perfect English. There was a tiny hint of an accent but not as thick as the kidnapper's accent. The inflections were somewhat different from a native speaker, but, other than that, there was no way of knowing this guy was from a different country.

I sat down gingerly on the chair and said nothing. I felt like I would feel if a vicious dog was barking his head off at me. I wouldn't look this guy in the eye and wouldn't say a word unless he asked me a direct question. And then I would only answer that question.

"You met Grigor, I take it," he said.

I looked behind me and saw the guy who kidnapped me was still standing in the room.

I turned back to look at the man, who I assumed was Sargis, and nodded slowly.

"Good. Good. I hope he treated you well. I told him he must. I told him you were a lady and must be treated as such." He paused. "I trust he treated you as a lady?"

I nodded, not knowing what else to really do.

He shook his head. "Oh, come come, you're a lawyer. You specialize in words. Words are how you make your living. Words and persuasion. You can use your words with me. Tell me how Grigor treated you. There will be an exam at the end of this and hopefully Grigor passes it well. So, tell me how Grigor treated you."

I took a deep breath. I didn't want to piss this guy off, so I'd go along with whatever he asked me. "Fine," I said in as strong a voice as I could muster.

"Fine," the man said. "As in? Did he lay a hand on you or call you an inappropriate name? He used to do that, you know. When he first starting working for me, he hit the women he brought here. Sometimes did even worse than that. And the names he would call them…" Sargis made a face and shook his head. "Vulgar. Needless to say, I trained him not to do any of these things. Now, I'd like to know, did my training pay off? Did Grigor treat you with respect and kindness?"

I nodded slowly. "Yes," I said. "Except he put a gun in my back."

"Good," the man said. "I'm very sorry about the firearm thing. It's necessary, you know. If he just said 'come along with me,' and didn't have the firearm, you would've laughed in his face. I consider the firearm to be a necessary evil. I think you'll agree once you've had the chance to really think about it."

I just stared at him, not reacting to that. I didn't know how I should've reacted to that. I could objectively and logically see his point – without that gun, I would've told him to fuck off and leave me alone. But since he had that gun...

I sat up straighter and crossed my arms in front of me. I had to show he couldn't intimidate me.

The man motioned to Grigor. "Grigor, bring us both a drink," he said. "Scotch rocks for me, scotch neat for her." Then he smiled. "You like scotch, don't you?"

I shook my head. I suddenly felt panic rise in my chest. Could I refuse this drink? And if I didn't refuse it, what would happen?

A part of me knew what would happen if I refused that drink. He probably would kill me. He was acting like a proper gentleman at the moment, but he was a powerful mob boss. The fact he lived in this palace told me that. Mafiosos didn't get this kind of money by treating people with respect. That was for sure. They get this kind of money by making their enemies fear them. By being ruthless. By dipping snitches in a vat of acid and burning people alive in cars.

I gripped the side of my chair as Grigor poured the two drinks. One for the man and one for me.

The man picked up his glass, raised it and winked. "Cheers," he said, nodding.

I reluctantly picked up my glass and raised it as well. My hand was shaking as I brought the liquid to my lips. I wondered if I could get away with not drinking it. However,

I saw him watching me intently so pulling a fast one wouldn't be possible.

The liquid was smooth as butter as it went down my throat with no hint of after-taste. I closed my eyes, waiting for it to take effect. A part of me craved this, wanted this. Especially now that I was faced with a life-or-death situation. I had no idea if I could get out of this room alive, so this alcohol calmed me down.

Another part of me was terrified about what this would do to me. I was tightly hanging onto my sobriety. I was grasping onto it as a desperate man might be grasping on the edge of a cliff right before he fell to his death.

I was falling, falling, falling into the abyss. It was a relief, really. I had the perfect excuse for taking another drink. It was either drink this scotch or die.

I never thought I'd be in this position yet here I was.

The man was smiling now. "Good, isn't it? Glenfarclas 60-year-old single malt scotch. $27,000 a bottle." He shrugged. "There are others more expensive than that, of course, but I save them for my senators. Not that you aren't as important as a senator, of course. I'm not saying that at all." He smiled again. "Drink, drink. You won't get another chance to drink something this smooth and robust. Enjoy."

I finished my glass and Grigor poured some more. "You see, this is how you do it," Sargis said. "This is how you get this young lady to imbibe. What Artur did was not the proper way of going about it."

I closed my eyes, suddenly understanding what happened. Apparently, Artur hit me on the head and poured whiskey down my throat. I had to admit, this man had a certain class and elegance. He was having me drink whiskey in a civilized way.

I finished the second glass as I noticed the man was still

nursing his first. *Slow down. Slow down. You need your wits about you.*

The man nodded at Grigor, who came and poured another glass for me.

"You like your scotch, I can see," the man said with a smile. "By the way, I'm so sorry I didn't tell you this up front. But my name is Sargis Gregorian. As you probably already knew. You know exactly who I am."

He paused.

"And I'll tell you a few things that won't be repeated. In fact, after you leave here, you will forget I exist. You will forget my name."

"And if I don't?"

He shrugged. "Then I will kill you."

And then he laughed.

Chapter Twenty-One

I DIDN'T LAUGH ALONG, of course. I would wait to see what he said.

"Okay," he said. "Where do I begin. First of all, I want you to know I did not kill Ezra Cohen." He smiled. "Believe me, I wanted to. I wanted to very badly. But apparently somebody else wanted to kill him even more." He poured himself another drink and sipped it. "It was disappointing, really. I wanted to make him die in a much more painful manner than what he did. What fun is that, slipping a little poison into his drink and having him die peacefully in his sleep? Not only that, he was on so many other drugs that night that he probably didn't feel his death coming at all."

He shook his head. "Very disappointing."

I felt mystified. "Then why am I here? If you didn't kill Ezra, why did you bring me here?"

"Oh, I knew it was only a matter of time before you started putting the puzzle pieces together, which would, in turn, lead you right to me. However erroneous your assumption would've been that I murdered that worm, I knew you would make that very assumption once you got into the specifics of this case. I've simply brought you here to disabuse you of that assumption before you even had the chance to make it."

That didn't make sense to me. I didn't believe him. He went through an awful lot of trouble bringing me here, trouble he wouldn't have gone to if he was squeaky clean on this issue. "What kind of information would I find out?" I asked.

"Well, I might as well tell you the entire story, so you know. Of course, this story can only stay in this room. If it doesn't…" He shook his head. "Well, you have two beautiful daughters. They would both be very valuable to me in what I do."

My blood chilled. "What do you mean?"

He cocked his head to the side. "You've seen the movie *Taken*, haven't you? If you haven't, go and see it. It's not entirely accurate – the Liam Neeson character wouldn't have gotten away with anything he got away with in that film. But the slave trade part…" He shrugged and smiled. "That's accurate, I have to say. And Rina and Abby, both 13 years old, both beautiful young dark-haired girls." He nodded and looked up at the ceiling. "I have some clients lined up for both, even as we speak."

My heart rate started to climb through the roof. "You wouldn't."

"No, I wouldn't. Not as long as you do what I say. Which would include keeping your beautiful lips shut about anything I'm telling you in this room. I hope I make myself perfectly clear, Ms. Ross."

I nodded. "Crystal."

My head started to swim, the result of those three glasses of scotch I chugged in rapid succession. I'd never tasted any scotch so smooth and full-bodied.

Keep your wits about you.

Keep your wits about you and nobody will get hurt.

"Very well. Let me just tell you the connection I had with Ezra Cohen. He has a brother-in-law who has been one of my long-time…acquaintances. His name is Rafael Petrossian. He's married to Ezra's sister, Ariel."

It was then I realized I didn't bother to ask Ariel what her husband's name was or what he did. "Ariel's last name is Rossi," I said. "I assumed she was married to an Italian man."

"Rafael isn't Italian, I can assure you. He's Armenian. He legally changed his name to Ralph Rossi." He shook his head. "A man with as poetic a name as Rafael Petrossian changing it to Ralph Rossi, just to fit in with American culture. I never understand that kind of self-loathing. You were born with a proud Armenian name, perhaps you should continue on with that same proud Armenian name. But that's neither here nor there."

"I spoke with Ariel. She doesn't seem to know anything about this."

"Yes, that's true. Willfully blind, that one. So, Rafael is somebody I have known for quite awhile. I make it a point to know most people who live in my neighborhood. In my old neighborhood, I guess I should say. Rafael has never worked for me, though. He has always worked on the docks in shipping. He receives goods from overseas, inventories them, and sends them on. Menial work compared to what he could be doing for me, but it's all important, isn't it?"

I nodded, seeing Grigor pour me yet another glass of scotch.

A part of me wanted to wave him away, but a bigger part of me wanted him to keep on pouring.

It was like the story of the two wolves. One wolf is evil – angry, sorrowful, greedy, arrogant, self-pitying. The other wolf was good – joyful, peaceful, loving, kind, compassionate, faithful. They're fighting, and a young boy asked which wolf would win. The answer was "the one you feed."

Those two wolves were fighting within me. One wolf was telling me to keep on drinking. The other wolf was begging me to stop. I was trying desperate to feed the second wolf, but the first wolf seemed to be winning.

I took a sip of the new glass and closed my eyes. "Go on."

"Well, Ezra met me through Rafael. And I could tell in Ezra's eyes and the way he spoke that he was longing for a different existence. Longing to become somebody new. Somebody important. Somebody wealthy. Somebody who would command respect. So, I made a business proposition with him. A couple of business propositions with him, really."

"What were these business propositions?" I knew about them, but I wanted him to tell me.

"I lent him money for a beautiful apartment project downtown. Those apartments were brand-new, high-rise. Lovely, really. I knew I would get that money back because Ezra assured me his grandfather was very wealthy. I looked into it and found out it was true. Ezra's grandfather was fabulously wealthy and in the latter stages of Alzheimer's."

Sargis shook his head and looked out the window. His eyes were misting lightly, as if he were fighting back tears. "My own grandfather died after suffering from Alzheimer's for ten years. I wouldn't wish that on anyone. He didn't know anybody by the end. That broke my mother's heart, of course. I would see her crying after she visited him."

"So you hastened Ezra's grandfather's death, didn't you?"

He nodded. "It was merciful, really. His grandfather was put out of his suffering and Ezra came into the money to pay me back for the apartment financing."

"Merciful? The car went off a cliff in the rain. How was that merciful?"

"Oh, dear, is that what Ariel told you about Ezra's grandfather?" He chuckled. "Ezra told me Ariel enjoyed telling stories. Embellishing things. Making things seem much more dramatic than they actually were. But no. Ezra's grandfather died peacefully in his sleep. He was given an overdose of morphine and Seconal. He closed his eyes and drifted off."

"I'll look up this story when I get home, you know. I'll find out what really happened to Jacob Cohen." Jacob was the name of Ezra's grandfather.

"Be my guest," he said, handing me a computer. "Why wait? You can look that up right now."

I took a deep breath and logged onto the computer Sargis gave me. I Googled the name "Jacob Cohen, millionaire, Ezra, Ariel, Daniel, Eli, California." The computer immediately brought me to different articles about Jacob's death.

I clicked on each of the articles, and, sure enough, they all said that Jacob died in his sleep of natural causes. None of them said anything about his car going over a cliff.

I looked up and saw Sargis was smiling smugly at me. "Are you satisfied? I wouldn't have done something like that to an elderly gentleman such as Jacob. Not after what I went through with my own grandfather."

"Natural causes," I said. "He didn't die of natural causes. You killed him."

"Yes," he said. "I did. It was a mercy killing."

"But you did it to get Ezra to pay you."

"That was a bonus, but, really, I knew that poor old gentleman was suffering."

"And then Ezra didn't pay you…"

"Right. He didn't. No matter how many warnings I gave him, he didn't pay me. And then I heard from Rafael that not only was Ezra unethical enough not to pay me the money he owed me but he cheated his brothers and sister out of all that money." He shook his head. "Ezra was immediately put on my list." He smiled. "I have a long list."

"I'll just bet you do." I was finding my courage with every glass of scotch. I found over the years that liquid courage was always the best kind. "So you killed Ezra."

"No. I didn't kill him. I told you that from the beginning. But, I admit, the facts on the ground do look poorly. I can see why you would automatically assume I killed him. But I did not kill him."

I sighed as I sipped my scotch. "Then why did you go through all this trouble to kidnap me? And why did you tell me that whole preamble about kidnapping my girls and selling them into white slavery if I breathed a word about this meeting to anyone? Why go through all that?"

"Because I know attorneys. I know how they operate. They fixate on somebody and try to bring them to heel. They desperately flail around to find somebody else to blame for what their client has been accused of. They'll cast their net wide and deep until they find the most likely culprit. I'll admit I've looked like a likely culprit to you, but I am not the person you're looking for."

"But you're getting your money now from the others.

From Daniel, Eli and Ariel. You're getting that money from them now."

"Yes, of course I am. They're much more reasonable to do business with than Ezra ever was. They're less venal, less greedy. Much less likely to cheat. They paid me what Ezra owed me plus $2 million and everything became settled. Just as I like it. None of them are at all likely to do business with me anymore, and that is fine with me. I do not do business with people who do not want to do business with me. I'm really quite reasonable when you get to know me."

"But you're telling me you wanted Ezra dead, right?"

"Right. He was on my list. But, as I said before, I wouldn't do it quietly like that. Ezra deserved much harsher treatment. I was disappointed I didn't get the chance to do to him what I really wanted to - burn him alive in a warehouse. So I guess what I'm saying is this. If you find the person who did that to him, I would really like to know his name. Or her name, as it were. I would like to speak with him. Or her. Because I am disappointed Ezra didn't meet his proper end. I would like to express that to the person you uncover for this."

I sat up straight. "And why should I believe you about this?"

He shrugged. "Because my dear, why would I lie? Even if I told you I murdered Ezra, there would be no way to prove it. Plus, there would be no way you could go there in your theory of the case. You would never, ever present me as an alternative theory for the person that killed that slime, because you'd know what would happen if you did. On that note, you know what will happen if you ever breathe a word of what I just told you. Not that I told you about any crime I committed, but people might look askance at what happened to Jacob. It was a mercy killing but not everybody will understand that."

He laughed. "I'm very sorry for having you drink with me. I know you have a problem with alcohol. But I hope you understand one thing."

"And what is that?"

"I would like for Ginger Perry to be convicted for the murder of Ezra Cohen."

Chapter Twenty-Two

IN MY PARTIALLY DRUNK STUPOR, SARGIS' words didn't quite register. "I'm sorry? What do you mean? Why do you want that?"

He shook his head. "Maybe that came out wrong. Here is what I'm trying to say. I hope you can figure out, without a shadow of doubt, who killed Ezra. If you can do that, then, by all means, you may use that as your theory of the case. You may use somebody else as your alternative theory for who killed Ezra. But if you cannot come to a conclusion that somebody else killed Ezra, then you must plead Ginger Perry for his murder. If Ms. Perry doesn't accept a plea agreement then you must do all you can to make sure she is convicted for killing Ezra. What I do not want is for Ms. Perry to be acquitted, which will cause the feds and state to start looking in my direction for the murder." He shook his head. "The heat must stay off me. As I told you earlier, I am innocent of any wrong-doing, but I admit my business dealings with Ezra make me look suspect."

I furrowed my brow. I was comprehending him, but not really. "I still don't understand."

"Let me make myself more clear. Either you make sure Ginger pleads to this murder or is convicted for it or you find another person who murdered Ezra. Not me. By the end of your case, I would like for the feds and the state to focus on somebody. They will either focus on putting Ms. Perry into prison for the rest of her life or they will focus on somebody else. They will not focus on me. I hope I've made myself perfectly clear."

I nodded. I still strongly suspected this guy was responsible for murdering Ezra. But what could I do about it? Seriously? What could I do?

I felt a sense of despair creeping up. It spread through my chest and down through my fingers. I started to shake. What could I do? I had to find *somebody* else to pin this crime on. I couldn't defend Ginger and try the case like I usually would when I didn't have an alternative suspect. Normally, I would put doubt in the jury's mind that my client killed the victim. I didn't always have to prepare a defense based upon SODDI – some other dude did it. I mean, I typically would prepare a SODDI defense but I didn't always have an alternative suspect in mind. Sometimes I would get lucky and find the alternative suspect. That always made my defense easier - show somebody else had the motive, means and opportunity to do it and show the jury this other person was more likely to have done it.

I didn't always have that luxury, however, so I'd throw a lot of shit against the wall to confuse things. Try to confuse the facts enough so the jury had reasonable doubt my client did it. They didn't always know who actually did it, but they would have reasonable doubt it was my client, which was all that mattered to me.

That was what I planned to do with Ginger in this case. If I couldn't figure out an alternative suspect, I'd go for broke showing the jury Ginger wasn't the one.

Now Sargis was warning me that I literally couldn't try the case that way. If Ginger was acquitted, the investigation on who killed Ezra would intensify and probably lead right to Sargis. If she was found guilty, the dogs would be called off.

I bit my lower lip. "Marissa, the lead investigator for the murder. She suspects you. She was the first to tell me about the Armenian Power and how Ezra was indebted to you and the Power. How will I keep her off your trail?"

"Marissa Leoni isn't a problem," he said. "I've spoken with her. She explained to me that her office is under pressure to get a conviction on this case. It's very high-profile, you see, because of who Ezra was. How powerful he was in that studio. The police are under pressure to make sure *somebody* is punished for this crime. We have an understanding, Ms. Leoni and I. As long as somebody ends up serving time for Ezra's murder, the LAPD and the feds won't look at me for it. But if Ginger goes free and there isn't an alternative suspect for the LAPD to pursue..." He shook his head. "That would be very bad. Ms. Leoni couldn't call off the investigation against me at that point. That's how it was explained to me."

"But aren't you involved with a lot of murders? Haven't you been?"

"Of course. My fingerprints are on several murders in the city. All of them were people the cops were anxious to see dead so I've been clean all these years. All the murders I've commissioned were generally members of other organizations who...betrayed me. Crossed me. Nobody shed a tear for any of them. But Ezra is a different story, of course.

The LAPD must have this case resolved one way or another."

I looked at my empty glass, realizing I wanted it to be filled again with that scotch. Within a few minutes, my wish was fulfilled, as Grigor brought back the bottle of scotch and poured me another glass. He poured Sargis one as well and Sargis put the glass to his lips and sipped it lightly.

"What I'm saying is this. If you don't have a solid alternative suspect for this killing, you must make sure Ms. Perry is convicted. That's all I'm saying."

"And if I don't make sure?"

"Then you die and your girls become my property. It's really as simple as that." He smiled. "I hope that's clear enough for you."

I nodded. "It's plenty clear. Couldn't be clearer, really."

"Good, good. Well, I think our little talk has crystalized a few things. You may leave."

I looked at my now-full glass and hastily drank it down. Since it was my fourth (or fifth?) drink in a matter of hours, I was feeling wobbly, unsteady on my feet.

"Grigor, take her home," he said. "I know her car is elsewhere. At a coffee shop on Sepulveda. But as you can see, Ms. Ross is not fit to drive herself home from that coffee shop. So drive to that coffee shop where Ms. Ross' car is. Take Artur along with you so he can drive Ms. Ross' car to her home." Then he smiled. "You see, Ms. Ross. I can be a very reasonable man. Very easy to work with. Just remember that. And also remember I don't like being crossed. I can be a very unreasonable man when I've been betrayed. So don't betray me."

Don't betray me. Don't betray me. Don't betray me. Those words dance around in my head as I got unsteadily to my feet. Grigor didn't have a gun sticking into my back, but, rather, his arm was linked through mine. It was as if he was making sure I didn't stumble.

This was an odd encounter, to say the very least. Sargis was charming, articulate, cultured and mannered. He was a vicious thug who expressed a desire to burn Ezra alive and admitted to murdering people in cold blood, but he certainly was a dapper fellow.

We got to Grigor's car and he opened the back door and gently laid me down on the seat. Then he got behind the wheel, while another guy, whom I guessed was Artur, got in the passenger's side.

And we drove off, presumably towards my car.

Chapter Twenty-Three

THE TWO MEN chatted in the front seat. They were speaking in a different language – it sounded similar to Russian, but I imagined it was Armenian. They were speaking animatedly, gesturing with their hands and laughing often.

Artur looked at me and smiled. "Don't worry," he said with a thick accent. "I will take care of your baby."

"My baby?"

"Your car. I will drive your car from the coffee shop to your home. Just like Sargis told you about."

There was a part of me that remembered Sargis said something like that, but there was also a part of me that had a hard time comprehending. My brain was completely foggy and everything was a blur. "Now, why are you driving my car home?"

"Because you can't drive," Artur said. "Obviously."

"Why can't I drive?" Nothing was making sense for some odd reason.

"Because you're too fucked up," Artur said and laughed.

Then he turned his attention back to Grigor and the two men started speaking Armenian again.

My stomach was starting to turn. It was starting to do backflips and frontflips and flips all over the place. The enormity of my talk with Sargis hadn't sunk in. He told me that either Ginger was convicted or I had to find out, without a shadow of a doubt, who killed Ezra. It couldn't just be an open case, like the OJ Simpson case ended up being for all those years after OJ was acquitted for Nicole Brown Simpson's murder. There had to be a solid culprit or else I would have to plead Ginger out.

That made me sick because it severely limited my options. That meant I couldn't try all the clever tricks I might've tried to make sure Ginger was acquitted. I couldn't look for a technicality that might acquit her, and I couldn't just try for reasonable doubt. No, I would have to ensure her conviction unless I found the actual person who did it and could show the jury that other person did it beyond the shadow of a doubt.

I could throw her case like I did to Michael Reynolds. Michael Reynolds was an earlier murder case I deliberately threw because I wanted to see him get convicted. He raped me in college, he wasn't remorseful for what he did so I wanted him to pay. I agreed to defend his case because I *wanted* him to fry. I deliberately did a terrible job at trial for just that reason.

I knew how to throw a case. I did.

But I didn't want to here. Not if Ginger was innocent. She was a good person underneath all her bluster. She didn't deserve prison.

Yet what choice did I have?

I would have to work overtime to find out who really killed Ezra.

IN ABOUT A HALF HOUR, I was home, sweet home. Artur dropped off my car, and then got into Grigor's SUV and the two of them sped away.

Mia was busy making dinner while the two girls were sitting in the living room watching something on Netflix. Nobody seemed to notice there was anything amiss, and, when I looked at the clock, I realized why.

It was only 6 PM.

God, it felt later than that. I was afraid I'd get home at midnight again and the girls would be panicking. But that wasn't the case.

So, I was kidnapped, lectured to by a sophisticated and mannerly Armenian gangster, got totally sloshed, and was brought home. All in the span of a matter of hours.

Surreal.

"I'm bored," Rina complained when I got home. "I'm so bored."

"Didn't you go down to the beach?"

She rolled her eyes. "Boring. That's all we ever do, Mom."

"Well, I see you're watching a show on Netflix. Oh, it's that show *The Summer I Turned Pretty*. I know the person who developed that." Then I shook my head as I remembered that Patty didn't develop it, but wished she did. "Never mind."

"Yeah, it's a good show, but Mom, we have to get out of this house. Do something fun. You promised us this vacation would be fun. That we wouldn't miss our friends at all. Well, guess what, Mom? You lied. It hasn't been fun. I *have* missed my friends. I'm getting texts and Snapchats, and Emma and Haley are all over Facebook, Tik Tok and Instagram showing what fun they're having together. Together, Mom. We were all three tight and now they don't even know I'm alive. And they're always having parties and putting those pictures on Facebook and Tik Tok too, Mom. I'm telling you, I want to die. I want to die, Mom. It's the end of the world."

"Of course it is," I said, "It's always the end of the world when you're 13. And that's not a dig. I've been there. But you'll get back to Kansas City and your friends before you know it. In the meantime, you're right. We all need to get out of the house."

I couldn't drive yet, however, so I asked Mia to drive.

"Yay, Mom," Rina said excitedly. "Where are we going? What will we do?"

"Well, let's find a dog-friendly restaurant and go out to eat, and then we can all go walking on the Hollywood Walk of Fame. I even know of some shopping areas where we can take Stella and Sue, so, if it's early enough after we do all that, we'll go shopping."

Abby started jumping up and down and Rina soon joined her. "Oh, thank God, we've been so cooped up here," Rina said. "You just don't know. Me and Abby were just about ready to die."

"Well, don't die," I said. "Mia, I hope you don't mind driving."

"No, I don't," she said, looking at me strangely. "Rina, Abby, go get ready. Take a shower. I was making dinner, but I'll put it in the fridge and we can have it tomorrow for lunch."

The two girls ran into separate bathrooms as Mia got out some Tupperware to put her food in.

"I'm sorry," I said. "I saw you making dinner so I shouldn't have suggested getting something eat."

"Not a problem," she said. Then she cocked her head. "But you've been drinking. Is that why you wanted me to drive so badly?"

I shook my head. "I don't know what you're talking about. I'm really tired and really stressed, but I haven't had a drop."

She looked at me skeptically and shook her head. "If you say so."

"I do. Anyhow, thank you very much for driving. Thank you in advance."

"You pay me to be a full-time nanny, so where you go, I go. I hope you know what you're doing, though."

"I do. And I haven't been drinking. I promise."

Abby and Rina came running back out of their respective bathrooms. They looked at each other and giggled. "I win," Abby said. "I came out first."

"You did not," Rina said.

Both girls had wet hair and were dressed in bathrobes. "Girls, go and get ready," I said.

"We will," they said in unison.

I turned to Mia. "I did the right thing in bringing them out here, I think. They seem to have really bonded."

"Yes," Mia said. "And they really are having fun out here. But they've been down to the beach every day this week and they're going a little stir-crazy. I might take them to the Zoo tomorrow. I think they would really like that."

"Well, maybe this weekend I can get tickets to go on a movie studio lot," I said. "Maybe even go to Universal Studios. I know the girls would love that."

"Oh, they would," Mia said. "Let's do that. And don't let them down. If you suggest going there this weekend, keep your promise."

"When have I not kept my promise?" I asked her.

"Never I can think of," she said. "Just don't start now."

"I won't."

The girls came out in sundresses and baseball caps. "We're ready," Abby said.

Chapter Twenty-Four

WE ENDED up at a restaurant that faced one of the beaches and had a patio where dogs were welcome. It was a simple place that served hamburgers, salads, sandwiches and pasta. It wasn't anything special, but it was a chance for me to decompress after the scare I had with Sargis.

I picked through my french fries and burger while Stella and Sue begged on the floor next to us. Cute boys walked on the boardwalk past the patio, and Rina and Abby would stare at them and giggle. One in particular paused and smiled. He was a kid of about 14 or 15, with longish hair that covered one of his eyes, a dark tan and dimples. He was lean, as kids of that age usually were – he was beginning to fill out, because he was starting to get tiny muscles in his arms, chest, and abs, but his legs were skinny. He was dressed in board shorts and no shirt.

"Hi Rina," he said, in a voice that sounded like it was just about to mature, but wasn't quite. "And Abby."

"Hi Seth," they both said and giggled.

I gave them a look that said "and you know this kid?"

"Mom, this is Seth," Abby said. "We've been hanging out with him and his friend Noah at the beach."

Just then, another kid came up. He was tall, a bit taller than Seth, with longish black curly hair, dark eyes and a big, bright smile. He, too, was shirtless, and he, too, was skinny yet muscular. He looked about the same age as Seth.

"And this is Noah," Rina said. "It's so funny seeing you guys here," Rina said.

"Would you like to join us?" I asked the boys.

"Nah," Seth said. "Mrs. Ross. We don't have shirts to put on."

I nodded. "Well, okay then." I looked over at the table next to me. The people at that table were drinking from a bottle of wine, and my mouth started to water. "It was nice meeting you."

The boys made no move to leave, and I looked around and saw that everybody had already eaten their food. This seemed like as good a time as any to sneak away and get a shot or two at the bar.

"Excuse me," I said. "I need to use the ladies' room."

At that, I went inside the restaurant and went right up to the bar. "Hello," I said. "I would like a double scotch rocks please."

The bartender poured my drink and shot it over to me. "That will be $15."

I gave him a $20 bill and told him to keep it. I looked towards the patio and saw Rina and Abby were still busy talking to the cute boys, while Mia was busy looking at her phone. I could probably sit at the bar for a few minutes more, so I downed that drink and asked for another.

The bartender gave me another, and I gave him another $20 and had him keep it.

Then I drank down that scotch as well.

I put the empty glass down at the bar. "Thanks," I said. "Those were good."

And I walked out to join everybody on the patio.

A HALF HOUR LATER, we were in the car and heading towards the Hollywood Walk of Fame, something the girls were looking forward to seeing. I was too because I was interested in knowing who got their stars on the Walk. We went up and down the sidewalk looking at different stars. The girls would, from time to time, go into one of the shops that lined the walk. They would buy a little trinket or a t-shirt or something and come back out.

I stayed on the sidewalk with Stella and Sue.

"So, how are things going with your case?" Mia asked as we walked along the sidewalk looking at the stars.

"It could be better," I said. "But it could be worse, too."

"What do you need to do?"

"I need to figure out if my client is lying about not murdering Ezra. I have no margin for error here. None at all. If she's guilty, I need to plead her out."

"Well, of course," Mia said. "That goes without saying. Doesn't it?"

"Not necessarily. My duty as an attorney is to give my client zealous advocacy. No matter what. Even if I believe they're guilty. If they tell me they did it, but they still want to try the case, I'll try to talk them out of it. But if I can't talk them out of it, I need to try it and give the case all I have. I can't leave anything on the table. That's my job. My duty. Anything less than that, and I'm guilty of ethical violations and possibly malpractice."

"So, with Ginger..."

"With Ginger, I need to figure out what happened. That's all. I need to figure out, 100%, if she's guilty or innocent. If she's innocent, I need to figure out who did it. I have no margin for error on this one," I repeated.

As I walked along, I thought about my options on Ginger's case. What if she demanded a trial and I couldn't figure out who did it? What then? If she demanded a trial, I had to find a way to lose it. I didn't want to do that. I wanted to win the case for her.

But in order to win her case, I'd have to dig deep and figure out the culprit. That was always tricky. Sometimes it worked out and I could show the jury that X did the crime, not my client. The evidence was strong enough that X would be arrested for it and my client would go free. Everybody was happy – except X, of course.

Other times, though, I didn't have an alternative suspect. What would happen if that was the case here? I could drag somebody under the bus. Maybe Sasha, Ezra's ex-wife. Maybe I could figure out who that Angel Cody person is.

Or maybe it was somebody else. Somebody I hadn't yet heard about.

THE GIRLS, Mia, Stella, Sue and I had fun the rest of the evening. We went to the Santa Monica pier. The girls rode the Ferris wheel while Mia and I went shopping in the stores that dotted the boardwalk. We got ice cream and cotton candy and watched the night surfers down below.

Then we drove home. The two girls were asleep in the back of the SUV and I got sleepy just watching them. I was still buzzing from the two double scotches I had at the restaurant, not to mention all those scotches I had earlier, so I fell asleep in the passenger's seat.

We got home, I put the girls to bed and then passed out on my own bed.

And had a brutal nightmare. I was laying on the floor, my throat slit, while the two girls were kidnapped and both sold as sex slaves.

When I woke up in a cold sweat, I was terrified.

Could I get through this?

Could I survive this?

Could the girls?

I didn't know.

What I did know was I desperately needed a drink.

Chapter Twenty-Five

I GOT in my car that morning, intending to see Ginger and pick up more clues on who killed Ezra. But, before I did, I walked to the liquor store just down the street.

"What would you like?" the guy asked while I stood there looking at all the top-shelf liquors in a glass case behind his head.

"I'd like a bottle of your Glenfiddich," I said, pointing to the expensive bottle of scotch in the glass case.

He got it out of the case and put the booze into a brown plastic bag. "That'll be $35.00," he said.

I swiped my debit card, took the bag from him and put it in my car.

I wasn't sure what to do. I was more responsible than drinking and driving. I was craving this liquor, yet I couldn't bring myself to down a few shots and get behind the wheel.

But I couldn't take it home with me. That would never do. Mia already suspected I was drinking again. She knew I was a recovering alcoholic because I told her I was. I couldn't let her see me drinking. She'd call me out, bigger than life.

As I deserved.

Just then, I got a call coming in. Axel. "Hey baby," I said.

"Hey, lass," he said. "I wanted to see how you were. How is your case going?"

"Oh, fine," I said, looking at the bottle of booze next to me on the seat.

Step One. Admit you are powerless over alcohol and your life has become a mess. Or something like that. Those weren't the exact words, but the sentiment.

I was certainly at that step. My life was spiraling out of control or was about to. And I certainly was powerless over alcohol.

"Fine, mate?" he asked me. "You don't sound fine."

"Well, it's going okay," I said. "I need to do a lot more work though. I need to know who did it. Then I can try this case."

"Of course," he said. "That's always the case, isn't it, mate?"

"Yeah. But it's really the case this time." I cleared my throat. I couldn't tell him anything about Sargis and Sargis' threat. It might spur him into action which would be absolutely disastrous. I couldn't chance that Axel might hop the first plane to LAX, go over to Sargis' house and tell Sargis to back the hell off. Then what would happen?

My girls would be in danger. I would be too.

"I have a few days off," he said. "I'd like to visit."

I closed my eyes. If he came to visit, what would I do? I couldn't hide my drinking from him, could I?

Step one. Admit you are powerless over alcohol and your life is out of control. I was considering turning down a visit from the love of my life, Axel, because alcohol was more important to me.

"I'd love that," I said. "Come on out."

"I can be on the next plane tonight," he said. "Meet me at LAX at 11:45? I'll be flying Delta."

I laughed. "Sounds like you had it planned in advance."

"I did, love. I just hoped you were as raring to see me as I was to see you."

"I'll meet you at LAX at 11:45 tonight."

I got off the phone and looked longingly at my bottle of scotch. What would happen if I drank it? I couldn't see Ginger. I couldn't pick up Axel. I'd be helpless.

Powerless.

Admit you are powerless over alcohol and your life is in the shitter.

I threw my head back on my seat and closed my eyes. I wanted that bottle of scotch. I craved it. I'd gone on a mini-bender twice now on this vacation and I didn't know how much longer I could stay strong. How much longer I could resist that siren song.

With white knuckles, I went to the back of the SUV and lifted up the console. I put that bottle of scotch in there and drove off.

Admit you are powerless over alcohol and your life is nuts.

Chapter Twenty-Six

"HARPER," Ginger said. "What are you doing here?"

I went to the studio, but they said she was at home. So I drove over to her home. She was sitting on the couch and then a guy and girl came out of one of the bedrooms. I didn't know if that bedroom belonged to her roommate or to her.

The guy handed Ginger a hundred dollar bill and a bag of white powder. Then he left.

Guess that answered my question. "I wanted to talk about your case. You and I have to work together to figure this out. Time is a-wasting on it."

"Harper, I don't know who did it. I thought your job was to figure that out."

"It is my job, but Ginger, you have to help me. Now, I need to go back over what happened that night. Piece by piece. Frame by frame."

"I told you," she said. "I sucked his whiskey dick. That's all."

"But you brought him that glass of scotch," I said. "That poisoned glass of scotch."

"Yeah, I did. I brought it to him." She shook her head. "I told you all that."

"But who gave you that glass to give to him? Who did that Ginger? Who?"

"Nobody," she said. "I don't know who gave me that glass. I told you that. I don't know. I don't remember."

I sighed. "Ginger." I took a deep breath. "This act is growing thin. I need to go in a certain direction. If I don't find a good direction, I'll have to plead you out or withdraw from your case."

I was threatening to withdraw from her case, but I knew I couldn't. I was pretty sure I'd be violating the promise I made to Sargis if I withdrew. If I did that, I was doomed and so were my girls.

No pressure.

"Harper, no. I don't remember. All I know is I got to the party and somebody told me to see Ezra. They said Ezra requested me. That Ezra had seen me in a movie and wanted to meet me. That's what they said, Harper. That's what they said."

"Ginger," I said. "I think you're telling me a lie. Or you're not telling me the entire story. One of the two. I can't figure out which one it is, though."

"I'm not telling you a lie."

I sighed. "What's going on with Mario and your new boss? I'm so sorry, what is the name of your new boss?"

"My boss at Dark Angel studios? The big boss there?"

"Yeah."

"His name is Mathew Newton."

"Mathew Newton. That's the studio boss at Dark Angel?"

"Yeah."

I furrowed my brow. That didn't sound right. That name was different from the name she'd given me before. "Well, what's going on with Mario? I forgot to ask you about that. You used to talk about Mario getting into it with your new boss. And you were mad at Mario because Mario wasn't paying you. Right?"

"Mario is dead," she said. "He was found dead last week in the street."

"Oh. Why didn't you tell me?"

She shrugged. "I didn't know how that mattered."

I made a note on my paper. That didn't seem to matter, really.

Or did it? Was Mario's death significant?

I didn't know. I made note of his death and went on.

"Okay. Mario is dead. And your boss' name is Mathew Newton. But that's not the name I was thinking of. There was another name you told me before. Another guy who'd recruited you to the porn business. What was that name?"

Ginger looked perplexed. Then her face brightened. "Oh, yes. Dale. Dale Thompson."

I wrote down the name "Dale Thompson," and then looked at that name.

Something stirred in me as I looked at that name.

I didn't quite know what it was.

"Harper?" Ginger was asking me. "What are you doing?"

"Huh?" I asked her. "I'm not doing anything. Why?"

"You've just been staring at that piece of paper for about ten minutes."

"Oh. I got lost in my head for a moment. I'm sorry."

"That's okay."

I looked at that name for several minutes more. It seemed so familiar….

"What do you know about Dale Thompson?" I asked Ginger.

She shrugged. "I don't know about what he did before he went to the Dark Angel studio. All I know is he found me and said he'd make me a star. He saw something in me."

"And where did you meet him? I guess I never heard this story before."

"I met him at a party. At an industry party."

"An adult film industry? Or a mainstream film industry?"

"At a mainstream film industry. Why?"

"Okay. Do you remember what this party was? Where it was? Who held the party?"

She paused and looked at the ceiling. "What party was it? I don't know. I go to so many. I work a lot of parties, you know. I'm the in-house entertainment, they call me."

"When was it? This party where you met Dale Thompson?"

"I don't remember," she said. "Why are you asking me all these questions about him?"

"Because," I said. "I'm brainstorming. I'm onto something, but I don't know what it is. So I need to ask you more questions about how you know Dale Thompson so I can figure out why that name sounds familiar to me and why I have a feeling Dale Thompson is significant."

"What is brainstorming?"

"It's where you think about a lot of thoughts to find out how the thoughts are connected." I put the name "Dale Thompson" in the middle of the yellow sheet of paper and then drew lines emanating from the name.

"You're brainstorming on Dale's name?" Ginger asked me. "Why are you doing that?"

"I don't know yet," I said, putting a pen in my mouth. "Now, take me back to the night you met Dale. How did he approach you?"

"I was sitting on a couch with some other girls," she said. "He sat down next to me and was talking to me and all the girls. He was talking to us and wanted to know if we were interested in making a lot of money. We all said we were. Those other girls were also working for Mario and were unhappy like I was. Mario wasn't paying any of us girls. At least he didn't pay regular. He owed us all a lot of money. So the other girls told Dale they were interested in more money and more regular pay. He gave us his card and asked us to call him."

"And you called him," I said. "When? The next day?"

"Yes. And Mario got mad at me for calling him. He wanted me to only work for him. But I told him I couldn't work for him if he didn't pay me regular. I signed a contract with Dale right away."

"What did you know about Dale when you started working for him?"

"I didn't know nothing about him."

"Nothing at all?"

"No. Nothing at all."

I became agitated but didn't understand why. I was getting closer to figuring it out although I wasn't sure if I'd be happy when I found the answer.

"I'll do a background check on Dale Thompson," I said. "Just as a fair warning."

"Why?"

"Because. I have a feeling Dale is shady."

"Go ahead and do a background check, Harper. I think he's shady too."

"Now, I remember you said Mario got you the gig at Ezra's house. Now, Mario is dead. Does anybody know how he became dead?"

"Yeah. He was found dead in an alley, a needle in his arm."

I wrote that down. Mario overdosed. Typical for guys like Mario. I never met him but knew he was involved in shady stuff. Anybody who'd get a girl out to Los Angeles to do porn work, then not pay that girl, had to be shady.

"Why are you asking all these questions?"

"Because. I just am following up on a hunch." I didn't want to tell her the truth – I was desperate to find the culprit in this case. Somebody who I could 100% pin this murder on. I really didn't want to throw Ginger's case. I didn't know if I could do it. Doing that to Michael Reynolds turned my stomach. I hated knowing I couldn't do my job properly.

"What hunch do you have?"

"It's a hunch I'm getting about Dale Thompson. By the way, is there any way I can meet with that guy?"

"He's at the studio, in the main office."

"Can you get a message to him that I'd like to speak with him?"

"Sure."

I didn't know if he'd speak with me. He probably wouldn't. Especially if he had something to do with Ezra's murder, which I increasingly thought was likely.

Ginger left to make a call and came back in five minutes. "I talked to Dale's assistant and she said you can come back tomorrow at 2 if you want to talk to him."

"Will do."

AFTER I LEFT GINGER, I took my laptop to a bar, sat on a patio and ordered some scotch and sipped it while I did my research. This felt like home. Like I'd never left. This was what I used to do when I was a functioning alcoholic – go to a bar that had wi-fi, get a stiff drink, and do research. This was calming. There was a problem with my psyche these past few years because I was always anxious. I always felt I wasn't good enough. Like I was messing things up in my life. Those nagging insecurities were always in the back of my mind.

But alcohol took those nagging insecurities away. Alcohol gave me courage. Made me feel things weren't as bad as I thought. Made me believe in myself.

And it really opened my mind.

I got out the guest list from the party. I'd reviewed that guest list 100 times. Patty, who worked at Paramount and knew most people in the business, had reviewed it too. Everyone on there seemed clean except the one guy – Tom Dale. She didn't know him. Never heard of him. I didn't know him, either. I didn't know anybody on that list, but I found a web presence for all of them except Tom Dale.

He was a mystery man.

How would I figure out who he was and if he was significant?

Could I figure that out?

As I sipped my drink, the waiter asked me if I wanted another.

"Yes," I said.

He nodded, went inside the restaurant, and came out in a matter of minutes, a glass of scotch in hand. He sat it down on my table and I immediately picked it up and sipped it.

"Smooth," I said. Then I looked at him. "Matt," I said, looking at his name tag. "You're working in Los Angeles as a waiter. Can I ask you a few questions?"

"Sure," he said. "It's not busy right now as you can probably tell."

"Are you in the movie business? I mean, trying to break into the movie business?"

He grinned. "How did you know?"

"Well, I know it's a stereotype that most waiters and bartenders are really struggling actors, going on auditions in their free time. Like in that movie *La La Land*, although that girl was working in a coffee shop on a studio lot. Great movie, by the way."

"I know. I loved it."

"Me too. So…" I paused. "Did you know Ezra Cohen? The development head at Paramount?"

"I didn't know him. I knew of him, though. Everybody knew of him. Everybody who's anybody did, anyhow."

I nodded. "Do you know the name of the person accused of killing him?"

"Ginger Perry," he said without hesitation. "Everybody's talking about her."

"Right." I nodded and sipped my drink. "Everybody's talking about her. Free publicity, isn't it?"

"Yeah. You couldn't buy that kind of publicity."

"One more thing. Does the name Tom Dale ring a bell?"

He shook his head. "No. Why?"

"And you know a lot of people in the movie industry?"

"Oh yeah. I do. I'm constantly networking, trying to get invited to as many parties as I can. I make it a point to know just about every name I can. All of us trying to break in are doing that. But the name Tom Dale doesn't ring a bell."

"Would it surprise you to know a guy named Tom Dale was at Ezra Cohen's party the night he was killed?"

"Yeah."

"And why is that?"

"Because those parties are usually only open to industry insiders and others, like myself, who are trying to become industry insiders. They don't usually let randos into those parties and it sounds like this Tom Dale might've been a rando."

I narrowed my eyes and sipped my scotch some more. "Thanks," I said to him. "You've been a big help. There'll be a big tip for you."

"You're welcome," he said, "Although I don't know how I helped you."

"You did. Help. Thanks."

I sipped my scotch and stared at the guest list some more.

And then called Ginger.

"Hey," she said. "Harper, what's up?"

"Ginger, your boss, Dale Thompson, does he have any aliases by any chance?"

"Yeah," she said.

"Do you happen to know what they are?"

"He's got one alias. Just like I have several. You know about those though."

"Yes I do. But what is Dale Thompson's alias?"

"Tom Dale."

Chapter Twenty-Seven

OF COURSE! Of course Dale Thompson was the same guy as Tom Dale. That made perfect sense. He just reversed his two names and shortened his last name to "Tom." Why didn't I see that before?

But what did that tell me?

It told me Dale was at that party. And Ginger had neglected to tell me he was at that party.

Why? Why was Ginger hiding that particular ball? Was she covering for him?

Or was she in on it somehow?

Damn. I'd been drinking. I couldn't drive to her house and confront her.

I called her again. "Ginger," I said. "Are you working still?"

"No. I'm at home. Why?"

"I need you to meet me at this bar. Do that within the next hour."

"Oh, Harper, I can't. I have to go back to my other job in a couple of hours. I need the rest."

"Other job? What other job?"

"I'm turning tricks at another party. I'm getting paid to go to that party and get money for every trick I turn. I gotta make as much money as possible, Harper. I won't be this hot for long. Dale told me to make as much money as I can because I'm gonna be on my ass again in a couple of years."

She was more self-aware than I'd given her credit for. "I need you to come to this bar. I can't come to you right now because I've been drinking."

"I can't-"

"You will come and visit me in an hour. Within the hour. Or I'll withdraw from your case and head back to Kansas City."

I was bluffing. I couldn't withdraw from her case. Sargis was relying on me to either throw Ginger's case or find the real culprit.

If I withdrew and left Ginger's case to chance, in the hands of another attorney, I'd be screwing up my end of the bargain.

I gave her the place where I was. Then I hung up and called David.

"Harper," he said when he picked up the phone. "Have you come to your senses?"

"Yes," I said. "I have. About Sargis, anyhow. Listen, I have another lead on this Ezra case. I wanted to run it by you."

"What's your new lead?"

"Ginger's boss, Tom Dale, I mean Dale Thompson, was at the party that night. I'm trying to figure a few things out about that."

"Yeah? So?"

"So? Listen, there was one name on that guest list that

nobody could figure out. I couldn't find the guy's name on the internet, and Patty had never heard of him. I even asked a waiter and struggling actor who knows most people in the industry. He'd never heard of this guy, either."

"I'm still not following."

"I think he's the one who put poison into that drink and gave it to Ginger to give to Ezra. But now I'm thinking Ginger is also dirty. She never told me her boss was at the party that night. I don't know why she never told me that. And I think she lied about when and how she met Dale Thompson. There's something about the timing of what she said that's not sitting right with me."

"Hmmmm…" David said. "Go on."

I drummed my fingers on the table as I thought about what Ginger told me about Dale. When she first called me, she said she was working for this Mario character but Mario wasn't paying her. Then, when I got to town, she had a new job with Dale Thompson's studio, Dark Angel. Mario was pissed because Ginger was wanted to exclusively work for that studio and Mario wanted his cut. Now Mario was dead from an overdose, Ginger was working for Dark Angel studio, and everybody knew her name.

Was there a through-line?

And was Ginger really an innocent party in all this?

"I wonder if Ginger is as innocent as she seems."

"Why are you wondering about that?"

"Well, here's the thing. How is this for a theory? I'm throwing this out to you, and, since you're on her case as well, you owe her just as much loyalty as me. It goes without saying you won't advance this theory to the LAPD or anybody in authority."

"Of course that goes without saying," David said. "I took an oath, same as you."

"Right. Okay." I took a deep breath. "Okay. So what if Ginger and Dale were in on the murder of Ezra. Ginger did it because she wanted to be famous. And Dale…"

What was Dale's motive for killing Ezra? That was the sticking point. If I could figure that out, I could figure out what happened.

And then it would be a matter of telling Ginger I knew what happened, we'd lose at trial, and she was better off taking a plea agreement since she was guilty. And then call it a day. Everybody wins and I go home without the shadow of Sargis Gregorian following me.

Ginger wouldn't win in that particular scenario but at least I wouldn't feel bad pleading her out.

"Dale…" David said. "Finish your thought."

"Dale's motive was…" I paused. "That remains to be seen. That's the snag. I'm getting closer, but, I'll admit, that's a snag."

"Look closer," David said. "Look closer, and maybe you'll figure it out."

"Ginger's supposed to meet me here," I said. I didn't tell him I couldn't drive because I was drinking. I didn't want him to know that.

Admit you are powerless over alcohol and your life is circling the drain.

"Where are you?"

"I'm at a restaurant in Malibu," I said. "I'm trying to get my head together while I figure this out."

"A restaurant or a bar?"

"A restaurant," I said, feeling exasperated. He knew. How did he know? I guessed alcoholics could always tell when a fellow alcoholic had fallen off the wagon.

"Okay, then," he said. "Listen, I know you don't have a sponsor yet for your AA meetings. Do you need one?"

"No. Listen, I'll get a sponsor when I get back to Kansas City. A long-term sponsor. I don't need one here. I don't know what good it would do to get a sponsor and then go home to Kansas City and ditch the L.A. sponsor."

"It will do you some good. Trust me on this. You still have to get through this trial and that'll be stressful for you."

"I'll think about it."

"Okay."

I hung up the phone and looked at my watch.

Ginger would be here any minute.

I hoped.

Chapter Twenty-Eight

DAVID

I HUNG up the phone with Harper and there was something nagging me about how she sounded. I hated what Artur had done to her. It was so ham-handed and stupid. He shouldn't have done it that way. I wanted Harper to fall off the wagon because I wanted her to fuck up Ginger's case.

But I didn't want that anymore.

I'd talked to Sargis, who told me he'd straightened everything out with Harper. He gave her some direct threats. Threats he'd make good on. Sargis knew Harper had gotten the picture and there was no longer a reason to sabotage her.

And then he told me he sabotaged her anyhow. Maybe unknowingly. He had Harper kidnapped and plied her with high-dollar scotch. Sargis knew she was weak when it came to alcohol. Sargis knew everything about this case, including everything about Harper herself. He knew she'd want to drink with him and knew he was piercing her weakness when he did that.

He had to know he'd push Harper off the wagon again. However, I didn't think he cared. After all, if she was drinking, she'd likely want a short-cut on Ginger's case. And if she took a shortcut, it would end up with either Ginger taking a plea agreement or Ginger losing at trial. The latter would probably happen, anyhow, if Harper continued to drink. Drunks tended to not do so well in court. They usually end up drinking instead of working up their case and go into trial either sloshed or hungover.

I didn't want either of those things to happen to Harper. Since Sargis had set her straight, I didn't see the need for subterfuge anymore. That would mean that, if Harper was drinking again, I felt the need to get her to stop. Again.

But, then again, Harper would have to take a dive on Ginger's case. She would have to take a dive unless she figured out, without a shadow of a doubt, who killed Ezra. And that person had to not have ties to Sargis. That was important to Sargis. If Harper found the alternative suspect, he needed to have a clean break from Sargis and all of Sargis' dealings.

Morally, I thought it wrong not to help Harper.

Pragmatically, I wanted to let her sink.

Then again, she seemed to have another interesting theory. This Dale Thompson guy, Ginger's studio boss, might've done it. And Ginger herself might've been in on it.

I called Sargis to run all this by him.

"Yes?" he said when he answered the phone. "I have some clients coming in, so please make this quick."

"I will. Does the name Dale Thompson mean anything to you?"

"No."

"How about Tom Dale?"

"No. Why does this concern you?"

"I just wanted to ask. You told Harper you wanted somebody air-tight to go down for Ezra's murder. If it wasn't Ginger, you wanted to make sure it was somebody else air-tight. Harper is working on a theory that might satisfy you."

"Good."

"I'll talk to you later."

"Goodbye."

I took a deep breath and wondered if this would work out anyhow.

Even if I didn't sabotage her.

Chapter Twenty-Nine

HARPER

GINGER CAME TO SEE ME, just like I asked. "This better be good," she said. "To drag me all the way out here."

I was starting to sober up so I knew I'd be good to drive home soon. Not that Ginger cared about that. "I assure you, I'm not wasting your time. Sit down."

Ginger sat down. She looked worried. I wondered why.

I cleared my throat as I looked at her worried blue eyes. "Ginger, what do you know about Dale Thompson? I need the truth here."

"I told you, I met him at a party. He was looking for girls to work for him. He chose me and some other girls from that party."

"And when was that party again?"

"I don't know. I don't remember."

"Was that party before or after Ezra was found dead?"

"After."

I bit my lower lip knowing Ginger was lying to me. "It was after? Not before?"

"After."

"Let me ask you this, then. When you met Dale Thompson, did he look familiar to you at all? Like you'd seen him before?"

She shook her head. "No."

"You didn't see him at the party where Ezra was found dead?"

"No."

I sat back in my chair. I wondered if I could believe her. Ginger, thus far, had always been honest with me. Yes, she was a grifter and a cheat. She'd stolen people's identity. She ripped Ezra off the night he died. She'd posed as the wife of an Alzheimer's patient in an attempt to get his fortune. She'd done all these dishonest things.

Yet I didn't think she'd lied to me before. Was she lying now?

"Why are you asking me these things?" she asked me. Her blue eyes were still looking worried.

"Because Dale Thompson was at that party. That party where you were. That party where Ezra was found dead. He was at that party, Ginger. I can't help but suspect that somehow, someway, Dale gave you the poisoned drink and you gave it to Ezra. Maybe you gave it to Ezra because he promised you fame if you killed Ezra and was arrested for his murder. Famous enough that you wouldn't have to do anything on film you didn't want to do. You could name your price. Because, let's face it, you name your price, haven't you? How much are you making at that Dark Angel studios right now?"

Ginger was just looking at me, her blue eyes a mixture of hurt and question. She shook her head and tears came to her eyes. "Harper, you're my attorney," she said. "You're my attorney. How can you be talking to me like this? How can you not believe in me? I don't understand. I told you the truth. Why are you questioning me?"

"I'm questioning you because I have a strong suspicion that the person who gave you that drink to give to Ezra was Dale Thompson. I think that because Dale Thompson was at that party. He was the only person at the party unknown by an industry insider. I think Dale Thompson won't check out once I start digging into his background. I'll find he had motive to kill Ezra. I think that'll be the case. And if that's the case, I'm sorry, Ginger, but you'll have some explaining to do."

She continued to shake her head, tears spilling down her cheeks. "I don't know what you're saying," she said. "I don't know why you're doing me like this."

"You never answered my question," I said. "My other question. How much are you making at that studio? How much is Dale Thompson paying you?"

"I get paid by the scene."

"How much do you get paid for each scene?"

"$2,000 a scene for me with a guy, $1,500 a scene for me with a girl, $4,000 a scene when I do things like anal and gang-bangs. If I agreed to do things like bondage or let a guy beat or pee on me, I get paid $10,000."

"I see," I said. "So you get paid twice what other established actresses are making for their scenes. And you're a brand new actress. Why are you getting paid twice what other actresses are making?"

"I don't know. I mean, I do know, and it's because everybody knows my name in town. Everybody is curious about me. Everybody wants to know about me. That's why. I didn't make that happen, though. I didn't, Harper. Why would I do something like that? Why would I do something that might mean I to go to jail? Harper, if I ended up in jail, I won't be making any money. I'll be making license plates."

She was convincing. She made an excellent point. Why would she do something that would end her up in jail just for short-term gain? Would she take a risk that huge just to be famous? With Ginger, it was possible. She'd literally do anything for a buck.

"Well, I'll speak with Dale," I said. "I'll make an appointment to speak with him tomorrow. And I'll figure out why he wanted Ezra dead."

At that, I called Dale's assistant. She picked up.

"Hello," I said. "I'd like to make an appointment to speak with Dale Thompson," I said. "My name is Harper Ross, I'm an attorney, and I need to speak with him as soon as I can."

"Just one second," she said. "Let me look at his schedule." She paused. "You can come tomorrow at 3 to speak with him. Would that work?"

"That'll work." I felt excited about that. I'd get a chance to speak with Dale, face to face. I'd find out why he wanted Ezra dead. I wouldn't ask him, straight up, if he killed him. However, I'd ask him about any relationships he had that would mean he wanted Ezra dead. I hoped I could figure that out.

After all, he probably knew Ezra. If he didn't know Ezra, he wouldn't have been at that party. It seemed Ezra didn't let people into parties he didn't know.

Or did he? I would have to ask the bouncers at the party before I spoke with Dale.

So much to do, so little time. I was sobered enough to drive by that time, so I could do some more investigations before I spoke with Dale tomorrow.

"Okay," I said to Ginger. "You can get back to work.

But know this – I'll find out if you had anything to do with this. And if you had something to do with this, you'd be a fool not to take a deal. I don't know if that 20-year manslaughter deal is still on the table. I think It won't be because it has expired. But I might get something decent for you. And if I figure out you played a part in Ezra's murder, I'll pressure you to take a plea agreement."

"I won't take a plea agreement because I didn't do nothing."

"I know you say that. Believe me, everybody always says that. Everybody is always innocent as a baby bird. In real life, though, it stands to reason that *somebody* is guilty. Somebody did the killing. Usually, it's my client. This isn't my first rodeo, Ginger. That's all I'm saying."

She shook her head. "I didn't do nothing wrong. Honest."

"Okay." I looked at my watch. "Well, I have to go. I'll go to the security firm that works Ezra's parties. I need to see what their procedures are to keep random people from getting through the doors of these parties. I have a feeling their procedures are stringent. And I also have a feeling these individuals knew Dale. I have a feeling they knew him well. Otherwise, I don't know how he could've gotten in under an assumed name."

I gathered my stuff together and put it in my bag. I stood up. "I'll see you later."

Ginger still sat in her chair, her shoulders slumped. She looked up at me. "Harper, you believe me, don't you? Don't you?"

She had tears in her eyes.

She's an actress. An actress.

"Ginger," I said. "What is your ultimate goal in life? Once this all goes away, once you are no longer the hot, fresh face on the porn scene and you have to do Philly Slides for a cut-rate just to keep your head above water, what will you do?"

"Philly Slides?"

"Yeah. When somebody poops on you and smears it around."

"Cleveland Steamers."

"Cleveland Steamers. What will you do when that happens? When you have to let people beat and shit on you on screen so you can still have a career? Because you know that's next, Ginger. You know what's going on right now can't last. What do you want to do after it all goes away?"

"I want to be an actress. A mainstream actress. Like Margot Robbie."

I nodded. "Everybody wants to be Margot Robbie. But how will you ensure that happens? That you can find work in the mainstream movie industry? And you know there hasn't been an adult film actress to make that transition. Right?"

"I'm taking acting classes," she said. "Every chance I get."

I nodded. Ginger's acting classes were the last things I wanted to hear about. "Those classes teaching you how to cry on cue?"

"Yeah," she said. "That's like one of the first things they taught us."

"Thought so." I put on my sunglasses. "I'll talk to you later."

I left, got into my SUV, and tried to put Ginger's tears out of my mind.

She could be innocent. It was possible she innocently took the glass of poison-laced scotch to Ezra, not knowing what was in it. That was possible.

Then again, maybe Ginger was a really good acting student. Maybe she nailed the art of looking innocent and crying in her first class.

The horrible thing was, I didn't know which scenario was true.

Chapter Thirty

THE SECURITY FIRM employed by Ezra was called Addington, Incorporated. They were billed as one of the largest security firms in the city and provided personnel for most of the large Hollywood parties. Ezra had employed them, and nobody but them, for all his parties.

I went in there. It was a huge glass structure located in the Valley.

It was stifling hot day, or it was shaping up to be that way, and I was regretting my choice of pantsuit. I really should've gotten with the program and wore a simple sundress with fabric that breathed, and sandals, instead of my usual get-up of pant-suit, complete with jacket and silk shirt. I was always determined to look professional. To look the part of a high-powered successful attorney. I never quite felt the part, but I was determined to look it.

Of course, when you're sweating like a fat guy in a sauna, like I was on that day, you don't quite look professional. It didn't help that my red hair was getting frizzy in the humidity.

I hated summer.

I went right up to the young girl manning the phones. She was behind an enormous marble desk, a headset on her head. "I'll have him give you a call. Thanks!" she said enthusiastically into the phone.

She looked at me. "Hi, welcome to Addington. Can I help you?"

"Yes," I said. "My name is Harper Ross. I'm an attorney. I'm trying to do some investigation into the murder of Ezra Cohen. If I may, I'd like to speak with somebody knowledgeable about the security procedures used in Mr. Cohen's parties."

There was a chance somebody had snuck into the party without getting on the guest list, which would make my job that much more difficult. If there was a rando in that party, how would I ever figure out who did it?

"I'll call Grayson McNeill," the receptionist said. "I'm assuming you would like to know about the procedures used at Mr. Cohen's party on May 25, correct?"

"Correct. Thanks." I was glad this receptionist or assistant was smart enough to read my mind.

At the same time, I was slightly concerned about myself. I was leaving out pertinent details. My brain was foggy and I was craving a drink like I'd never craved one before.

Admit you are powerless over alcohol and your life is crappy.

I looked down at my fingers and saw them twitching. I soon would start shaking. My head would start pounding and I would start sweating worse than I already was in this suit. The nausea would start. I would have to drink more to stop myself from feeling so crappy.

And the vicious circle would begin. When would I ever learn?

What was Step Two? Acknowledging there was a higher

power who could step in and help me take control of my life? Something like that. Was there a higher power who could do that for me? There must be. Millions of drunks all over the world worked those 12 Steps to help them stay on the wagon for years.

I rocked back and forth on my heels as I waited for Grayson McNeill to make his appearance.

He finally did. He was tall, about 6'3", and was dressed in a three-piece suit. Blue eyes, craggy face, butt-chin. He looked like a typical Hollywood guy as I understood Hollywood guys to look.

"Hello," he said. "Harper Ross?"

"Yes," I said, nodding. "Thanks for seeing me on such short notice."

"Of course. I'm always available to help. Especially on this case. Ezra Cohen was a friend of mine. We worked security for his parties for the past two years."

He looked over at the receptionist. "Hold my calls," he said. "Thanks." He turned back to me. "Follow me to my office," he said. "And we can talk."

I followed him through the maze to his office. It was a large office that looked out into a small forest behind him. He had a bird feeder hanging from a hook behind his window and there were rabbits hopping around in the grass. It looked like a peaceful scene. It was the kind of scene where you could swivel your chair, watch and feel your blood pressure coming down.

He smiled as he saw me watching the rabbits and birds. "What can I do for you?"

I looked down at my shaking hands, fixating on how I needed a drink. Badly.

Admit you are powerless over alcohol and your life has become unmanageable. That was it. Those were the words. The actual words I was supposed to commit to memory. That would become my mantra from that point on.

"I need a picture of your security procedures for Ezra Cohen's parties. In particular, I'd like to know the security procedures for Mr. Cohen's party on May 25 of this year. The party where Ezra Cohen was murdered."

"Of course. Now, you've been to his house, I take it?"

"I have"

"So, you know how many different entrances there are into the house. There are five different doors – the door that leads in from the pool, the front door, and three different side doors. Our security firm provides a bouncer for every single door. They check IDs for everybody who comes through that door."

"They check everybody's IDs?"

"Yes. They check everybody's IDs."

"Even the people they know by sight?"

"Even the people they know by sight."

"Can I get two things from you?"

"Sure, anything. What would you like?"

"I need the names of the people working the doors of Ezra's party that night and I need a guest list for all of Ezra's previous parties. He hasn't been in the industry all that long, so it wouldn't be too difficult to get, would it?"

"Not at all. I have all that on my computer right now. I'll print it out for you."

"Thanks."

Grayson looked at his computer, clicked it a few times, and the printer behind me whirred to life. He stood up, got the papers out of the printer and handed them to me. "Here's the guest lists for all of Ezra's previous parties. You're right, he hasn't been in the industry for long, only about two years as an executive, so he hasn't had that many large parties." He handed me the guest lists. "And here are the names of the bouncers working the party that night."

I looked at the material he gave me. "Thanks," I said. "I appreciate that."

He nodded. "Is there anything else I can do for you?"

"Yes. I need to ask you a few more questions."

"Go ahead."

I got my yellow pad and pen out. "I'd like to ask you how you started working for Ezra."

He shrugged. "He hired us from a referral."

"A referral?"

"Our name is very well-known in the industry. We supply door personnel and security for most large industry parties. Ezra found out our name from asking around. It would've been unusual if he didn't hire us for his parties to be honest with you. That's not arrogance. That's a fact. Our reputation is stellar."

"You didn't know him personally before he hired you?"

"No, but I know him personally now." He paused. "I mean, I knew him personally before his death."

I knew what he meant. "He was a personal friend?"

"Yes. Yes he was."

"Do you know a person named Tom Dale?"

He shook his head. "No."

"How about Dale Thompson?"

"Dale Thompson is the studio head for Dark Angel as I understand it. It's an adult film studio in Van Nuys. That's a studio becoming well-known even in the mainstream film industry. Why do you ask?"

"Do your door men and women know Dale Thompson?"

"He's well-known to all our door men and women. They would know him by sight."

"They know him by sight because…"

"We've worked his parties as well. He uses our services frequently. He's been around for a number of years, so we've worked hundreds of his parties over the years."

"But he hasn't been to many of Ezra's parties?"

He shook his head. "You'll have to double-check the guest lists on Ezra's parties, but I don't believe Dale Thompson has been at any of Ezra's parties." He looked perplexed. "Why do you ask these questions about Mr. Thompson?"

"I just needed to know, that's all."

"Okay. Is there anything else I can do for you?"

"Nothing at the moment. Thanks for seeing me on such short notice."

"Certainly. If you have any other questions, I'll be happy to help you."

"Thanks."

I left his office and went back to my car.

I looked at the guest lists from all of Ezra's previous parties.

No Dale Thompson on any of them.

No Tom Dale, either.

That was significant. Why it was, I didn't yet know.

I only knew it was.

Chapter Thirty-One

I PICKED Axel up at LAX when his plane landed that night. I was dying to see him. We had been Zooming every night, but that wasn't the same. I needed his arms around me. I needed to hear him say everything would be okay. That I wasn't a screw-up. That I was doing the right thing.

Whatever that right thing happened to be in this case. Unfortunately, I didn't really know what the right thing was. I didn't know if Ginger was totally innocent. I didn't know for sure if Dale Thompson was guilty. All I knew was that my head was pounding, my stomach was turning, my legs and hands were shaking, and I was dying for a drink.

Admit that you are powerless over alcohol and your life has become unmanageable.

One step at a time…

Step by step. I needed to work that first step and really believe it. Really believe I was powerless over alcohol and my life had become unmanageable. Internalize it. Say it over and over and over until I believed it in my heart.

I waited in the short-term parking lot of LAX for his plane to land. I was watching on my app for it to land, and then I'd go into the baggage claim to meet him.

In the meantime, I waited in my car and drank from my bottle of scotch. I brought it with me, and even though I was determined I wouldn't take a drink, I had to. I was feeling too shitty not to. My stomach was burning. My head was about to explode, even though I took five Advils. Every muscle in my body felt like it was on fire.

I didn't want to feel this shitty on my first night with Axel in about a month, so I had to do something to take this feeling away.

I had to do anything to make this feeling go away.

I was going to admit to myself that I was powerless over alcohol and that my life had become unmanageable. I really was.

But I'd work that step tomorrow. Get some rest tonight, drink a ton of water and about six Pedialytes, eat a lot of protein, and then start fresh. Water, Pedialyte and protein were my go-tos for hangovers.

But, for now, I couldn't feel this shitty, so I had to take a drink.

I finally saw on my app that his plane had landed, so I walked into the airport and went to the baggage claim.

The place was a zoo, unlike any place I'd ever seen. It was a busy airport, I knew, but the chaos was barely controlled. There were people everywhere. Flights were landing and people were streaming out of their gates and descending on the baggage carousels like hordes of locusts.

I didn't care. As long as my Axel was one of the ones streaming out, I would be happy.

Finally, I saw him. And he saw me. He ran towards me and I threw open my arms.

He embraced me the second he got to me and kissed me on the lips.

And then he immediately pulled back.

I closed my eyes. Embarrassed. Humiliated. Ashamed. I couldn't believe I thought I could get away with it. I thought I could get away with taking a drink in the car right before I saw him. I didn't even think to cover it up with mouthwash, gum, a Tic Tac or something.

I wanted to get caught.

He narrowed his eyes, said nothing, but took my hand. "Let's go and get my things, lass, and then we need to talk."

Admit that you are powerless over alcohol and that your life has become unmanageable. And you might lose the best thing that's ever happened to you just because you're weak.

We went over to the baggage claim and Axel's small suitcase immediately came up. "Is this all you have?" I asked him.

"That's it. I can only stay for a few days." Then he smiled. "And I hope it'll be a nice few days indeed."

"It will be. I have one interview I need to do tomorrow with a pertinent witness, but, other than that, I'll have time to show you around. We'll go to the beach, out to eat and just have fun."

He nodded as he held my hand and dragged his bag behind him. "Fun."

We walked to my SUV and put his bag in the back. Then we both got into the SUV. I put my key in the ignition, but Axel stopped me. "Lass, you need to talk to me."

"About what?" I would have to play dumb here.

"About the fact that you're drinking again."

I tried to laugh. "I'm not-"

"You are. Clearly, you are. I could smell that grog on you a mile away."

"Grog?"

"That piss. That swill. That alcohol."

"I think you're mistaken." Here I was, lying. Lying, just like I always used to. Lying to myself, lying to Axel. Just lying.

"Lass. If you can't be straight with me, if you can't be honest with me, what are we doing? Seriously, what are we doing?"

"We're not doing anything." I looked at him. "But I was wondering if you would drive. I suddenly don't feel very good."

"I'm driving because you can't. You can't drive because you're pissed."

"I'm not angry. Why do you think that?"

"No, not pissed as in angry. Pissed as in drunk."

"I am not." I looked out the windshield. "Listen, somebody will have to drive, because every minute we spend in this parking lot is another five dollars. I don't feel like driving. I'd like you to drive."

At that, Axel got out of the car and came around to the driver's side. I got out on my side and went around to the passenger's side.

We drove home in an uncomfortable silence. Axel was angry with me for lying. I was angry with myself for lying and being so goddamned weak. I was powerless over alcohol. That meant I was weak. So weak. And if I was weak, then what? Could I get through Ginger's case? Would I crawl into a hole when it came time to try it? Could I concentrate on what the witnesses were saying in that case, what the opposing counsel was saying, and all of that? Or would I be sitting in that courtroom thinking about nothing except how much I needed a drink?

That was powerlessness. That was a life that had become unmanageable.

That's what that was.

Chapter Thirty-Two

WE GOT HOME, and the girls were more than thrilled to see Axel. "Axel!" Abby screamed, running towards him and his open arms. Even Rina was excited, because she also ran into his waiting arms. "We missed you so much," Abby said.

He hugged both girls and grinned. "I can only stay for a couple of days, but I hope we can pack about a month's worth of fun into these two days."

The drive home had been strained, to the say the least. Axel didn't say a single word to me. I didn't say a word to him, either. Mainly because I didn't know what to say. I wanted to keep lying. I didn't want to admit the truth. I didn't want to go back to AA this time. I wanted to keep on drinking. I had two relapses in a short period of time. After the first relapse, I felt a bit stronger. But this was my second relapse, and I didn't want to stop this time.

Neither of those relapses was my fault, of course. But that didn't matter. What mattered was I was drinking again and had no desire to quit. That's what mattered to me.

Mia was hanging back while the girls were mobbing

Axel and excitedly telling him about all the fun they were having living on the beach and Boogie-boarding and going to the Zoo and, and, and…

At some point, the girls dragged Axel over to Mia. "And this our nanny, Mia," Rina informed Axel. "And she's just the coolest nanny ever. I mean she's as cool as Sophia."

Mia put her hand out with a smile. "Nice to meet you."

"And you."

Axel sat down on the couch and Stella and Sue leaped up next to him and put their head on his lap. I smiled. The dogs ordinarily wasn't welcome on the couch, and I hoped the dogs didn't see getting on the couch as useful precedence, but I knew they would. They were dogs. They would try to get away with whatever they could.

I sat nervously next to him. He gave me a look that told me he was still pissed and I looked away. "Abby, Rina, show me your patio. Maybe we can go down to the beach?"

Abby nodded rapidly and grabbed Axel's hand. "You won't believe how close the beach is," she said. "We've had so much fun."

At that, the three of them, plus Mia and the dogs, went out to the patio and then walked onto the boardwalk and to the beach. Axel didn't care to invite me, and the girls were so excited they didn't notice I wasn't going with them.

Mia came back in. "You coming?"

"Sure," I said. "If I'm welcome."

"Of course you are." She looked perplexed. "Why wouldn't you be?"

"Axel isn't happy with me," I said. "And that's putting things mildly."

"I noticed that. What's wrong?"

"I guess we got into a fight on the way over," I said. "He's pretty angry with me."

She nodded. "What was that about? Can I ask?"

"Sure, you can ask." I took a deep breath. "He's pretty angry I lied to him about something important. And I don't know how I can tell him the truth."

"It must be something big," she said. "If he's that angry with you."

"It is." My buzz was wearing off and I went into the fridge and got out one of my Pedialytes. I filled a huge water bottle with ice water. "I'll go to the beach with you," I said. "I love going there at this time of the night. There's something about standing in the dark, with the only light coming from many bonfires, that comforts me. I'll miss this more than anything when I get back home."

I sipped my Pedialyte and my water bottle as I took off my shoes and walked slowly through the sand. I saw Axel and the girls next to the water, and Axel had a toy he kept throwing in the water. Stella and Sue excitedly went into the water every time he threw it, and one of the dogs brought it back and barked.

I got close to the shore and sipped my water and Pedialyte. If I could just get past the horrible hangover maybe I could power through until I had the chance to get to another AA meeting. In the meantime, I would have to keep working through that first step.

Admit you are powerless over alcohol and your life has become unmanageable.

I put my head down and felt a sense of relief when Axel came up to me and put his arm around my shoulders. He pulled my face into his chest and stroked my hair. I wrapped my arms around his back and nestled him. I hoped this meant he forgave me. I hoped this meant he'd give me another chance.

I felt the tears coming. The tears that were threatening

ever since I'd fallen off the wagon – twice – came tumbling out. I was so afraid Axel would leave me alone to deal with my problems. I was so stressed over what I was up against with this case and I needed his support. I knew there would be huge risks, no matter what direction I took. I didn't want to take a dive for Ginger if she was truly innocent. Yet I had to build such a good case against somebody else that nobody looked at Sargis for Ezra's murder. If something went wrong and Ginger was acquitted and the cops started to sniff around Sargis, I was dead. And so were my kids.

"It's okay, lass," he said. "Just tell me the truth. I'm here to help. I'll do whatever it takes to help. But you have to be honest."

I nodded. "Yes," I said. I looked over at the girls and saw they were busy throwing the toys to the dogs so I hoped to speak frankly to Axel. "I started drinking again." I didn't tell him why I started drinking again. I didn't tell him because I didn't want to complicate everything. I didn't want him to find Sargis and kick his ass. That was the last thing I needed.

He looked me in the eye. "Thank you." He kissed my forehead. "I'll help you stop."

"I've been to a couple of meetings," I said. "But I'm having a hard time with the very first step. I've been having a hard time admitting I'm powerless over alcohol and my life has become unmanageable. I know It's true. I've just been having issues with internalizing that. And then the next step, where I'm supposed to give my problems over to a higher power…I just don't know about that at all."

"It's okay, lass. Step by step."

"And then, after I do all that, I have to make a moral inventory. I need to admit my defects in character. I need to make amends. It all seems so painful and difficult."

"You've gone through AA before, haven't you?"

"Yes. I have. I've been through it before. I've gotten the chip for not drinking. But I never really worked through the steps. I went through the motions. I white-knuckled my sobriety the entire way. I didn't do the work. I know I now have to and I'm scared."

"You can do it. I'll be with you the whole way."

"I know." I cried some more. "I love you."

"And I love you." He took my hand. "Now, let's enjoy the beach a bit, and we'll go inside and I'll hold you all night. Sound good?"

I nodded. "Like you wouldn't believe."

Chapter Thirty-Three

THE NEXT DAY, I was feeling crappy, but I was determined *not* to reach for my bottle of scotch. I made myself two eggs and forced myself to eat them. I put another Pedialyte into a large glass and another huge glass of water.

"What are you drinking?" Rina asked when she saw my pink Pedialyte drink in my glass.

"It's Pedialyte," I said. "What you give to babies when they're not feeling good." *And what you give to drunks trying to overcome a hangover.*

"Why are you drinking that?" Abby asked. "Are you not feeling good?"

"No," I said. "I'm not feeling good at all. But I will be. Hopefully soon."

Axel put his hand on mine and smiled. "What are you doing today?"

"I'll see that shady Dale Thompson and talk to him. And then I'll try to piece together a good case for Ginger. Time is ticking down. Down and down and down." I picked up my briefcase and put on my sunglasses. "I'll try to be home by 5. In the meantime, I need to go somewhere, do my research and try to figure out the direction I need to go."

I went to my SUV and got an idea. I called Patty to see if she had time to meet me for lunch. I could use some support for my latest relapse, and I wanted to ask her a few questions about Dale Thompson and the people working the doors at Ezra's party that night. It didn't sit right with me that Dale Thompson could enter the place under an assumed name. That told me somebody either wasn't doing his or her job or somebody was dirty.

Or maybe I was barking up the wrong tree. Maybe Dale Thompson and Tom Dale weren't the same people. Never mind the fact that there wasn't a web presence for Tom Dale and Patty had never heard of him. Never mind that the waiter, Matt, hadn't heard of him, either. Or, for that matter, Grayson McNeill, the head of Addington Inc.

No, Tom Dale didn't exist. That had to be a pseudonym for Dale Thompson. Why did these bouncers allow him to sign in under an assumed name?

I got into my SUV and, still drinking my water, I called Patty.

"Hello, this is Patty Miller," she said.

"Patty, this is Harper Ross," I said.

"Oh, hey, Harper. How are things going?"

"Not so good. You free for lunch today?"

"I am. Would you like to meet?"

"I would. How about you and I meet at The Water Grill?" The Water Grill was a seafood restaurant downtown on Grand Ave.

"Would one work?"

"One would be great."

"See you then."

AT ONE, I went to the Water Grill and saw Patty was already waiting for me and looking at a menu. She looked up when she saw me and smiled. "Hey, Harper," she said. "It was good to hear from you."

"Thanks for meeting me."

The hostess came around and sat us, and, within a few minutes, the waiter took our orders. After the waiter left, I sipped my water. It seemed like I had drunk a gallon of water that day and was gradually feeling better. My headache was going away, I was no longer shaking, and my stomach had stopped doing the mambo.

"So," Patty said. "What's going on?"

"Two things," I said. "I might as well get it out of the way. I fell off the wagon again."

She nodded. "I figured it was something like that. I'm sorry to hear that. Is there anything I can do?"

"No," I said. "I just wanted to talk about how much I'm having problems just working that first step. I've gone through AA in the past. Back home, I went. I even got a sobriety chip. But I just don't think I've internalized the lessons. Took those twelve steps into my heart and soul. How do you do that? How do you say those words and believe them?"

"It's hard. It's even harder when you get past a certain point and then start drinking and have to start all over again. That's the worst. Maybe you should skip ahead to the 11th Step – do meditation and pray to God for his will and pray for the power to carry out his will. I never understood why that's the 11th step and not the first. Because you have to look within in you to find the strength and that's where you'll find it – through meditation and prayer."

"I need to find a sponsor," I said. "But I need to find somebody back home in Kansas City. It's kinda pointless to find somebody here."

"I'll be happy to be your temporary sponsor," she said. "You can call me anytime of the day or night and I'll answer the phone. We've all been where you are. We've all struggled. You're not alone. I don't want you to think that."

"Thank you." I paused. "I also wanted to pick your brain about a few things."

"Shoot."

I gave her the list of the bouncers were working Ezra's party. "Do you know these people? Are you familiar with them?"

She looked at the list. "Sure. They're all security personnel with Addington, Inc. Why do you ask?"

"Are all of these people trustworthy?"

"I think so. I don't know any of them all that well. I just know they work for Addington. Everybody uses that security firm so it's very reputable. They do a great background check whenever they hire people, so I don't know why these people would be dirty in any way."

I sipped my water and took the list back. I wasn't quite sure what else to ask.

"Why do you ask?" Patty asked.

"I'm trying to figure out how Dale Thompson got through them under an assumed name. Grayson McNeill, the head of that firm, told me everybody has to show an ID. Even the people known to the bouncers. Dale Thompson got in the door under an assumed name. That sounds fishy to me."

"Let me look at the list again," she said.

She studied the list of bouncers that night and then looked at me with a puzzled look on her face. "Well, there's one person on here you might check out. Her name is Elizabeth Ellis. I don't know her at all. The others work the door on lots of parties. I don't know them personally, however. But Elizabeth Ellis...I mean, I know she works for Addington but I think she's new. She's not somebody who commonly works industry parties."

I wrote down the name Elizabeth Ellis and nodded. "Well, this is helpful."

"Is it? In what way?"

"It's always helpful when you can narrow down suspects. Not that Elizabeth Ellis is a suspect, but it helps when you can pinpoint who's possibly trustworthy and who possibly isn't." Of course, just because Elizabeth Ellis wasn't known didn't make her a suspect. But she didn't have much of a reputation around the industry while the other bouncers did.

"I hope that gives you some kind of information you can use."

"You did."

AFTER LUNCH, I went back over to Addington, Inc. to inquire about Elizabeth Ellis.

Grayson McNeil was in his office again, so I went back to talk to him.

"What else can I help you with?" Grayson asked me.

"I was looking over your list of bouncers at Ezra's parties, discovered that four of the bouncers who working that night were well-known, but one, Elizabeth Ellis, seems to be new. Can you give me any information about her?"

Grayson narrowed his eyes and clasped his hands in

front of him. "What kind of information are you looking for?"

"How long has she worked here?"

"One month. But she no longer works here."

"She was fired? Or she quit?"

For the first time, Grayson looked suspicious. Like he wanted to get rid of me. "Personnel information is confidential. I think you, as a lawyer, would know that."

"I know that. I also know that…"

"You do know what?"

"Nothing. I thank you for your time."

"Of course." Grayson seemed to relax. "If you need anything at all, just let me know."

"Sure."

I left the office and realized that getting information about this Elizabeth Ellis would be the job for one person.

Anna.

Chapter Thirty-Four

"HARPER," Anna said. "Long time, no hear. I miss working for you."

Anna was my computer hacker. She could get any record for anybody as long as said record was on the internet. Dark-haired, beautiful, with tattoos and piercings everywhere, Anna would've been a possible girl-crush if she didn't work for me. She saved my ass on more than one occasion because she found people I didn't think were possible to find.

I could never forget the time she finally found a key witness in my self-defense case. If not for Anna, Heather Morrison would be serving a life sentence in prison this very moment. But because Anna tracked down Louisa Garrison, Heather was acquitted. Louisa was found just in the nick of time, too. A few days later and there would've been no way to get Louisa to testify.

Now Anna would be called upon to find out a few other key things for me. "I need you to give me all the information you can about Elizabeth Ellis," I said. "She lives here in Los

Angeles, I think, but she was an employee of Addington, Inc., which is a security firm. I also need to find out the attorney for the will regarding Jacob Cohen. His heirs were Ezra, Daniel, Eli and Ariel. Ariel is currently married to a man by the name of Rafael Petrossian." I had a hunch the attorney involved in that mess was as dirty as they come.

"Will do. When do you need this?"

"As soon as you can get it to me."

I was driving while talking to Anna. I was anxious to get back to Axel and the girls but had that meeting with Dale Thompson at 3. I needed to kill some time. Not a lot of time, just about an hour, so I went to the Griffith Observatory on Mount Hollywood. I'd take pictures of the Hollywood sign and look at the view. I'd always heard it was spectacular.

Plus I wanted to think. I had a hundred things bouncing around in my head and needed to get them all straight. I needed to get away from all the bars, restaurants and people and try to get my head on straight.

So, I drove up the mountain, winding around the roads until I got to the Griffith Observatory. I didn't go into the Observatory. It wouldn't really pay for me to do that, since I had that meeting with Dale in just over an hour, and, with L.A. traffic, I wouldn't have a lot of time to myself. But as I got out of the SUV and looked over the expanse of the city, and breathed the air, I knew I'd made the right decision.

Get centered. Learn how to meditate. Step 11 – through meditation and prayer, connect with your higher power. Find out His will for you and seek his power to help you. I was paraphrasing this Step, but that was the gist. Patty was probably right – it was better to skip ahead to that step because you need to establish a connection to your higher power before you can communicate to Him about what you want from life.

I closed my eyes and listened to the sounds of nature as I stood by the edge of the cliff that looked down. I breathed in through my nose and out through my mouth. I did that several times, trying to feel the relaxation coursing through me. Tried to establish some kind of connection between myself and the universe. Tried to get to some level of higher consciousness. Some level of peace. Serenity.

I let my mind flow freely. Thoughts came into my head but didn't stay. The negative thoughts were immediately chased away. The positive ones came in, briefly, and then left again. I tried to bring back the positive thoughts. Tried to make them stay. The positive thoughts about my girls, about Axel, about my family, about my career.

Always, though, there was that negative voice. That negative voice I could never quiet no matter what I did. No matter how many times I tried to get rid of it, it was there.

I opened my eyes when I saw Anna was calling me.

"Yeah, Anna," I said, picking up the phone. "What can you tell me?"

"Elizabeth Ellis is actually related to Ezra Cohen. She's apparently the daughter of Jacob Cohen's illegitimate son. That's what I found out. Her father's name was Aaron Samson. Aaron is dead, though. You can take from that what you want, but it sounds like she would've been Ezra's half-niece."

That actually made some sense. And it immediately made me think she would've let Dale Thompson into that place under an assumed name. I wondered how she could pass the necessary background check. "I see. And how long did she work at Addington, Inc.?"

"It looked like she only worked there a week. And, before that, she was working as a project manager for a software tech firm. She apparently is back with that tech firm."

"And what is the name of the tech firm?"

"It's Dark Angel, Inc. It's apparently a tech firm that's involved-"

"In the adult film industry," I said. "It sounds like it's associated with the Dark Angel studios in Van Nuys. The studio where Ginger works."

"Yes. Actually, it is associated with that studio. Dark Angel, Inc. is the tech division of that studio. It handles the web presence for the studio – all the webcams, streaming movies and websites are handled through Dark Angel, Inc. She's been working there for about ten years. As I said, she worked for Addington for only a short period."

Damn it. Why would Grayson hire her? The innocent explanation was simple – Elizabeth was an industry insider, in a way, and nothing in her background would've raised red flags.

Then again, she obviously wasn't experienced in the security field. That was unusual. A professional firm such as Addington, Inc. had a reputation to uphold. If I gave Anna the names of all the other security guards in that firm, she would no doubt tell me that they all had a background in law enforcement or security. They all were probably trained in firearms and conflict resolution, at the very least.

I gave Anna the name of the firm and asked her for a background check on the rest of the security personnel working for Addington.

"I'll get right on that. Oh, and, by the way – I found out the name of the attorney for Jacob's will. As you probably know, two wills were filed. One was filed five years ago and the most current one was filed about six months ago."

"Right. One of the wills said the four children would split Jacob's inheritance evenly. The other will said only Ezra would inherit Jacob's fortune. Is that correct?"

"Yes," she said. "The attorney for the first will was a different attorney than the one for the second will, of course. Anyhow, the attorney for the first will was named Jamal Hudson."

"And the attorney for the second will? What was that attorney's name?"

"The attorney for the second will...let's see. I wrote it down....oh, yes, here it is. His name is David Jenkins."

Chapter Thirty-Five

"DAVID JENKINS." *Now, now, Harper, don't jump to conclusions. Don't assume your David Jenkins is the same David Jenkins as the guy who drew up that phony will.* "What can you tell me about David Jenkins? Did you do a background check?"

"Yes. I did. He's not an attorney that does wills, estates and trusts for a living. He's not like Tammy, in other words. His main practice is white-collar and organized crime criminal defense. And he didn't sign off on the will. I only know he prepared that will because his name was on some of the supporting documents that aren't available to the public. The attorney who signed off on that will was another person, not the attorney who prepared the will. That's what I gathered from all the documents I could hack into."

I nodded. David was obviously covering his tracks. He didn't want his dirty fingerprints on that phony will. If his fingerprints were on that will, at least publicly, it would be only a matter of time before I figured out his dirty deed and cut him loose. He didn't know I had a girl who could hack into any database. If there was a paper trail for a document,

Anna would find it, especially if it was uploaded to the Cloud. Which I imagined these documents were – they were probably "securely" uploaded to the Cloud. Never to be seen by the public.

"What's the name of the signing attorney on that will?"

"That person's name is Julian Wellsely. That's an attorney in Los Angeles who apparently prepare wills and trusts for a living."

I wrote that down. "I'll have to have a talk with Mr. Jenkins," I said. "I don't know what his deal is, but he's up to no good. Obviously."

"David Jenkins? How do you know him?"

"He's an attorney in town here. He's working with me as local counsel. I should've known there was something up with him because he's working for me so damned cheap. That should've set the alarm bells off. But, of course, it didn't." I started to mentally kick myself. "It didn't."

What was his game? There were pieces of the puzzle laying all over the table. I needed to put them together into a coherent whole.

"What do you mean? Do you mean you hired David Jenkins to help you with your court case and you didn't know he…" She paused. "What? So, he drew up the phony will Ezra used to dupe the grandfather into signing. What does that mean for your case?"

"I don't know. There's obviously something to it. And I'll have to find it out."

At that, I hung up the phone.

I looked at my watch and saw it read 1:45. Time to get on the road and over to Van Nuys to talk to Dale Thompson.

I didn't know if he could give me any pertinent information, but I would try.

Chapter Thirty-Six

I WENT to see Dale at the Dark Angel studio. I would try to get the information from him that would hopefully help me put this entire puzzle together. It had a hundred moving pieces. I just needed somebody to help me put them all together.

Unfortunately, when I got to the studio, the receptionist informed me Dale wasn't in the studio anymore. "I'm very sorry," she said. "I forgot to tell him you were coming. Totally my fault. I have you down on my schedule and everything."

I wanted to jump down her throat when she told me that. That was unacceptable to me, of course. I needed to speak with him. I knew he poisoned Ezra. The question was why. He obviously got into the party with the help of Elizabeth Ellis. I needed to find out how Elizabeth Ellis could get a job with a security firm, considering her lack of knowledge or experience in the field.

I also needed to know if Dale Thompson was behind the death of Mario, Ginger's former "manager." Not that

Dale would tell me that, but I could ask him pertinent questions to find that out. Questions that would indirectly tell me what I needed to know.

"When can I come and see him?"

She looked uncomfortable. "He said he won't ever talk to you. I told him who you were. He said you could come and see him a hundred times and it wouldn't do any good. I'm so sorry. When you called I didn't know who you were. You told me you were Ginger's attorney, but I guess that didn't ring a bell."

"Well, then, fine. Fine." I would have to subpoena him for trial and have him answer questions under oath. He couldn't avoid a subpoena unless he got an attorney who quashed it for him. But I also knew there would be no grounds for quashing a subpoena. Good luck with that, Mr. Thompson. Good luck with quashing that subpoena.

"That's fine? Really?" the receptionist said. "You're okay with walking away and letting him not speak with you?"

"Oh, of course. Of course." I made a note to subpoena this bastard as soon as I could. "Well," I said, giving her my business card. "Tell him I sent my regards."

At that, I left. It wasn't over. In fact, it was only beginning. The way he was acting told me he was guilty as hell.

The only thing – was Dale connected to Sargis in any way? Would my pointing the finger at Dale implicate Sargis? If so, my life would be in danger. So were the lives of Rina and Abby.

If I rolled the dice on my theory and was wrong, I could be dead and Rina and Abby could be kidnapped and sold into white slavery.

No pressure.

"DAVID," I said, getting into my car. "We need to talk."

"Sure, Harper," he said. "Where are you?"

"On my way to your office," I said. "I'll be there in a half hour."

"I have…"

"If you have a client meeting, then please reschedule it. If you have a court appearance, I would appreciate it if you could get somebody to cover for you. This is important."

He was quiet for a few minutes. "I was just going to say that I have clients coming in this afternoon. But I'll be free in a half hour. Come visit my office."

I drove along the freeway towards his office. My mind was racing 1,000 miles per hour. What was going on with him? He'd been involved with Ezra all along. He composed that phony will for him. Why did he do that? What did that mean for this case? I was so confused, I didn't know what end was up.

I got to his office and took the elevator to his suite.

He was waiting for me.

And so was Sargis Gregorian.

Chapter Thirty-Seven

SARGIS SMILED at me when I walked into the office. "Hello, Ms. Ross," he said pleasantly, holding out his hand to shake mine. "So we meet again."

I looked from David to Sargis and back again. "What's going on?" I asked David suspiciously.

Sargis looked hurt. "Is that any way to treat an old friend? Where's my warm welcome?"

I just shook my head. "I don't have a warm welcome at the moment. I'm trying to figure out what the hell is going on."

"Sit down," David said, pointing to a chair. "And I'll tell you everything."

I sat down and Sargis was standing next to David's desk. His arms were crossed and a sly smile was playing across his face.

"Go ahead," I said, "I guess you somehow know exactly why I'm here. You somehow know just what I'm going to ask you. I don't know how you know but you seem to. So, go ahead. Go ahead and tell me what's going on."

"I could tell by your tone of voice on the phone that you know."

"I know what?"

He just stared at me. I could tell he was trying to feel me out. He was trying to figure out exactly what I knew about him. He certainly wouldn't volunteer any information.

I looked over at Sargis. "Mr. Gregorian, if you don't mind, I really need to speak with Mr. Jenkins alone."

Sargis smiled but made no move to leave.

"Harper," David said. "Sargis will stay and listen to anything you have to say to me."

I was intimidated by Sargis' presence. I didn't want to say a word in front of him. Yet I had to get to the bottom of why David lied to me. Deceived me. Betrayed me.

"Okay," I said. "I found something out about you that has disturbed me. To say the very least."

"Go on," he said. "Tell me what you found out."

"I found out about the will, David. The phony will presented to the probate court. Jacob Cohen's last will and testament that gave Ezra Cohen the whole enchilada. Jacob's estate went entirely to Ezra because of that phony will. That will was drawn up just days before Jacob breathed his last. So I see a connection between that will being drawn up, Jacob dying, and Ezra's murder. It's a perfect throughline. You were behind it all."

David looked at Sargis. Sargis, for his part, was still smiling. He looked at David and shrugged.

"Yes," he said, "I was behind that will. You found that out but you can't do a thing about it. Sargis told me he has you by the short-hairs. I assume you know you can never tell anybody about what I did in this case."

I sighed. "That goes without saying. I already have an agreement with Sargis. I play his game and he lets me live. I do what he says, and my girls are safe. I don't play his game and all bets are off. So, yes, I won't breathe a word about your deception. Especially since it's related to Sargis. But I'm trying to figure out why you did it."

Sargis interjected. "Ms. Ross, David has been my attorney for many years. Not on the books, of course. But he has been my advisor for many years. He facilitated that project for me. Ezra owed me $35 million for that apartment project. He was coming into an inheritance but it was only $50 million. It wouldn't have done for him to have split that inheritance four ways. $50 million divided by four is only $12.5 million apiece. If he didn't get that entire inheritance, he wouldn't have had had the money to pay me. I hired David to fix that issue. That is all."

I nodded. "I see. Parts of that deal were in place from the beginning, weren't they? From the time you made that deal with Ezra, you put into motion the entire plan that would ensure Ezra would give you all that money. You fixed it so that Jacob met his untimely end right after you made that agreement, but not before you got David to make that phony will that ensured Ezra would get all the money. The fix was in from the beginning."

"Right," Sargis said. "You can't do anything about that. You not only cannot tell anybody a word about David's deception but you also must keep him as your co-counsel. He will make sure you stay in your lane. He will make sure you do what I ask."

I bit my lip. I saw no way out. David was dirty. He was working with Sargis. Sargis had warned me he would kill me and kidnap my girls unless I did things his way.

I was stuck with this whole scenario.

I felt sick.

Chapter Thirty-Eight

August 29 - the day of the trial

I FELT SICK. Sicker than usual. The last six weeks had been a whirlwind. I stayed off alcohol even though I hadn't yet internalized the 12 steps. I got through the first step – admitting I was powerless over alcohol and my life had become unmanageable. I finally broke down one day and admitted I had no power over alcohol.

The trickier part, of course, was every step that came after it. I had to somehow turn my life over to a higher power and the problem I had. I just couldn't turn over control to another entity – let alone an entity I didn't quite believe in. I was Catholic and took the girls to church, but the doubts about whether or not there was a God watching over us was something I still struggled with. Faith was always difficult for me.

Even though I was stuck on the first step, I made as many AA meetings as I could handle. That was the best I could do for the moment. My plan was to go to Kansas City and find an AA sponsor and really do everything right. For once. I wouldn't white-knuckle it anymore. I'd absorb the lessons of AA and be fundamentally transformed.

Even if it killed me.

The only possible good thing about all of this was I'd came up with a trial strategy David approved of. We had decided, together, to focus on Dale as the culprit of the crime. I had done enough investigation that I knew exactly why he would've killed Ezra. Since Dale wasn't associated with Sargis, this was also acceptable to the mob boss.

Of course it wasn't fool-proof. In any way, shape or form. This made me nervous. I had to convince the jury that Dale was the true killer. If I didn't and Ginger went free, my life would be in danger. That would leave the case unsolved, which would mean the police would keep looking. And they would inevitably be led straight to Sargis.

But if I could build an air-tight case against Dale, that would be ideal. Ginger would be free and the evidence would point to Dale. That would make Dale the number one suspect to the LAPD, which would take the heat off Sargis.

I managed to get David on my side on this trial strategy. After I figured out his game he was much more honest with me about his end-game. Protect Sargis Gregorian at all costs.

I convinced him of Ginger's innocence and of Dale's guilt. That was good enough for him.

"Keep the heat off Sargis. If you do that, you've done your job."

The pressure was on. I would have to carefully build such a good case against Dale that the police could never ignore it.

Otherwise everything would fall apart. And everything I

held dear would be in danger. My life and the life of my girls.

I GOT into the courtroom and sat down. I had my jury questions prepared for voir dire and was ready to pick a jury. I had my research done, my discovery done, and I was ready to go.

I was ready for this as I ever was for a trial. Trials were always super stressful. No matter what. I always had so much riding on them.

But I had never had this much riding on the outcome.

"Harper," David said. "I think we have a winning strategy. It takes the heat off Sargis, and, if it goes well, it'll exonerate Ginger."

"And if it doesn't go well?"

He shrugged. "Ginger loses the case. We lose the case for her. If we can't convince the jury that Dale did this, that has to be the only outcome."

"But she didn't do it." I had become convinced that Ginger was an innocent pawn. A dupe. I had my doubts about her all along – I vacillated between thinking Ginger was truly innocent, and that Ginger knew what she was giving Ezra in that drink. Maybe she did it to become famous and to get a leg up on the other girls. To have the chance to maybe segue into a better career in the mainstream movie industry just because her name was so well-known.

But, along the way, I came to believe this theory wasn't correct. Because of that, I knew that if I took a dive on her case, it would be an injustice.

"I know she didn't do it," David said. "But if we can't convince the jury that Dale did it, then us losing the case is the only outcome that will be acceptable."

The only outcome that would be acceptable.

No pressure.

Chapter Thirty-Nine

IT WAS on the second day of the trial when it happened. The first day of the trial was pretty routine. We each did our opening statements to the jury. Adrian told the jury how Ginger as the only person in the world who had the opportunity to kill Ezra Cohen. "She was in the room with him when he was poisoned, ladies and gentlemen. You will hear evidence from the medical examiner who will confirm that Ezra Cohen was poisoned between 11:45 and 12 AM on the night of May 25. You will hear evidence from witnesses who will confirm that Ms. Perry was with Mr. Cohen from 11:10 PM to 12:15 AM on that night. These same witnesses will confirm that nobody else was in that room with him during this period of time. She was the only possible person who could've killed Mr. Cohen, ladies and gentlemen. The only possible person."

I, of course, had my own opening statement to make to the jury. "I do not dispute that Ms. Perry was in that room with Mr. Cohen during the hours of 11:10 PM and 12:15 AM," I told the jury. "But what I do dispute is that my client, Ginger Perry, had any knowledge that she was administering poison to Mr. Cohen. She simply handed Mr. Cohen a scotch. She didn't know there was poison in it. You heard the prosecutor say she would present evidence of opportunity. But she can't produce evidence of motive, because there is none. My client had nothing to gain by killing Mr. Cohen. She didn't even know him. No prior interaction with him. Mr. Cohen was nothing but a client. She will admit she performed a sex act on him. She'll even admit she stole cufflinks and a ring from him. But that's it. In her mind, she had a reason to steal from him because she needed the money. But she didn't have a reason to kill him."

I continued on. "I will, however, present you an individual who had reason to kill Ezra. His name is Dale Thompson, and you will hear testimony from him today. You will hear that Dale Thompson had a motive to kill Ezra Cohen, and that motive was greed. Pure and simple. Greed. One of the oldest impulses in human nature. You'll also hear evidence of a conspiracy to murder Ezra that involved several different players, all of whom managed to get a cut of Ezra's fortune after he died. Two of these players were related to Ezra – his sister, Ariel Rossi, and his half-niece, Elizabeth Ellis. They both had motive to kill Ezra because Ezra did something to make them very angry. When his grandfather, Jacob Cohen, was desperately sick with Alzheimer's Disease, and was not in his right mind, Mr. Cohen hired an attorney to draft a phony will that left every penny to him. Only to him."

I had done my due diligence on this case and could find the trail that ran through all of these individuals. I planned on making that trail known to the jury through my questioning of these witnesses. When I was through with my side, I knew I could fit all the puzzle pieces together for the jury quite nicely.

The only thing was, I couldn't tell the jury who truly drafted that phony will. Julian Wellesley was the signing attorney for it, so Julian Wellesley was the person to finger for it. David's fingerprints weren't on that will, at least publicly, so he had plausible deniability on the whole thing.

I wanted to get rid of David and make him a witness when I found out what he did. As far as I was concerned, he was dirty. He might not have been in on Ezra's murder, but he certainly was a part of the scheme that led to Ezra's murder. That meant he had a clear conflict of interest in this case.

I couldn't get rid of him, however. Sargis informed me that David was to remain on the case. I was taking my orders from Sargis simply because Sargis had the ability to kill me and make my two girls his property. I couldn't feel safe unless I did things exactly as he wanted. He had to sign off my trial strategy every step of the way. It wasn't how I wanted to try this case. It wasn't how I wanted to practice law. I wasn't in the habit of having outside parties dictate trial strategy. But I made an exception with Sargis. He terrified me. I could handle the threat on my own life. What I couldn't handle was the threat to my girls.

Sargis was delighted when I told him my suspicions about Ariel, Elizabeth and Dale. Ariel and Elizabeth were fairly easy to pin down. They both had connections with Dale. Ariel and Elizabeth were working together and had been for a long time.

Now, I just needed to show all this to the jury. All while somehow convincing them that Ginger was nothing but a dupe. That would be the hardest part. Dale had given her that drink. This meant she'd lied to me all along. She told me, repeatedly, she couldn't remember who gave her that scotch to give to Ezra. I found a witness, who knew both Dale and Ginger, who told me differently. It was Dale who gave Ginger that drink to give to Ezra. Ginger knew Dale at that time. Ginger had actually met Dale a week earlier, and Dale arranged for Ginger to be at that party. Not Mario.

She lied to me about all of this. Why did she lie?

"Because I didn't want you to think I did that on purpose," she told me. "I didn't want you to think I poisoned that man for Dale and I knew I was poisoning him for Dale. That's all, Harper. I didn't want you to think that."

I *did* think that. I still kind of thought that. But I certainly wouldn't convey to the jury that I thought that. As far as I was concerned, Ginger was still an innocent dupe. That was all the jury would hear about. Ginger had never told me differently, thank God. If she told me differently – if she ever told me she knew what was in that scotch she gave to Ezra – then I would've approached her case very differently. In that case, I couldn't put her on the stand. And I probably would've put much more pressure on her to take a plea bargain.

THE SECOND DAY of the trial was my chance to put my case on. The first day was the prosecutor presenting her evidence. Her evidence consisted of the coroner's report and the witnesses who testified they knew Ginger was with Ezra when he died. I wasn't disputing any of this testimony. I had the toxicology reports and I knew the prosecution witnesses were solid.

Those were the only witnesses she had, so she rested after the first day.

The second day was the day for my witnesses to give testimony. They would get on the stand and lie, so I would have to treat all of them as hostile. All of them except Ginger, of course.

"Ms. Ross, call your first witness."

"The defense calls Ginger Perry."

At that, Ginger walked to the stand, took the oath and sat down for questioning. I went over my questions with her before the trial so I was reasonably certain I knew what her testimony would be. I also asked her to tone down her look just a bit. She did as I asked – her hair was a more natural color of blonde, her makeup was more subtle than usual and she wasn't dressed trashy. She had on a simple navy dress with navy and white shoes. At the moment, she looked more mainstream than ever before.

"Please state your name for the record."

"Ginger Perry."

"Ms. Perry, you're the defendant in this trial, correct?"

"Yes." She looked nervous. "I am."

"Let me take you back to the night of May 25. You were at Ezra Cohen's party, correct?"

"Yeah. I mean yes."

"Did you know Ezra Cohen prior to this party?"

"No."

"Then why were you at the party?"

"I was at the party because Dale Thompson asked me to go."

"Who is Dale Thompson?"

"He's my boss. I work at Dark Angel studios. I'm an adult film actress."

I nodded. "And why were you at Mr. Cohen's party?"

"I was at his party because Dale told me I could service Mr. Cohen. He told me I could maybe become a regular girl for Mr. Cohen and that Mr. Cohen paid very well."

"At around 11 PM, did you go into Mr. Cohen's bedroom?"

"Yes."

"Did you give him anything?"

"Yes. A glass of scotch."

"And who gave you that glass of scotch?"

"Dale Thompson."

"Dale Thompson gave you the glass of scotch which you then gave to Ezra Cohen. Is that correct?"

"Yes."

"Were you aware this glass of scotch had poison in it?"

She shook her head. "No."

"I have nothing further." It was pointless to ask Ginger more questions. The details of what happened would be filled in by the prosecutor on cross-examination. Unfortunately for Ginger.

"Ms. Jackson," Judge Woo said. "Your witness."

Adrian approached Ginger. "Ms. Perry," she said. "Isn't it true that the glass of scotch you gave to Mr. Cohen was laced with arsenic?"

Ginger shrugged. "Yeah, but I didn't know that at the time."

"You didn't? Your lawyer had argued you didn't have motive to kill Ezra Cohen, but you had motive, didn't you?"

Ginger shook her head. "No. I didn't have no motive to kill him."

"Actually, you did. You wanted to become famous, didn't you?"

"No. I never thought about becoming famous."

"You're an adult film star, correct?"

"Correct."

"And are you aware that the average career span of an adult film star is less than one year?"

"No. I didn't know that."

"You wanted to beat those odds, didn't you?"

Ginger looked confused. "Beat those odds how?"

"Well it's pretty simple. You kill a high-powered studio executive and become famous. Once you're famous, you become a popular adult film star. And that's what happened, isn't it? You became a very popular adult film star."

"I'm popular, yes."

"And you actually get paid twice what other girls in the industry get paid, don't you?"

"I don't know."

"I do. I know. Isn't it true you get paid $2,000 for every scene you film between you and a man?"

"Yeah."

"And $1,500 for scenes between you and a woman?"

"Yeah. So what?"

"You get $4,000 for scenes considered more niche – anal sex and group sex. Isn't that correct?"

"Yeah, but I don't see how-"

"And you command $10,000 for really specialty scenes, such as bondage, simulated rape, and scenes where your male co-star urinates on you. Correct?"

"Yeah. That's right. I get paid a lot of money for golden showers. Having somebody pee on you, that's pretty gross, so I get paid a lot of money for that. So what?"

"The 'so what' is that other actresses get exactly half for all those scenes."

I stood up. "Objection. Unless the prosecutor is planning on bringing in these other actresses to testify about their salaries, or the prosecutor is planning on bringing in a certified document that details the average income for adult film actresses, this line of questioning is objectionable. Lack of foundation."

Judge Woo nodded. "Sustained. Move along Ms. Jackson."

Adrian continued. "And you testified that Dale Thompson gave you that glass of scotch. Is that correct?"

"Yes. That's right."

"And Dale Thompson is your boss, correct?"

"Yeah."

"And did Mr. Thompson ever tell you you were getting more money than other actresses because you were famous?"

I didn't object to that as hearsay, as Dale would testify on his own behalf later on.

"Yeah. He told me that."

"And he told you exactly why you became so famous?"

"Yeah. Because I supposedly murdered Ezra Cohen."

"I have nothing further."

I sighed. The prosecutor did a pretty good job of establishing motive. It was up to me to rehabilitate her.

"Ms. Ross, do you have any follow-up questions for this witness?"

"Yes. Thank you." I approached Ginger. "Ms. Perry, did you knowingly poison Mr. Ezra Cohen on May 25 of this year?"

She shook her head. "No. I wouldn't do that. Why would I do that? Why would I risk going to jail just to become famous? If I'm in jail, I'm not making movies. If I'm in jail, it don't matter how famous I am, it does me no good. Fame does me no good behind bars."

"I have nothing further."

We got through that testimony without Ginger drawing a rebuke from the judge. A win in my book.

"Ms. Ross, call your next witness," Judge Woo commanded.

"The defense calls Dale Thompson."

This would seal the deal, in my book. I would corner him, keep him off-balance and hopefully he would crack. This being California, I couldn't deposed him, so he didn't know what I would ask. He had no clue why he was called to testify. Exactly how I wanted it.

The only problem was I didn't know what he would say. A fundamental rule of trial work was you should never ask a question you don't know the answer to. I was violating that rule but sometimes it couldn't be helped. Sometimes you just had to take a big risk and hope it panned out.

If only trial work could be as tidy as I was always taught in law school. If only I could stick to strictly asking questions to which I knew the answer. That was a luxury I couldn't always afford.

Dale made his way to the stand. He sat down and crossed his arms in front of him, a sure sign he was defensive. No matter, I would have to break down those defenses.

Dale was sworn in and I got right to it.

"Please state your name for the record."

"Dale Thompson."

"Mr. Thompson, could you please tell the jury what your job is?"

"I am the executive director of Dark Angel Studios in Van Nuys, California."

"And Dark Angel is where Ms. Perry is employed, correct?"

"Correct."

"And you recruited Ms. Perry to work for your studio, is that correct?"

He made a face that told me he was thinking. He squinted one eye and, with the other eye, he looked towards the ceiling. "Yes," he said. "I am."

"Now," I said. "On May 25 of this year, were you at Ezra Cohen's party?"

"No."

I nodded. "Permission to treat the witness as hostile," I asked Judge Woo. I had to treat Dale as "hostile," otherwise I couldn't ask him leading questions. Since Dale told his first lie, when he said he wasn't at Ezra's party, I had grounds to ask these leading questions.

"Permission granted," Judge Woo said.

"Mr. Thompson, you were at Ezra Cohen's party. You were there under an assumed name, Tom Dale. Isn't that correct?"

"No," Dale said, shaking his head. "That's not correct."

I was determined to shake him down. Elizabeth Ellis was another person on my list, and I had interviewed her. I scared her enough that she agreed to testify against Dale and tell her part of story, so I would have to carefully lay a trap for this bastard. Elizabeth was a credible witness. She would bring Dale down if I played my cards right.

"Mr. Thompson, does the name Elizabeth Ellis mean anything to you?"

"No. Why, should it?"

"It should. Isn't it true that Elizabeth Ellis actually works in the tech division of your company, Dark Angel?"

"I don't know. That's a separate division."

"And you got her that job, isn't that right?"

"I told you, I don't know. I don't know her."

"I've got Elizabeth lined up to testify differently. Do you care to revise your statement?"

He suddenly got pale. "Elizabeth will be here to testify?"

"Yes. Elizabeth will be here to testify."

He shifted uncomfortably in his seat. "Well, her name does ring a bell, come to think of it."

"It does, doesn't it? Isn't it true that you discovered Elizabeth was angry with Ezra Cohen because Ezra created a phony will that gave him all of his grandfather's money and cut out all the other heirs, including Elizabeth, so you decided to use her to help you get into Ezra's party the night of May 25?"

All this was true. Elizabeth had motive to kill Ezra because she was an heir. She was illegitimate, so would have to prove her birthright before she could cash in on her part of Jacob Cohen's fortune. She eventually would do just that and get her cut of Jacob's fortune.

"No, that's not true."

I rolled my eyes. "Again, I have Elizabeth ready to testify. Do you care to revise your statement?"

Dale's eyes shot daggers at me. "Yes. I asked her to let me into that party."

"And you used the name Tom Dale, didn't you?"

"Yes." He looked ready to kill me.

"And Tom Dale is an assumed name, isn't it?"

"Obviously. My name is Dale Thompson."

"So, Mr. Thompson. You're telling the jury you were at Ezra Cohen's party on the evening of May 25 of this year and you got in the door under an assumed name. Is that what you're telling the jury?"

"Yes. That's what I'm telling the jury."

"Isn't it true that, when you found Elizabeth Ellis was

Jacob Cohen's rightful heir, you went to her with a plan for her to claim her inheritance?"

This was also true. Dale concocted this whole scheme when he found out Elizabeth Ellis was Jacob Cohen's heir. He found that out when he overheard her speaking with other co-workers at her Dark Angel tech job. He was also friendly with Ariel, as he'd been working with her husband, Ralph Rossi, for some time. It turned out Ralph Rossi had a penchant for working girls and Dale ran a prostitution ring on the side. Ralph was one of his best clients.

All of this would come out one way or another. That was always the way I played multiple witnesses who were rolling on one another. Simply let each witness know the other witnesses were coming to testify and that witness will tell the truth most of the time. They don't generally want to attract a perjury charge and they figure they're done for anyhow.

That strategy worked most of the time. It seemed to be working well with Dale.

"No, that's not true. I didn't plot anything with Elizabeth Ellis."

Time to pivot quickly. "Do you know Ralph Rossi?"

"Sure," he said.

"How long have you known Ralph Rossi?"

"For about seven years."

"How do you know Ralph Rossi?"

"He's a long-time client."

"By client, you mean he's hired many of your call-girls over the years. Is that what you mean by client?"

He nodded. "Yes. I got nothing to hide. I provide a valuable service. Nothing wrong with that."

"And you know Ralph Rossi is married to Ariel Rossi

who is also an heir unjustly cut out of Jacob Cohen's will. Correct?"

"I guess so."

"Isn't it true you, Elizabeth Ellis and Ariel Rossi all got together to concoct this plan to poison Ezra?"

"No, that's not true."

"Isn't it true you wanted to specifically use one of the actresses at your studio to carry out this plan because you knew you could get tons of free publicity for your movies?"

"No, that's not true."

"But do you deny that Ginger Perry has been a supreme money-maker for your studio ever since she was arrested for Ezra's murder?"

"I-"

"Isn't it true that Ginger Perry has brought almost $20 million in rental and streaming revenue into your studio in just a matter of months?"

"Yes, that's true but-"

"But what? Has any other girl brought in even a fraction of that amount?"

"No, but-"

"And do you deny my client has become nationally famous because you've been courting the nationwide and on-line media about her case?" This was something else I had found out – Dale Thompson was constantly goosing the story in the media. He was constantly planting different clues and twists in the story so the media never lost interest in it.

"I don't know what you mean."

"I mean you've been artificially keeping this story alive in the media. You've been planting stories about this murder daily on-line and you've been constantly calling the 24-hour news channels with different tips and leaks. You've made sure the story has stayed fresh in everyone's minds."

"Well, yeah, I've done that. That's part of my job. Getting publicity for my studio and my girls is part of my job description."

"And a big story like this is something that has given your studio a lot of publicity. Isn't that right?"

"Of course. Ginger's name is in the news so people are curious about her."

"People are so curious about her that they're streaming her videos and renting her DVDs at a record pace, isn't that right?"

"Yes. That's correct."

"So, your studio is really benefiting from Ginger Perry's notoriety." I nodded. "And isn't that why you specifically gave Ms. Perry that glass of poison to give to Ezra that night?"

"I didn't do that."

"Let's see. You know one of Jacob Cohen's ousted heirs because she works for you. You know another of the ousted heirs through her husband. Both of those ousted heirs, Elizabeth Ellis and Ariel Rossi, stand to gain millions out of Ezra's death. And your studio has been reaping the benefits of Ginger's notoriety in the form of millions of streaming and rental revenue. Those facts are not in dispute, do you agree?"

He crossed his arms but said nothing.

"Mr. Thompson, do you agree?"

"Answer the question, please," Judge Woo said from the bench.

"Yeah. I guess."

"And isn't it true that both Elizabeth Ellis and Ariel

Rossi agreed to give you $2 million if you agreed to kill Ezra Cohen?"

"No. That's not true."

At that, I got out a copy of his bank statement. I subpoenaed this so it was proper to introduce as evidence.

"Mr. Thompson, I would like to provide you a copy of your bank statement. This is a statement from Bank of America. Do you bank at Bank of America, Mr. Thompson?"

"Yes."

"And is this a true and accurate copy of your statement for the month of June of this year?"

He looked at it, his face getting white. "Where did you get this?"

"Answer the question please."

"Yes. This is a true and accurate copy of my bank statement of June of this year."

"I would like to enter this bank statement as Exhibit A," I said.

"No objection."

"The bank statement is entered into record as Exhibit A," the judge said. "Please proceed."

"Does this bank statement show a transfer of $1 million from Ariel Rossi?"

"Yes."

"And isn't it true that, as soon as Elizabeth Ellis shows she is the true heir of Jacob Cohen, she, too, will transfer $1 million to you?"

"No. That's not true."

"I have nothing further."

At that, Adrian stood up. She had her work cut out for her. I almost felt sorry for her. "Mr. Thompson, did you poison Mr. Ezra Cohen?" she asked.

"No. Of course not. I wouldn't do something like that. I know that other attorney made me look bad, but I wouldn't do that."

She shook her head. It seemed like she was unable to question Dale further without completely undermining her case against Ginger.

Then she appeared to try a different strategy. She had no loyalty to Dale. As far as she was concerned, Dale could go down for Ezra's murder along with Ginger. As long as she got Ginger on the hook, she did her job. "Now, isn't it true that when you gave that poison to Ginger, you told her what was in that glass of scotch? Isn't it true you told her you would make her a star if she poisoned Mr. Ezra Cohen?"

Adrian was the epitome of trying to make lemonade out of lemons. I didn't think her strategy would be sound, though. I figured it would backfire.

"What's with you people?" Dale asked. "I just told that other lady I didn't give no poison to nobody. I guess I have to tell you that, too."

"Nothing further," Adrian said and then sat down.

Adrian's question to Dale told me all I needed to know. She was properly convinced that Dale conspired to kill Ezra. I had a feeling Adrian would pursue charges against Dale the second this trial was over.

I did my job, and I did it well. I got the prosecutor on board with my theory of the case. Now if the jury acquitted Ginger, everything would fall into place. Dale was being hung out to dry.

I looked over at David, smiling. He knew we were on the right track.

MY NEXT TWO witnesses were Ariel Rossi and Elizabeth Ellis.

Ariel was first. As with Dale, I sought permission to treat her as hostile. I knew I would have to do that because she wouldn't tell the truth, either.

"Ms. Rossi, isn't it true that Ezra Cohen drew up a fake will for your grandfather to sign?"

"Yes, that's true."

"And, Ms. Rossi, isn't it true that in this fake will, you and your brothers didn't get a single dime?"

"Yes. That is true."

"Now, of course, you'll come into your rightful inheritance. Isn't that true?"

"Yes. Of course. Ezra died without a will of his own, so I inherit one-third of Ezra's estate, along with my two brothers, Daniel and Eli."

"You inherit one-third of the estate or one-fourth?"

"Well, I guess one-fourth, assuming Elizabeth Ellis can establish her birthright. That's up in the air, though."

"You're actually close with Elizabeth, isn't that true?"

"Yes. She's my half-niece. I found out my grandfather had an illegitimate son who passed away. When I found that out and found out my grandfather's illegitimate son, Aaron Samson, had a daughter of his own, I checked her out. We became close."

"You were close because the two of you were the only females left in the extended Cohen family, isn't that right?"

"Yes. We women have to stick together against the men." She chuckled a little.

"Ms. Rossi, how did Jacob Cohen die?"

She looked uncomfortable when I asked her this question. "He died in his sleep of natural causes."

"Ms. Rossi, did you in fact tell me that Mr. Jacob Cohen

died when a car he was riding in went off a cliff in Big Bear?"

She looked embarrassed. "Yes. I said that."

"Isn't it true you told me this because you wanted Jacob Cohen's death to seem suspicious?"

"No. That's not true."

I had actually figured out why Ariel told me that lie about Jacob. She wanted me to suspect that Sargis Gregorian killed Jacob because she wanted me to suspect Sargis of killing Ezra. If Sargis could kill an old man like Jacob to get what he wanted, then he was certainly capable of killing Ezra too. That was her logic, as far as I could tell.

But I couldn't go there in this trial. I couldn't bring in Sargis' name at all.

"Isn't it true you wanted to point me in the direction that somebody murdered Jacob Cohen in cold-blood, hoping I would also come to believe this same person murdered Ezra Cohen?"

"No."

"You know Dale Thompson, isn't that correct?"

She looked uncomfortable. "I don't. My husband does."

"And how does your husband know Mr. Thompson?"

She looked even more uncomfortable. "My husband…"

I finished her sentence. "Your husband used Dale Thompson's prostitutes."

Her face got beet red. "Yes." She turned to the jury. "It's not what you think, really. I was diagnosed with a sexual disorder several years ago and I could no longer keep him happy. Please don't judge me."

I felt sorry for poor Ariel. If it weren't for the fact that I was so certain she was in on Ezra's murder and was okay with Ginger taking the fall, I would've had even more sympathy for her. Still, I pressed on.

"So, Dale Thompson is your husband's acquaintance and he was at Ezra's home the night of the murder. Isn't it true you, Elizabeth Ellis and Dale Thompson all conspired to kill Ezra and let Ginger Perry take the fall?"

"It certainly isn't," she said, but her voice said she was lying. Her speech was tremulous, her outrage feigned. She needed to take acting classes with Ginger.

"I have nothing further."

Two witnesses down, one to go.

"Ms. Jackson, your witness," Judge Woo said to Adrian.

Adrian asked about five or six cross-examination questions but her heart wasn't in it. As with Dale Thompson, Adrian probably figured it wasn't any skin off of her nose if this whole conspiracy was proved to the jury. As long as she got a conviction against Ginger as well, she would be happy.

And since she couldn't ask Ariel about Ginger, seeing as Ariel didn't know Ginger, her cross-examination questions were perfunctory and ineffectual.

Elizabeth Ellis was my next witness. This would be the final nail in the coffin.

She approached the witness stand when I called her. A tall and thin brunette, she was dressed to the nines in a dark blue Chanel suit with white piping and matching shoes. She had the kind of lithe and thin body that could carry off just about any look, however.

She took her oath and sat down.

"Could you please state your name for the record," I said.

"Elizabeth Anne Ellis."

"Ms. Ellis," I said. "I'd like to take you back to May 25 of this year. On that evening, where were you?"

"I was working the door at an Ezra Cohen party."

"You were. For whom were you working?"

"Addington, Inc.," she said.

"When did you start working for Addington, Inc.?"

She cleared her throat. "On May 20."

"Just five days before the party," I said. "Are you still working for them?"

"No."

"When did you stop working for them?"

"May 26."

"Did you quit or were you fired?"

"I quit."

"You quit. You worked for them a week. Actually less than a week. Six days."

"Correct."

"Was that supposed to be your full-time job?"

"No."

"What was your full-time job?"

"I work in project management for Dark Angel, Inc."

"Dark Angel, Inc." I nodded knowingly. "Dark Angel, Inc. is a subsidiary of Dark Angel studios in Van Nuys. Is that correct?"

"It is."

"So you know Dale Thompson, then."

"I do."

"And on the night of Ezra's party, the night he was murdered, you were working the door of his party. Is that your testimony?"

"It is."

"And when Dale Thompson came to the party you let him in the door. Is that right?"

She shifted uncomfortably in her seat. She looked like she didn't know how to answer my question. I had gone over this with her beforehand and it seemed like she would tell the truth. Now, as I looked at her, I wasn't so sure.

"Yes," she finally said. "I let him in the door."

"In fact," I said. "You let her in the door under an assumed name. Tom Dale. Is that true?"

"Yes." She looked down at the stand. "That is true."

I nodded. "Is that standard protocol, to let people in under assumed names?"

"No," she said.

"In fact, it's standard protocol for Addington security personnel to check everybody's ID thoroughly and not let people in unless they had the proper identification. Is that right?"

"Yes," she said. "That's correct."

"Why did you let Dale Thompson in under an assumed name?"

"I don't know."

"I'll ask you again. Why did you let Dale Thompson in the door of Ezra's party when he did not have the proper identification?"

"I knew him," she said. "And I figured it would be okay to do that."

"But he was using an assumed name. Is it fair to say you were breaking protocol by allowing him in the door of that party using an alias?"

She shrugged.

"Please answer the question verbally," Judge Woo said.

"I guess I was breaking protocol."

"I have nothing further."

"Ms. Jackson," Judge Woo said. "Your witness."

This time Adrian opted not to ask Elizabeth anything. There was little to be gained by cross-examining her. Adrian appeared not to have any actual information about Ginger. Ginger was her target, and, as with the other witnesses, Adrian was happy to have them hang themselves. It gave her more reason and ammunition to go after them when this court case was said and done.

"I have nothing for this witness, your honor," Adrian said.

"Ms. Ross, please call your next witness," Judge Woo said.

"Your honor, the defense rests."

"Ms. Jackson, do you have any rebuttal evidence?"

"No, your honor."

"Very well. We'll take a fifteen minute recess, and then the prosecution and the defense will give the jury their closing arguments."

The jury filed out and Adrian approached me. "I guess it goes without saying I'll make sure the LAPD arrests and presses charges against Dale, Ariel and Elizabeth after this. You made a pretty solid case against them. But, fair warning, I'm going after your client in my closing arguments.

"Of course," I said. "I would expect nothing less."

Adrian walked out of the courtroom and I turned to Ginger. "It's looking pretty good," I said. "I think we got this."

"No," she said. "We don't got this. That prosecutor still wants to make sure I fry for this murder. She might want those others in on it, too, but she still wants me."

"All we need is reasonable doubt," I said. "And I think I met that burden."

David smiled and nodded. "You're doing great," he said. "I think you're right. I think we'll win this. And keep Sargis happy as well."

"We'll see. We'll see."

Chapter Forty

THE JURY CAME BACK IN, and it was time for closing arguments.

"Ladies and Gentlemen of the jury," Adrian began. "You heard a lot of arguments in this courtroom today. A lot of smoke and mirrors. Now, the defense would've you believe that the murder of Ezra Cohen was a grand conspiracy between Elizabeth Ellis, Ariel Rossi and Dale Thompson. That they all were in on murdering Ezra because they were greedy and they wanted to make sure that they got Ezra's money. I admit, the defense told a compelling story. Even I was taken in by the evidence presented. In fact, there's reason to believe that the defense was right – Elizabeth, Ariel and Dale probably were in on it."

"But we're not talking about Elizabeth, Ariel and Dale right now. No, we're talking about Ginger Perry. Ladies and gentlemen of the jury, I would like you to not lose sight of an important fact - just because somebody else is guilty of murdering Ezra does not mean that Ginger isn't also guilty of the murder. It does sound like there was a conspiracy, but you cannot, and I mean cannot, lose sight of two facts. Two undisputable facts. One, Ginger Perry was the person who gave the poison to Ezra Cohen. That's a fact that hasn't been disputed at all. Mr. Cohen consumed the poison while he was alone with Ginger Perry. Ginger Perry was the last person to see him alive. Those are facts. They might be inconvenient facts for the defense, but they are facts all the same."

She paced around and addressed each juror, one by one. "And, ladies and gentlemen, here's another fact. It is not in dispute – Ginger benefitted greatly from Ezra's murder. She's a new adult film actress, yet she's making twice what other film actresses make. Everybody knows her name. She has a notoriety that would've been impossible for her to attain otherwise. If it weren't for her being involved in Ezra's murder, she would've been just one of thousands of porn stars trying to make a name for themselves. She would've been out of the business, used up like every other generic porn star out there, in less than a year. She would then be out on the street. What would she have done if she was treated like so much cattle? I don't know, that's one thing Is an unknown, but I would imagine she would be working the streets again."

"But she's not working the streets. She's not. She has this cushy job, making thousands of dollars for doing things she apparently enjoys doing. She has a big name in the adult film business. She might even be able to parlay her adult film career into a mainstream movie career. All because she is accused of murdering a studio executive. All because her boss, Dale Thompson, has gone out of his way to keep her name in the papers, on-line and on television. In fact, right now, even as we speak, there are thousands of conversations out there about Ms. Perry. She's gone viral. Good for her." She clapped her hands. "Good for her."

"This whole case would be great for her except for one thing. A man is dead. And Ginger Perry killed him. Please don't lose sight of that. Please don't lose the forest for the trees. And I ask you to return a verdict of guilty to the charge of murder in the first degree. Thank you very much."

As I stood up, my heart was pounding. Adrian's closing argument was good. It was very good. Mine was just going to have to be even better.

I stood up and paced over to the jury. "Ladies and gentlemen of the jury," I said. "You heard evidence about what really happened in this case. You heard solid evidence that Dale Thompson, Elizabeth Ellis and Ariel Rossi conspired to kill Ezra Cohen. They all had motive to do it. Elizabeth Ellis and Ariel Rossi both were motivated to kill Ezra Cohen, because they both were cut out of their grandfather's will. Since Ezra inherited all of the grandfather's estate - $50 million – and Ezra died without a will, his siblings got all of his money. That gave Elizabeth and Ariel good reason to murder Ezra."

"As for Dale....he knew both Elizabeth and Ariel. You saw that Ariel Rossi transferred $1 million into his bank account recently. So, his motive to kill Ezra – greed, plain and simple. But it was more than that. He also wanted to make one of his actresses a viral superstar. He wanted one of his actresses to put his studio, Dark Angel, on the map. He knew if he duped one of his actresses into killing Ezra, he would get his viral superstar. He would make his chosen girl so notorious that everybody would know her name and everybody would be curious about her movies. And it worked. With Dale behind the scenes, pushing Ginger's case in the news every single day, Dale got his viral heroine."

"That's what happened in this case, ladies and gentlemen. That's what happened. That's what the evidence showed in this case. What the evidence didn't show, however, was that my client, Ginger Perry, had anything to do with the murder. The evidence didn't show that Ginger knew that the scotch she supplied to Mr. Ezra Cohen contained poison. The evidence didn't show that Ginger gave the poison to Ezra knowingly. The evidence did show she had no idea she was giving Ezra a drink laced with arsenic. from her testimony. The prosecutor didn't really give you any counter-narrative to this, except to say that Ginger was in the room at the time that Ezra died, therefore she must have done it. That's the only evidence that the prosecutor showed in this case. The evidence against Ginger was completely circumstantial."

"Ginger is not guilty of murder in this case. You heard her testimony. She gave Ezra a drink of scotch. She serviced him sexually. And then she left. She didn't know she was giving Ezra poison. She had no clue. She was a dupe. Yes, she benefited from her own notoriety. That's indisputable. But that fact alone is not evidence to convict her for Ezra Cohen's murder. Not enough evidence at all."

"Now, if you have reasonable doubt that my client knowingly gave Ezra Cohen arsenic poison, then you must acquit. The law states very clearly you must give the defendant the benefit of the doubt. In this case, the prosecutor clearly didn't meet the burden of showing that Ginger is guilty beyond a reasonable doubt. There's no way that the prosecutor can meet that burden with the evidence she presented. Therefore, you must vote to acquit. Thank you very much."

I sat down. The judge then gave the jury instructions and sent them on their way.

And the waiting game began.

"SO," Ginger said. "What do you think? Do you think that the jury will come back soon?"

"I do. I think that the prosecutor's case was so weak, I think that the jury will come back sooner than you might think."

"You think they didn't make the case?"

"I think that they didn't make the case. To say the least."

She nodded. "I hope you're right," she said. "I really hope you're right."

I WAS RIGHT. The jury came back after only two hours. I was surprised, but not really. I presented a pretty open and shut case for them. I personally thought I did better in presenting Ginger's case than I had done in a long time.

I wondered if I was feeling more confident because I had finally been able to stay off of alcohol for an extended period of time. Not I felt like I was over it. I did feel, however, I could maybe, finally, stay off the sauce for awhile. At least until I got back to Kansas City and I could get a sponsor and attend regular meetings.

"Has the jury reached a verdict?" Judge Woo asked.

"We have, your honor."

"Will the defendant please rise."

Ginger and I stood up. I held her hand and closed my eyes.

"On the charge of murder in the first degree, how does the jury find?"

"Not guilty."

"Is that the final verdict of the jury?"

"Yes, your honor."

"Very well." Judge Woo banged his gavel. "The defendant is free to go."

I smiled and Ginger hugged me. "I knew you could do it. I knew it."

"Well," I said. "This is freedom for you. Don't waste it. You have a good career and you won't be spending time in prison. You're making a lot of money. Save it. You're in too volatile of a business not to. You're the flavor of the month. Never forget that."

"Aw, Harper, why you gotta be so negative?"

"I'm not being negative. I'm being realistic."

She shook her head. "I know. But thanks all the same. I owe you."

I had to smile. "You don't owe me a thing."

I went over to the prosecutor. "So," I said. "You going to pursue charges against those three?"

"Of course," she said. "You made a good case against them. I'll be putting together charging documents today."

"Thanks."

Next in the Kansas City
Legal Thrillers series

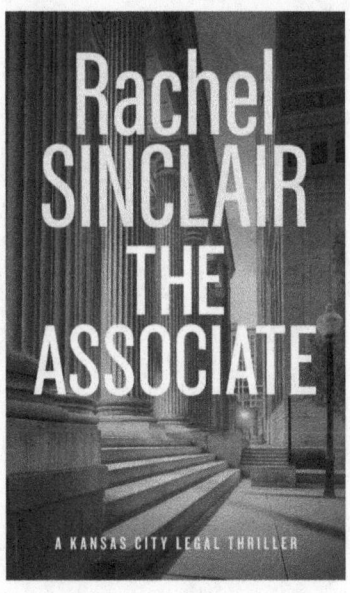

vinci-books.com/theassociate

When an Armenian mobster's son is accused of murder, Harper must win the case or lose her life.

Defense attorney Harper is forced to represent an Armenian mobster's son accused of murder. With her own life hanging in the balance, failure is not an option. Enter Damien Harrington, Harper's enigmatic new associate with a secret that could shatter their partnership. As they navigate the treacherous waters of the trial, Damien takes the lead, battling his own demons while trying to uncover the truth behind the murder.

Turn the page for a free preview…

The Associate: Chapter One

HARPER

ERIK GREGORIAN WAS CURRENTLY my client. Against my will, of course. It turned out that Sargis Gregorian, Erik's father, was not as good as his word. Who knew that a gangster and a thug would be somebody who wasn't a man of honor? I had to laugh a little when I asked myself that question. Of course Sargis would go back on his word. His son was in trouble. He also was a cheapskate because he apparently didn't want to pay for an attorney to represent the kid. No, he wanted his legal representation for free. Since I was intimidated by his threats to my girls, I would do what he asked. I wouldn't try to cross him. I might never be rid of him. I knew that for a fact. I might have stepped into a mess of quicksand, and I couldn't get out of it.

"Erik is coming in," Pearl informed me. "At 2 PM."

I sighed. My little interlude in Los Angeles somewhat helped me in that I finally got a break and got my alcoholism under control. Hopefully for good. I came home and found an AA sponsor. Her name was Katie Wright, and she had been on the wagon for 20 years. She talked me off the ledge more than once in the past few weeks, and I was finally working through my 12 Steps.

So, I was in a better place, mentally, than I was before I went out to LA. I was more relaxed because I finally had an associate, Damien Harrington, helping me out. Liam McNeil, the associate I hired before I went to Los Angeles, returned to his large firm. That was my fault, of course – I threw him into the deep end and didn't give him a life raft. Since he worked for a large firm, he knew very little about the nuts and bolts of practicing law. He thought he wanted to get right in the courtroom but had little stomach for the clients he had to deal with. I thought Liam was the right person, but if he wanted to stay in his ivory tower and not get his hands dirty, he wasn't the right person for my firm.

Damien, on the other hand, was perfect for what I needed. He had experience in criminal defense because he had worked for the Public Defender's Office. He was used to trying cases. I was lucky he was willing to become an associate instead of a partner, although he and I had discussed the possibility that he would become my partner in the future. I wanted to make sure he had what it took before I made him a full partner.

So far, he was doing stellar. He was bringing in cases. I told him he could eat what he killed, meaning the cases he brought were his. He could work them, and he could keep the fees brought in. In addition to those cases he brought in, I had him help me out with my cases. So, I had somebody who could cover for me in court when needed, and I had somebody who could second-chair me in trials. In short, I had somebody who could back me up when I really needed it.

I was much more relaxed because of Damien, and I was also more relaxed because I finally hired an investigator. I had one before, but I have been doing my own investigation for the past few years. That put additional pressure on me and it seemed there needed to be more hours in the day. But Damien convinced me I needed somebody to do the shoe-leather work, and he and I worked together to find Tom Garrett. Garrett was an ex-con who became a private investigator once he got out of the joint. He was very good at what he did because he was a part of the criminal underground, so he knew many players in that world. He could bring me information because his buddies from the streets knew he was working for a criminal defense attorney and they were eager to help their friends.

Damien would help me with Erik's case, too, as would Garrett. It would have to be all hands on deck to figure out exactly how to win the case for this kid. He was accused of killing a journalist. Her name was Shelly McMason, and she was working in the field, covering the kidnapping of a young girl sold into white slavery. Shelly was a brave reporter, not afraid to get her hands dirty, meaning she befriended many of Erik's gang members. The gang was a subset of the Armenian mafia, which controlled them from the headquarters in Los Angeles. Erik was the leader of that particular gang, so it was up to him to control his turf. As such, he decided Shelly was dangerous because she was getting too close to his operations. She threatened to expose him and his men, so he decided Shelly had to go.

This was a problem because, as Sargis found, the police tend to turn a blind eye when hits were turned onto thugs. Sargis had apparently killed many members of different gangs infringing on Sargis' turf. Since the people he killed were other criminals, he never got into trouble for these hits. The "victims" in these cases were vermin the cops wanted off the streets anyhow, so it was safe to say the cops were happy to be rid of these men.

It was the same in Kansas City. As Sargis explained, Erik ran his turf as a general might run his troops. He took care of threats swiftly and violently. Yet, he had never been charged with any of these murders. But Shelly was a different thing. She was a pretty young girl, only 23, a graduate of the University of Missouri's journalism school. She was a Delta Gamma alumnus, one of the best sorority houses at MU, and she had ambitions to work for a national presidential campaign. Her family was wealthy and considered to be old money. They owned a mansion in the Mission Hills area, where many old money people lived.

In short, Shelly was the kind of girl people cared about. She was the kind of girl whose murder would be a national story in ordinary times. She was the girl who might get an entire Dateline episode devoted to her killing. She wasn't just some low-profile victim who would get a small story in the *Kansas City Star* and nothing else.

The fact she was the victim in this case was a problem. Not just because she was a pretty young girl with a good family but also because she was a journalist. She was murdered doing her job, and because she was one of the press, the press took her killing very personally.

The upshot was I was stuck representing Erik, knowing he was good for the murder, with the spotlight of the media glare trained upon me. And I wasn't allowed to plead him out. Sargis made that extremely clear. I would have to try this guy's case and have to find a way to win it. As impossible as that seemed.

Damien came into my office and sat down across from me. Damien was my age, 35, and I knew little about his personal background. He kept to himself about those issues.

I knew he was married, although I didn't know how happily. I had heard him on the phone several times, talking in hushed tones, as if he didn't want anyone to hear what he was saying. I noticed he seemed slightly agitated and distracted after he got off the phone during those times. I didn't pry, however. I didn't know him well enough to ask about what was happening. It wasn't my business.

I also understood that he had two children – a son, Nathaniel, and a daughter, Amelia. He talked about them and had pictures of them in his office. Nathaniel looked a lot like Damien – dark curly hair cut short on the sides and slightly longer on top, green eyes, olive skin, lean. He was 8. His sister, Amelia, age 6, was the opposite of Nathaniel and Damien – she was small, blonde and pale. She had the same green eyes as her brother and father, however. I could see she was a Harrington by looking at her eyes. Other than that, however, I would have never guessed she was kin to Damien.

"So," Damien said. "You got that kid coming in, huh? The Armenian thug?"

"I do," I said. "The Armenian thug. I have no idea how I'm supposed to win this case. But I have to. Of course, I always give my clients my all, but on this one, I'll have to give him even more than usual. If I don't..." I sliced my hand across my neck. "Seriously, that Sargis guy scares the shit out of me. He's so strange. You meet him and you almost feel like you should hear classical music piping in through his walls. You can imagine him going to the opera and appreciating every note. You can see him reading Dostoyevsky and Proust in his spare time. He probably plays chess with his men. You get the idea. Yet, he's a thug, as sure as his son is. He personally killed people when he was coming up through the ranks, and even now, he personally kills people. Mostly he has his henchmen do it, but occasionally carries out the murders himself. I still have a hard time trying to square the outward image with the monster within."

Damien shook his head. "I don't know how you got roped into this bullshit, Harper. How do you get stuck with representing a guy for free? And forced into finding a way to win the case or else your girls will end up kidnapped?" He crossed his arms in front of him. "Personally, I think you should call his bluff. You can't give in to terrorists like that. That's common knowledge. You give in to terrorists and blackmail and it just never ends. Before you know it, you're representing the entire Gregorian clan and not earning a dime. That's not fair to you. You got a firm to run here." He smiled. "And now you got an associate to pay too. Don't forget that."

"It's okay," I said. "I mean, as far as the firm balance goes, I'm pretty flush. I've had some major cases lately. I'm not too worried about the money thing."

"You will be once this jackass starts monopolizing your time with his freebie cases. I'm telling you, this Erik case is only the beginning. You let Sargis get away with this and you open the door to being completely manipulated. Lucky for you I just brought in a wrongful death case that will give your bottom line a huge boost." He nodded his head. "It's a good one, too. I'm really lucky I found it."

"Tell me about it," I said. "And I'm assuming you're going to share it?"

"Of course I'll share it. I can't work it on my own. But it's a case I found yesterday afternoon while visiting my daughter Amelia in the hospital." He looked sad all of a sudden. "So, yeah, I was visiting Amelia in the hospital when I got to talking with this woman. She told me her son was in surgery. Amelia was also in surgery and other people weren't in the waiting room, so we talked and bonded."

I wanted to ask him where his wife was while his daughter was in surgery but didn't want to pry. "Go on."

"Her son was in the middle of a routine hernia surgery. She didn't seem all that concerned about it. It was in the oncology ward, though, where her son was having his surgery, so I figured the hernia probably wasn't all that was going on with her son. And it wasn't. He was also suffering from leukemia. But the mom, her name is Betsy Ward, said that her son, Austin was his name, was in remission. The hernia was being repaired by her kid's usual cancer doctors because the doctors thought the hernia might have resulted from an earlier surgery the doctors did on Austin, a bone-marrow transplant."

I wrote down what he was saying and wrote a question mark by my notes. I would have to come back to the questions I had for Damien. "So, Austin, the son, was involved in routine hernia surgery, and what happened?"

"Well, as I sat there, the doctor came out and talked to Betsy. I could tell by the way the doctor talked to her that it wasn't good news. Then Betsy started to cry and wail and she collapsed on the seat. The doctor didn't even try to put his arm around her. He just walked out of the room. So, I went over to her. She told me the doctor had just come out to tell her her son was dead. He died on the operating table." He shook his head. "The kid died during a hernia surgery. That kind of thing shouldn't happen. So, I got the mom's permission to get the kid's medical records, and I had an independent doctor review them. According to that other doctor, Austin apparently died because he was given Propofol in a high dose. Plus, according to this other doctor, Dr. Peter Wagner, Austin wasn't in remission at the time he had that hernia surgery. In fact, it looked like Austin's leukemia had advanced to the point where he was near death at the time he had his surgery."

"What's wrong with Propofol?" I asked Damien. "That drug has been commonly used in general anesthesia for quite some time."

"Nothing is wrong with Propofol *per se*," Damien said. "Except Austin was allergic to the drug. They used Propofol in his earlier surgery for the bone marrow transplant and he had an allergic reaction to the drug. They almost lost him during that surgery, and it was determined that Austin was allergic to Propofol. Yet the anesthesiologist used it on him again. That makes this whole thing a pretty open-and-shut case if you ask me."

I shook my head. "Yeah, but it's kinda a dog of a case. After all, according to Dr. Wagner, Austin was not long for this world no matter what happened in that surgery. That would mean the damages would be extremely limited." The way actual damages are calculated in wrongful death cases depends heavily upon what the lifetime earnings of the dead person would have been throughout an average life. Economists and actuaries are employed in the courtroom to testify about the earnings potential of the person in question. That was a complicated formula as it was – it was dependent upon the person's age, education, profession and income at the time of death. It sounded like Austin not only didn't have much income if he was a minor, but he also didn't have much potential income if he was dying.

"It's not that much of a dog case," Damien protested. "Austin might have only been 18, but he had been accepted at Harvard and MIT and was a mathematical genius. He was carrying a 4.4 GPA at Pembroke Hill, which, as you probably know, is the most exclusive private school in the

Kansas City area. He had a lot of potential. His vision in life was to work for NASA. He had the grades and the drive to do it. Not only that, but his mother had enrolled him in a clinical trial that hopefully would have helped him. His bone marrow transplant apparently didn't put him in remission, but this clinical trial sounded good. If we can convince the jury there was a chance Austin could have lived and gone on to fulfill his potential, then there's a chance this case might be a good one."

I sighed. I knew what he was saying, but I hated wrongful death cases. Especially wrongful death cases that involved medical malpractice. They were expensive to try – when you get all your experts lined up and paid, you typically pay $100,000 out of your pocket. That meant you better win the case. It wasn't like a criminal case where the expenses were nominal – you might have to get expert witnesses involved. You often had to do depositions, which cost some money. Still, you could try a criminal case with almost no money out of pocket if you do all the investigation yourself.

But medical malpractice cases were a different beast. You had to get actuaries, economists, and a team of doctors to testify. I tried to stay away from the usual suspect doctors – the hired guns that have built a cottage industry out of testifying for every medical malpractice case that comes along. They were way too easy for the other side to pick off and show the jury how biased they were. That meant I had to find other doctors to testify, doctors who aren't hired guns for anyone and everyone with a medical malpractice case. These doctors typically charged even more than the hired guns because they were going out of their way to give testimony.

"Okay," I said. "I won't talk you out of your wrongful

death case. If you believe in it, then, by all means, pursue it. I hope you know what you're doing on it, though. I'll help you as much as possible, but medical malpractice cases aren't my forte. I guess what I'm saying is you killed this. You can eat it. I don't really want to get too much involved."

He raised an eyebrow. "Your loss," he said.

"In the meantime," I said, "you'll have to have actual income. Contingency cases like medical malpractice won't pay off at least until you settle or it goes to trial, and if it goes to trial, it'll be nothing but a money sink for up to a year. The attorneys for the hospital will bury you with discovery requests, ask you to pay their attorney's fees if they win and do everything they can think of to make you quit this case. The only exception to that rule is if, somehow, someway, you find something that makes this case stand out. You find something that makes it likely a jury will hand the hospital its ass in trial. Then you can settle. But if this case is marginal, and the hospital knows it, then good luck."

"Giving the kid a drug he was allergic to – that's not good enough to make them settle?"

"No. Not if the kid would probably die anyway. I admit that it helps that he was so bright and had been accepted to Harvard and MIT. That he had ambitions to work for NASA. That shows his earning potential. But we have to understand that he wasn't in remission for his leukemia and would likely die before he could fulfill his potential. You find a way around that and we have a chance. But, from the facts, this case seems marginal enough that the hospital will turn the big guns on you to make you quit. It's not like you have one of the big medical malpractice names in the city."

Some attorneys in the city tried lots of personal injury and medical malpractice cases and won more cases than they lost. If Damien had a name like Cullan and Cullan, who were licensed physicians and medical malpractice attorneys, or Fowler and Pickett, a large firm that tried lots of these cases, the hospital would probably back down. But Damien Harrington was a nobody. He just got the case because he was in the waiting room with Austin's mother.

Damien shrugged. "Okay. Well, I guess if you're not in on this case, you're not in. I'll need a partner to help me out, though. I'll see if I can't find an attorney in town interested in trying this case with me." He looked disappointed, and I felt guilty.

"I'll think about it," I said. "Get some more discovery done on this case, find out what the weak spots will be, and I'll think about getting in on this case with you. But I can't help but think the two of us on this case will be blind leading the blind. I have little experience with medical malpractice, and you've been working with the Public Defender's Office since you left school. You have trial work, but it's all been criminal trial work. You have a steep learning curve on this case, and the hospital attorneys will eat you alive if they know you're a newbie."

"Think about it," Damien said. "That's all I can really ask. In the meantime, what do we know about Erik Gregorian's case?"

"I looked at the file the prosecutor gave me. According to the Statement of Information, Erik knew Shelly McMason personally. Shelly had successfully infiltrated Erik's organization. She had essentially become one of them. She was working as an undercover journalist for the *Kansas City Star* and was getting ready to publish a five-part story on Erik's organization and the practice of white slavery in the Kansas City area. Shelly died in a car accident but it turned out her brake lines were cut. Erik definitely had motive to kill Shelly. He also had the means and the opportunity, as he was friendly with her and often rode with her in her car several times. Obviously, the best way to try this case would be a SODDI defense – show somebody else could have killed her. Somebody else had motive to kill her. I will have to find out who that somebody else might be."

"I don't get it," Damien said. "Why does the prosecutor's office have such a hard-on for Erik? Yeah, he was the head of the organization Shelly would report on. That doesn't mean he killed her."

"Well, it doesn't exactly look good, either. Even if he got one of his men to cut her brake line, it still means Erik himself will get busted as a conspirator or as the instigator. As the leader of the local Armenian Power controlling the East Side of Kansas City, any violent end met by somebody in the Power will implicate Erik. That's the problem we'll have with this case. We have to show the jury that the person who killed Shelly wasn't involved in the Armenian Power at all. That will be tricky."

"Tricky but not impossible," Damien said. "We'll just get Tom Garrett to do a thorough background investigation on Shelly, including all the other people she was investigating, and show it could be any number of people who might have wanted her dead. If she was an undercover journalist, it stands to reason she probably pissed off many people along the way. Seriously, we have to find a way to throw the jury off. Even if Erik did it. Which he probably did."

"I know. That's the problem. I think Erik is good for this case all day long. I hate I have to get stuck with trying it. I really hate I could be in danger if I can't win this case. So will my girls. This Sargis guy has way too much power. I wish I never met him."

"That's what happens when you get tied up with these

mafia types. You can't just quit them. If you let him, he will intimidate you for the rest of your career. So don't let him. Hire a bodyguard and stand up to him. Show him you can't be pushed around."

I sighed. "Easier said than done."

Indeed.

The Associate: Chapter Two

DAMIEN

I WAS grateful for the chance to join Harper's firm. After the fucked-up life I had before I went to college and law school, I pretty much have woken up every day grateful. Not that any of what happened was my fault. Well, that's not exactly true – it was my fault and it wasn't. It wasn't my fault I was born into a wretched situation – my mom never actually knew my dad. I think he was one of her johns. Why she wasn't using birth control during her street-walker days, I'll never know. Or maybe she was, but it didn't take. Whatever. All I knew was my mom was a prostitute and then had me. I didn't exactly fit into her plans. To say the least. She couldn't work the streets anymore because she had a squalling infant in her trailer home, so she got on welfare and depended upon a variety of men to support us.

One of those men, Steven Harrington, actually stuck around for long enough that my mother gave me his last name. She married him and he adopted me. But he was an abusive bastard. He beat on my mother and me on the regular, and it got so bad I ended up running away. I ended up in a home for wayward boys, just like my idol, Steve McQueen. The Ozanam school was the place for troubled kids like me. It provided therapy and schooling and got me out of the house. It also introduced me to the kids who became my lifelong friends until all of us ended up in prison.

Actually, I didn't belong in prison. I truly didn't. It was guilt by association at its finest. The others – Tommy Arcola, Nick Savante, Jack O'Brien and his brother Connor – actually belonged in prison. They were all involved in a robbery that went very wrong. Connor - at 16, he was the youngest out of the bunch – got trigger-happy with an armed security guard who happened to be at that liquor store getting cigarettes. The security guard pulled his gun on Connor, who panicked and shot him in the leg. That wasn't a kill shot, and Connor didn't know much about firearms. He didn't mean to kill the guy, of course – if he meant to kill him, he would have shot him in the head or chest. And the security guard should have just been injured, but it was Connor's luck that the guard, whose name was Emilio Garza, contracted the MRSA virus while he was in the hospital and died a month later from his infection.

What that meant was that all four of the boys, who were my best friends from Ozanam, were put on trial for felony murder. Then, somehow, I got roped into the whole mess. I wasn't anywhere near that liquor store, and the boys told their attorneys that as well. Yet, I was put into a lineup, and an eyewitness fingered me as the one driving the getaway car. Tommy was actually the one driving that getaway car. He does somewhat look like me – we both have dark curly hair, and, at the time, we both were wearing our hair long. To our shoulders.

The five of us were tried separately, and we all were

convicted for the murder of Emilio Garza. Connor was still only 16 when we were put on trial, but was tried as an adult because of the nature of the crime. I was only 18, and so were Nick, Tommy and Jack. We were lucky we didn't get the death penalty. The jury opted for life in prison with the chance of parole for all of us, mainly because of our age and the fact that all of us came from really messed-up homes. We all were in the same school for troubled kids, and all of us had basically the same stories to tell the jury - chaotic and abusive parents, drug abuse and alcoholism in the home, etc. The same basic story that a lot of kids can tell. The same basic story that all of the kids in our school could tell. Most of them came from homes that never gave them a chance to have a normal life.

So, the upshot was I was 18 and in prison for a murder I had nothing to do with. For that matter, Tommy, Nick and Jack didn't really have anything to do with that murder, either. Especially Tommy – all he did was drive the getaway car. I personally have always thought that what happened was unfair to all of us. Yes, Connor was young and probably shouldn't have been given a gun to start with, but he never meant to kill Emilio. And, really, in a different situation, Connor could've claimed self-defense. After all, Emilio was the first person to draw his weapon and he pointed it right at Connor. It was basically kill or be killed in that situation. But the felony murder rule is very explicit – any killing done in the commission of a felony is murder. Period, end of story. Even if Connor would have gotten really stupid and accidentally shot one of the guys involved in the hold-up, the result would have been the same. Felony murder. And all the guys involved in the holdup would get the exact same charge, as they all were acting in concert. That was how it worked.

But, with me... that was a different thing altogether. I had done some jacked-up shit in my youth – I used to steal cars and, more than once, I helped the guys burglarize businesses after they closed. I never got caught for those things except one of the cars I stole. That theft was what landed me in Ozanam to begin with. That and the fact my mother decided she couldn't control me and told the judge in my car theft case she was afraid of me. Whatever that meant. My mother's testimony in my car theft case combined with the fact I stole the car in the first place meant I would be put into a special school where I could receive therapy for my anger issues, in addition to getting a decent education.

I belonged in Ozanam. I'll be the first to admit to that. But I didn't belong in prison.

Still, I tried to make the best of it. For five years, I made the best of it. I felt like my appellate attorney wasn't doing anything for me and I wanted a new trial. So, I went to the legal books in the prison library and studied them. I found some sample appellate briefs and some sample writs of habeas corpuses, and I worked on writing them. I only had a certain amount of time to file my appellate brief and I missed it. The notice of appeal could only be filed within 10 days of the judgment becoming final, and that judgment in my case became final when my motion for a new trial was overruled and my sentence was imposed. I missed that window of time. Or, rather, my lawyer missed that window. I then sought leave of court to file the notice of appeal late, but that was denied by the courts. I was out of luck as far as getting an appeal going. But I could file writs, and I did. I filed writ after writ, all of which were ignored by the courts.

At some point, I gave up filing writs, but, by then, I knew the law backwards and forwards. I became a jailhouse lawyer. All the other inmates came to me for legal help and help with writing their own appellate briefs and writs and other documents to try to get them out of prison. I was always very careful about timing issues, especially with the appellate briefs. I was always preparing motions for new trials and notice of appeals, and I often wrote entire appellate briefs for some of the inmates who couldn't afford an appellate attorney. Which was all of them. Some of the guys inside got lucky and got a court-appointed appellate attorney, but most of them weren't entitled to a special attorney and all of them wanted to try to get some kind of post-conviction relief. I wrote the briefs for them, they would get their chance for oral argument, and argued on their own behalf. Once in awhile, one of my "clients" would win the argument and get a new trial, and that was always a cause to celebrate.

When I was 23 years old I had given up hope I ever would see the outside of a prison cell. As unjust as it was for me to be in prison, and as angry as I was about being wrongly convicted, I had made peace by that time. I had come to understand I probably would spend the rest of my life in prison for something I didn't do, mainly because I happened to look like the guy driving the getaway car and the "eyewitness" couldn't distinguish me from Tommy and decided both of us were involved in the robbery. Tommy felt awful about the mix-up, and he apologized to me every time we met in the prison yard, but I always told him he had nothing to apologize for. All the guys swore up and down I wasn't involved, and nobody would believe them. I knew the guys weren't at fault for what happened to me – that stupid eyewitness was at fault. Not the guys. For that matter, the defense attorneys and the cops were also at fault, because they never listened to the guys when they protested I was nowhere near the crime scene.

Then, one day, I got a notice that the Innocence Project had taken up my case. As I understood it, the Innocence Project was dedicated to freeing the wrongly imprisoned. They specialized in using DNA evidence to get convictions overturned. They found out about my case when the *Kansas City Star* ran a story about my work behind bars helping other inmates get new trials and get cases overturned on appeal. I was interviewed for that article, and I emphasized I was innocent of the crime for which I was convicted. I told the reporter for the *Star* all about what happened – how my buddies were convicted for an armed robbery, how I wasn't anywhere near the scene, how I was still put into a lineup and an eyewitness identified me, and how the guys told anyone who would listen I wasn't involved in the crime.

There was a saving grace, one I never even thought about – I was never in the car used in the robbery. That was a car the guys had stolen and used specifically for the robbery. And the car was still available for DNA testing. That was one of the things the reporter had asked me – if I had ever been in that car. I told her I hadn't. I had never been to that liquor store, either – I hadn't been there before the robbery and I hadn't been there afterwards. That was the starting point for the Innocence Project. They managed to find the car used in the robbery – after we were convicted, the car was released as evidence and sold at auction. My lawyer on the Innocence Project, Chuck Riegel, tracked down that car, got a court order, and tested it for DNA. The DNA for all the guys was all over that car. Mine wasn't. They also went to the liquor store and tested the entire store for DNA. It was the same as the car – my DNA wasn't anywhere on the premises.

Chuck worked his ass off for little money and managed to get me a new trial. I was assigned a Public Defender for my new trial, and I couldn't have been more impressed by my new attorney's dedication. Her name was Colleen Sutton, and she looked like she had just walked off the boat from Ireland. Red curly hair, freckles, pale skin and big blue eyes. She was the first woman I had seen in awhile, and I thought she was the most beautiful female I had ever laid eyes on. She was a workhorse, and I found out she wasn't unusual in the Kansas City Public Defender's Office. She turned over every stone and made sure my case was adequately worked up. She tried the case and won it – the jury came back in less than an hour.

I felt ashamed I didn't have faith in the Public Defender's Office when I was a teenager. I didn't want a Public Defender for my case because I had the impression they were poor attorneys and only got a job with the PD's office because they couldn't get a better job. That they were the attorneys who graduated at the bottom of their class. That they were overworked, underpaid and would give my case short shrift.

I couldn't have been more wrong. The attorneys at that office were some of the most dedicated I had ever seen. They were passionate and intelligent and were working there because they were true believers in the Sixth Amendment – that everybody is entitled to representation, no matter what they did and no matter how little money they had. They were, in short, true believers. Many of the attorneys at the PD's office went on to become judges. Others went on to work for the federal government, defending people accused of federal crimes. Still others ended up making the big bucks for large defense firms in the KC area. But there were some who remained right where they were – representing indigent clients, making a fraction of what they could make in the private sector, all because they truly believed in what they were doing.

I fell a bit in love with Colleen, especially since she worked so hard to get my case overturned. I never pursued it, however. I was too embarrassed. She was an attorney and I was an inmate who didn't even have a college degree. I knew I was smart and, if I put my mind to it, I could also become an attorney. But I didn't have anything to offer her at that time, so, even though I thought she might also be into me, I didn't pursue her.

What I did do was go to college. My SAT scores were high enough to get into UMKC, and my Ozanam high school grades were excellent as well. I never got the chance to graduate from high school because I was convicted for that robbery before I could walk down that aisle to get my diploma. I got my GED and then went to UMKC and got my BA in Criminal Justice. Then I took my LSAT and scored in the top 2% in the country – a 172. That score, combined with my 4.0 undergraduate average, combined with my essay where I wrote about my experiences in prison and my work on behalf of other inmates, combined with letters of recommendation from my Innocence Project attorney and Colleen, got me into the University of Chicago Law School. UChicago is the fourth rated law school in the country, right below Yale, Stanford and Harvard. It's the school where Barack Obama taught Constitutional Law. I was shocked I got in and then had to figure out how to get the money together to go. I managed that with a combination of scholarships, grants and a lot of student loans.

When I got out of school, I went right to work for the Public Defender's Office in Kansas City. I never forgot the dedication and work ethic of the attorneys in that office.

How hard they worked on my case, how tireless they were... I never forgot that. And Colleen was still in the office. She was married, but we became great friends. I was also married to Sarah by the time I got out of law school. She was also a student at UChicago, but was in grad school, working on her Master's Degree in Art History. We fell in love, got married my first year in law school, and quickly had our two kids – Nate and Amelia.

That was then. This is now. And things were very different.

Grab your copy...
vinci-books.com/theassociate

About the Author

Rachel Sinclair was a criminal defense attorney for eleven years, so she doesn't scare easily. She graduated from the University of Missouri-Kansas City School of Law in 1998, and worked for the Public Defender's Office for several years before striking out on her own. She currently lives in San Diego, California, with her boyfriend, Joey, and her two fur babies, Annie and Toby. In her spare time, she likes to read, bicycle all over town, Boogie Board at the beach, and watch trashy television.

www.ingramcontent.com/pod-product-compliance
Lightning Source LLC
LaVergne TN
LVHW030241250326
834688LV00047B/1744